SEA STATION UMBRA

John Paul Cater

Oct 1, 2017

To Tom—

Enjoy the Story.

John P Cater

ISBN: 978-1-533-24323-2

TITLES BY JOHN PAUL CATER

FICTION

The Endlight Event
Endlight Dawning 2012
Satellite Lost
Pi Day Doomsday
Sea Station Umbra

NONFICTION

Electronically Speaking: Computer Speech Generation
Electronically Hearing: Computer Speech Recognition

ACKNOWLEDGEMENTS

I wish to thank my good friends and fellow authors Tom Johnson and his wife Ginger of pulp fiction fame for taking time from their busy writing and reviewing schedule to read and comment on this story as it developed in my mind and gradually bled from my fingers into words on paper.

Another high-five goes to the Jesh Art Studio of Fiverr for his visual rendition of a beautiful cover for this book that created several settings in the story. Without that image guiding my thoughts, much of this story would be just words rather than the textual imagery it offers.

Finally, last and foremost, I want to thank my lovely wife Jaye for tolerating the time I spend creating and writing books satisfying some inner drive for creative expression I can't quite understand. Possibly her unconditional love and unfailing support drives me forward as I try to impress her but that has yet to happen. Maybe next time.

*To my precious wife Jaye who again patiently
tolerated my mental ventures out of her life.
Still I drift away into new stories.
I love you with all my heart even though
I'm not always there (but I am).*

Chapter 1
O'Dark Thirty

It was four a.m. on a Monday morning June 13, 2016, when the bedside phone rang. I clicked on the lamp, looked at the clock then picked up the phone. Seeing Unknown Caller I rejected the call. Four hours remained until work started and there was no need for anyone much less an overseas telemarketer to call me this early. Seconds later, it rang again.

Lindy, my bride of barely six months roused from her sound sleep and growled:

"Answer it, Matt. It has to be an overseas call. Tell them to go away. We don't want whatever it is they're selling."

Now normally she's a doll of a woman; men swoon over her television news-anchor reports all day long but when she awakens it's Katy bar the door. My best option was to appease her back to sleep. And, since the phone ID again listed Unknown Caller I decided it best to answer the call and give them a piece of my mind if they spoke English.

"Hello. What in the hell do you want? It's four in the morning here in California," I grumbled, winking at my wife.

The usual automatic pause then several clicks followed before a voice spoke.

"And it's seven in the morning here in Florida. Good morning, Mr. Cross."

I had received calls at o'dark thirty before and they usually spelled trouble; the most recent came back in February when a Navy captain named Norton dragged me into a psychotic pi-day bomber's world. Although it was dangerous as hell and I almost died twice my part in solving that crime saved California from nuclear annihilation and netted me over a million dollars in pay. *Not again* I thought. Surely, it can't be as bad as the last time.

"Good morning, sir. To whom am I speaking?" I asked finally realizing it probably wasn't a telemarketer: there was no accent.

"My name is not important, Mr. Cross. My mission for you is. Do you know of my friend U.S. Navy Captain Tim Broward?"

"Yes, I do sir. I was aboard the RV/X Trident Tine under his command several months ago. Nice fellow. I really like him. The Navy did well putting him there."

"How was your experience with him?"

"I told him if I'd have been on his ship during my Navy tour, I'd probably still be in his Navy."

"Yes, Mr. Cross, that's what he said. He also told me that you're the best underwater expert he's ever seen in his long Navy career. Now I can understand your reluctance to re-up but we need your expertise again. This time in a similar capacity but with greater responsibility, more risk, and stranger circumstances."

My first instinct was to say no but it sounded mysterious. It drew me in.

"I'll need more information, sir."

"Mr. Cross, unlike your last involvement with the government this is not a civil matter. I can tell

you no more over an unsecure phone line. Do you have a scrambler line at work where we can talk?"

"Yes sir. Carlos, my boss, put one in one shortly after my last contract. He didn't like being out of the loop so he added it for future work. You can call me there later today."

"Well he was smart to do that. I have the number for MBORC. I'll call you around noon your time. Will that work?"

"Yes, it will. I look forward to your call, sir. Have a good morning."

As the unknown caller clicked off, Lindy opened an eye, looked at me, and mumbled.

"What is it now? Another one of your secret jaunts? How long are you going to be gone this time?"

It melted my heart when she asked but she was beginning to realize that I was obsessed with my work. She would always come second.

Looking into her gorgeous sleepy blue eyes pleading for an answer, I couldn't say. But I suspected for quite a while. Scrambled calls usually meant covert activities and those led to prolonged periods away from home in unmentionable locations.

I kissed her forehead gently and said, "I- I just don't know, honey. He didn't say, but he's supposed to call me back at noon today and tell me more. On the scrambled work phone."

"Well, who is *he* anyway? Jake from State Farm?"

I couldn't help but laugh at her waking sarcasm.

"No one I know, but he knew of my previous work. I guess I'm getting a reputation around the Navy as a modern-day Jacques Clouseau."

"Well goody for you Inspector but I think you mean Cousteau," she scoffed. "Anyway is it going to pay us another million dollars? We haven't even used up the last one yet. We've got a new car, a new house with a big screen TV, and new furniture. Do we really need more?" she asked with tears welling in her eyes.

"I just can't stand to have you gone, honey. I miss you so much. I'd throw it all away in a minute to have you stay home with me."

Sharing her emotion, I was up against a wall. Her words ripped at my heart. Fighting back tears myself I wondered if we really needed more money or was it just another of my self-indulgent ego trips? Of course had I told her that I saved southern California from nuclear devastation during my last 'secret jaunt' she might have understood. But I couldn't talk about it; that covert operation was hush-hush from start to finish.

"It's not just about the money, doll," I answered. "I won't accept a job unless I can help humanity: do something for our world no one else can do. Kinda like when I was in the Navy before I met you, I loved serving my country. I guess I still do."

She leaned up and kissed me.

"Well, Matt Cross, you're a good man. I guess I'll let you slide again. Just wake me up when it's over."

With that, she laid her head back on her pillow and resumed her soft snoring.

Chapter 2
Operation Deep Force

T hat morning after arriving at work, I found the news had preceded me. There on my desk was a handwritten note from my boss: Matt, see me when you arrive. It was curt: no pleasantries or anything. Just a short impersonal request. That usually meant he was pissed about something.

My walk down the long hallway to his office brought curious stares and murmured whispers from my coworkers. Everyone seemed to know but me. Wondering what I had done wrong, my mind churned but found nothing to regret. It had to be the phone call but how could they have known so fast?

His door was open so I walked in.

Looking out the window, he spun in his chair to face me.

"Come in, Matt," he said.

I loved Carlos. He was a jovial straight-laced businessman who treated his staff like family. Although he was brash, a few pounds overweight, and his thinning brown hair was over-dyed he would give us the shirt off his back if we asked.

Analyzing the tone in his voice, I relaxed realizing it was not his angry one. I sat down in the chair across the desk from him.

"What's up, boss?"

He paused, clearing his throat before speaking.

"I assume you got a call at some ungodly hour this morning as did I."

"Yes sir, I did. Caller wouldn't identify himself though."

"You know why, don't you?"

"No, not really. I've talked to a lot of navy people and they all told me *their* names."

He motioned to the hallway.

"Matt, you may have noticed a little more attention out there this morning. True?"

"Yes, I did. At first I checked my socks and then my shoes to make sure they all matched. Then I thought I might have had my shirt on inside out. I really had a guilt trip walking down here. Why is that?"

"The red phone rang ten minutes before you walked in. That's why."

"Your new secure phone line?"

"Yes, exactly. First time it's made a sound since it was installed. People rushed out into the hall to see what was happening. Thought it was a fire alarm. Turns out it has quite a distinctive ring, like a chain saw on cocaine."

That mental image tickled me. I couldn't stop chuckling but I continued, "Was the call for me?"

"No, for me. But about you," he snickered. Even he was caught up in his metaphor.

Leaning forward in my chair, I asked, "May I ask what was said?"

He paused in thought for a moment then sighed loudly and opened a small notebook from his desk.

"Matt, I've noticed a change in you since your honeymoon. Not a bad one but more of an interesting one. It's affecting your performance."

Sweat formed on my forehead and I felt my face redden with heat. Not one to accept criticism gracefully I could feel the hairs on my neck prickle.

Before I spoke, I sighed trying to control my temper.

"Yes sir, what have I done now?"

"Matt, you've been with us what... six years now?"

"That's about right."

"You came to us as a tenderfoot straight from the Navy. Back then, I wondered several times if we should keep you on. You plodded along following orders as well as you could but not much more."

I nodded grimacing ready for the next shoe to drop.

"Matt, calm down. I'm just getting started here," he said glinting a smile.

"Yes sir." More relaxed, feigning a grin, I armed my defenses. Carlos was a man of few words who usually saved them for reprimands.

"Now since your marriage last year you've given us nothing but stellar performances. You've just suddenly gotten smarter. Why is that? Have you been taking online courses? Attending college somewhere? If so I need to know for your promotion file"

"No, just wising up I guess but Lindy's gonna love your compliment. Knowing her she'll swear she did it herself," I said chuckling so forcefully my breath rolled a pencil across his desk. I was glad the tone of the meeting had changed; I was ready to walk out.

Smiling, he carefully moved the pencil back into place.

"The bravery and persistence you exhibited during the Fogner case brought nothing but praise from everyone you worked with in the Navy. Everyone! Even the Orange County Sheriff's Office couldn't say enough good things about your expertise in solving that heinous crime. Of course the DHS said you were worth every penny of their two-million dollar contract."

"Thank you for sharing that Carlos, but what does all this have to do with the chain-saw phone call?" As usual, my impatience got the best of me. Sometimes my words just came out unfiltered and I hated it.

"In due time, Matt," he said holding up a hand. "Now as I was saying you're rising in the company and bringing us more business with your work so I want to reward you for that. As of today I'm promoting you to Technical Vice President of MBORC a prestigious title with lots of responsibilities."

He reached into a drawer then handed me a short stack of business cards reading Matthew M. Cross, Technical VP, Mid-Bay Ocean Research Corporation, Moss Landing, CA 95039.

"How's that for a promotion?"

Blushing with humility I answered, "Well thank you sir. I'm overly honored. And yes I'll accept your offer." Even though I had just accepted I knew there was more. He just hadn't reached that part yet.

"Of course you'll get a fifty percent pay raise but I don't really expect that you'll need it."

"Oh? How's that sir?"

"Matt, you've just broken into the black ops community. Congratulations on that. There are tons of unaccountable Government money there."

"Really? I don't understand."

He glanced at his notebook.

"That scrambled call was from a Vice Admiral Sam Greenfield. I'd never heard of him."

Shaking my head, I agreed, "Me neither."

"Anyway he called from a U.S. Government agency: a black ops group. They can't identify themselves because they don't exist. In fact, in his group *he* doesn't exist. I'm not even sure his real name's Greenfield."

"I've been around that once before. During my SeaCrawler dives at Point Mugu I remember a location deep in the Pacific they called Poseidon's Palace. We were told it didn't exist. Must have been a black-ops thing. You think?"

"Well, Matt, you know that we deal with all kinds of government agencies and corporations in our marine salvage and recovery work. I've always assumed many were black ops agencies operating under commercial cover. That's the way the undersea world is: you don't know anything's down there until you bump into it and they don't want to be bumped into."

"Never thought of it that way but you're right."

Fidgeting the rolling pencil he continued, "I'm not going to lie to you Matt; they need your help with an incident... a big incident. He called me to okay your involvement with them. Faxed me a classified request for proposal too."

"What did you tell them?"

"I said okay. Then he told me if I would create a salvage contract for them he'd sign and accept it."

"Salvage? That's just a glorified trash collector job. Why would they need me for that?"

"It's a cover contract, Matt. Understand?"

His body language intimidated me. He sat up straight in his chair and glared into my eyes.

"Any more details?" I asked, not sure if I liked being a bargaining pawn.

"The contract's for 6.5 million dollars. They're hand delivering it today. They need you now, Matt."

I gulped loudly wondering what I was getting into.

"They've just performed an in-depth background security check on you which you passed with flying colors."

"I have noticed some back-suited men visiting my neighborhood over the past week. Is that what they were doing?"

"Yes probably."

"Without my permission?" I asked. I sat with my arms folded, feeling as if I had been betrayed. I hated when things involved me behind my back.

"Yes, Matt, that's the way they do it. Surprise visits so you can't warn anyone."

"Well that's just bullshit, Carlos!" Feeling that my privacy had been invaded I stood and paced in front of Carlos' desk.

His eyes widened at my anger.

"Now calm down, Matt. Sit," he said. "As our new Tech VP you'll need that security clearance. Almost every manmade object deeper than a thousand feet is classified one way or another.

Unless it's a wreck and then it could still be classified."

At his insistence, I sat back in the chair still smoldering.

"Well, I had a clearance in the Fogner case. Lived in secrecy for weeks aboard the Trident Tine. What happened to that?"

"That was a low-level Secret clearance Matt. Remember you're moving into the big time now with the black ops missions. Greenfield told me you're required to have a TSCW clearance for this mission."

"What's TSCW?"

"It means a Top Secret Code Word clearance specific to this mission."

"Did he say what the code word or mission was?"

"Only that the mission is called Operation Deep Force nothing more. My clearance doesn't extend into the black world yet so he couldn't tell me what the code word is or what you'll be doing."

I rubbed my eyes thinking it was too early. I must be dreaming. It was all beyond my comprehension so early in the morning.

"Oh, and he said the contracting company is called the Poseidon Corporation. Still interested?"

Stunned, my mind tried to absorb the information it heard. Usually bigger money meant a greater risk and mystery and there was that word again: 'Poseidon.' The word slammed my thoughts back to my Navy days at Point Mugu dodging Poseidon's Palace in the ocean depths talking around it rather than about it as if it didn't exist. Could it possibly be the same entity? It had been

11

over ten years since I last heard that name and it still sent chills up my spine.

Before I could answer, the towering eucalyptus trees out his office window began to blow wildly in a whirlwind like pompoms in a cheerleader's hand. Gradually a low rumble vibrated the room softly at first and then more violently as the landing gear and fuselage of a VTOL aircraft appeared through the window descending drifting down to the open field outside.

"That will be our contract," he said calmly. Turning to watch its props wind down he frowned.

"They sent another tilt-rotor craft just like the one that brought you back from the Trident Tine. Gotta repair that damn ball field again."

I had moved to the window and was standing beside him when I noticed a familiar sight. Carlos was right. It was an Osprey tilt-rotor aircraft like the one from before. Then I realized the tail number was the same: N0099. On further examination, I saw a familiar face staring out from the cockpit. It was Lt. Bill Harper the Navy pilot from that trip.

Recognizing him, I exclaimed, "My God that's Harper! It is the same plane and pilot as before. From the Tine. Wonder if he's still flying out from there."

Carlos stood and walked out into the hallway.

"Let's go find out. Follow me," he said.

Having to double step to keep up I wound several paces behind him through the halls toward the entrance. Ignoring the chain-saw catcalls that came from the offices we passed I knew my friends and coworkers were just razzing me. It was a ritual at MBORC to ruffle the feathers of anyone newly placed in the spotlight so it came as no surprise. I had done the same for most of them when they won or successfully completed contracts. This was my second time in the spotlight and it was growing on me.

Chapter 3
Rendezvous

We met them on the entrance steps before they entered our building. My old friend Bill Harper was the first to approach and extend his hand. I shook with him and noticed the shiny gold oak leaf clusters gracing his shoulders.

"Hey Bill, good to see you again," I said. "Congratulations, Lieutenant Commander, on the promotion."

Grinning from eye to eye he replied, "Thanks, Matt. Great to see you too. How've you been? Obviously busy."

Even though we were reuniting after only three months, it seemed like years since we together faced imminent death but by the grace of God lived through it. Those terrifying memories were bittersweet and reminded me that my tasks were often life threatening but controllably so. I lived for the excitement of days like that but I could never tell when they were coming. I expected this was one of those days.

"Yeah, I guess. Simple jobs but still busy."

Motioning back, I added, "I was just promoted to Tech VP of MBORC today after all this time. Guess we did good huh? But I'm not really sure if the promotion's for what I did or what I'm about to do."

He answered with a wink and chuckle.

"It's amazing what we have to do for a promotion isn't ---"

Carlos pulled on my sleeve dragging my attention to the two-star naval officer standing behind me.

"Admiral Greenfield, meet Matt Cross."

He was everything I expected in a high-ranking naval officer: tall, graying hair and beard, meticulous in his appearance and almost a spitting image of Sean Connery. As a commercial once said his dress whites were whiter than white. All that I needed was to hear him speak with a Russian accent completing my image of Captain Marco Ramius, commander of the Red October hunted by the USS Dallas in my favorite book.

"Good morning, sir. My pleasure," I said starting to salute. Then I caught myself and redirected my hand toward him for a handshake trying not to appear too obvious. The Navy routine I had recently endured rushed back to me attempting to change my civilian reflexes. I had a feeling it would become an even greater influence in the upcoming mission back aboard another naval ship or whatever vessel Operation Deep Force involved.

He shifted his briefcase to his left hand, shook my hand, and looked me over.

"Hello, Mr. Cross. So you're the genius diver that left our Navy and then outplayed us on that pi-day scenario. It's truly a delight to meet such a naval-minded civilian."

His comment confused me not knowing if it was a compliment or sarcasm. I did know that I detected a slight northeastern U.S. accent probably from Massachusetts or somewhere nearby and his was the voice on the phone from my early morning call.

Carlos laughed trying to break the awkward silence.

"Well Admiral, we have him now and I just promoted him within our organization. He's now a VP."

Frowning, the Admiral darted his attention to him.

"Now, Mr. Montoya, does that mean that he can no longer get his hands dirty with our work?"

"Oh of course not, Admiral. It means he now has to get every part of his body dirty," he scoffed.

Greenfield lifted his mood showing a sly smile.

"Good that's what I want to hear." Then looking back my way he said, "Well then, let's get down to business. Carlos, lead the way."

Standing with us Harper begged off the meeting excusing himself for some time on the beach.

"Gonna catch some rays and maybe a few seashells gentlemen. When you need me, Admiral, just buzz."

Greenfield nodded his consent as Harper saluted and walked away.

Meandering up the stairs and down the hall toward the conference room, I kept thinking *Why is the Admiral here now? He was supposed to call me at noon on the secure phone.* My lack of filtering reared its ugly head again but I couldn't help it.

"Admiral, you said on the phone this morning that you would call me at noon. Has something changed since then? I mean you're here in

California now and you were in Florida when you called right?"

He stopped and turned to me. With fiery eyes, he growled back.

"Now mister do you think I just flew over two-thousand miles across country in the back seat of a goddamned F-4 Phantom fighter jet at twice the speed of sound then suffered another hour on that damn vibrating whirly-bird out there just to save a phone call? Hell yes things have changed!"

Obviously, I had touched a nerve. I could almost see steam coming from his ears so I retreated hoping this was not a harbinger of things to come.

"Sorry, Admiral. I misspoke." I felt ten inches tall after his lambasting, wanting to disappear into a passing room as he turned and continued behind Carlos. Thinking *just a few more minutes and he'll sign the contract and be gone* I carried on waiting for his pen to mark the paper.

The conference room was dark, quiet, and cluttered with the last meeting's remnants: coffee cups, stirrers, and candy wrappers.

After we entered, Carlos set about clearing the table with a speed I had never seen before. The Admiral looked over at me and nodded toward him as if urging me to help. Unfortunately, I moved too slowly.

"C'mon, Matt, get your ass over here and help me out," he yelled. "Nobody around here cleans up after themselves anymore. You'd think my staff of genius scientists could pick up their own trash. After this I'm putting up a big damn sign in here that says 'your mother doesn't work here.'"

A chuckle from the front of the room reminded me that the Admiral was still waiting patiently watching our cleaning party. I thought it funny that my boss was so intent on cleaning the table ignoring the Admiral when we could have just used the uncluttered end to seal the contract. There were plenty of chairs for that and they were all clean.

"Now, Matt, for example look at that: a Payday wrapper," Carlos snapped. "I know you're the only one on our staff who eats Payday bars. Pick it up!"

As I swiped the wrapper and a nearby Styrofoam cup from the table, the Admiral spoke breaking his cleaning frenzy.

"Excuse me, gentlemen," he said. "I've been on planes, more planes, and automobiles without a head for hours. Can one of you please point me to the nearest one?"

Obliging his request, I walked into the hall and directed him two doors down to the right. Normally our visitors didn't carry their briefcases with them into the restrooms but he did. I wondered why.

Stepping away, he turned back to me.

"Oh Mr. Cross, would you mind having coffee served when I return? The flight attendant services in our Navy planes suck especially in fighter jets. I need some caffeine."

Smiling I returned to Carlos and relayed his request.

"Well get on it, VP Cross," he said to me. "You're now on a fast track to fame and fortune. Might as well work for it."

His tone of voice confused me; it didn't make sense that he would put me in this position then begrudge me the honor. Maybe he had been pressured to put me there. Maybe he was expanding the chain of command at someone's request and felt bitter. On the other hand, maybe he was just having a bad day. I couldn't tell. I let it pass and called his secretary for a pot of fresh coffee.

Chapter 4
Devil's in the Details

Admiral Greenfield returned to a spic-and-span conference room while we sat waiting as if nothing had happened.

"Coffee's coming," I said.

He smiled and sat beside me, then opened his briefcase and pulled out a cell phone.

"Got to check my messages. Excuse me a moment."

Five minutes later, having cleared his message queue he discussed his trip with us but avoided contract details waiting for the coffee to arrive. Soon Suzie entered with a coffee service, placed it on the table, and handed Carlos a manila folder.

"Here's the proposal with the emergency RFP mods submitted earlier by Admiral Greenfield's group."

"Let's get down to business," Greenfield barked. "I have a five o'clock tee time back in Florida with my boss at SOCOM. He'll want to know what happened here."

Carlos pulled the contract from the folder. By our standards it was thin probably only ten or fifteen pages. I had seen thicker ones for salvaging civilian wrecks for much less cost.

"Well, Admiral," he said, "it's quite unusual to have such a short turnaround time on a request for proposal but I think I've adequately covered your needs and the mods your office submitted from Florida this morning. It should be to your liking."

Sliding metal-rimmed reading glasses from his coat pocket, he took the contract and flipped to the last page.

"Eight million dollars!"

He recoiled then settled back in his seat paging to the Technical Objectives section.

"Hmm." Then came another "Hmm." Checking my watch, I noticed he continued for four minutes turning pages in between his almost irritating hums. Since I had never seen it but was told it was a dummy salvage contract, I was more than curious what all the humming was about.

"Well, it seems to be all here, Mr. Montoya, but why has the cost risen? It's not what we originally discussed."

"With all due respect, Admiral, the letters QRT in your RFP mods did that. Putting Mr. Cross on your quick response team will cost me lots of money; it means he will have to be replaced on his current contracts and then we will also lose his valuable expertise promoting new jobs."

My suspicions were being confirmed about my bargaining pawn status and I wasn't too pleased.

"How fast is the quick response?" I inquired afraid to hear the answer. "I mean when do I start?"

Carlos glanced at the Admiral and nodded then stared back at me.

"There is a dire emergency with an undersea government installation which needs your assistance now, Matt," he said. "They need you to travel out on the Osprey today to an undisclosed location and begin working your deep-sea miracles now."

Choking on the coffee I had just sipped I still managed to respond.

"Today? Now?" I asked, trying to remain rational. Rather than throwing a tantrum, as I wanted to do I bit my tongue and decided to talk it out.

"Now Carlos, Admiral Greenfield, I admit that I'm a driven man but this is ridiculous. I mean I need to tell my wife. I don't have clothes for a trip, not even a toothbrush. I---"

Greenfield held up his hand halting my objections.

"That is all taken care of, Mr. Cross," he said. "You will be given everything you need for up to a month's existence in our facility where you will live, work, and attempt to solve our crisis all at a thousand meters below the surface. As for your other concern, Mr. Cross, I'll personally call your wife on my flight back to Florida."

I was livid at not having been told beforehand that this was in the works but I had a feeling Greenfield was as surprised as I was at the new urgency. Besides calming my anger, the details of the task sounded interesting to me. I couldn't help it. What self-respecting deep-sea oceanographer would turn down an offer to live in an undersea habitat for a month? I had visions of a deep-sea space station and I would be an aquanaut living there: surely the height of my career.

"What's this facility called? Maybe I've heard of it," I asked.

The Admiral cleared his throat and sipped coffee.

"I highly doubt it but the onboard crew calls it Discovery One in honor of Stanley Kubrick's 2001 spacecraft; its code name is Sea Station Umbra. Heard of that?"

I thought back racking my brain for any association to the name but there was nothing.

"No, sir can't say that I have," I answered, "but it sounds interesting." I knew I'd hate myself in the morning for saying that but it just came out unfiltered as usual.

"What else can you tell me, Admiral?" I asked pressing further.

He looked at Carlos then slid the contract in front of him, took a pen from his breast pocket and signed it.

"We'll discuss that on the plane, Mr. Cross, since Carlos doesn't have the necessary clearance. I am duty bound though to tell you that only one-hundred individuals on this planet know of its existence and of those, only thirty six know why it's there and what it does. You, Mr. Cross, will be number thirty seven."

"I'll assume everything that I'm hearing is Top Secret and handle it accordingly," Carlos offered.

"That'd be a good assessment, Mr. Montoya. Going further into the description will require SCI codeword clearances. Matt now has those and will learn more of the mission later today."

He poured himself another cup and pulled out a bank's checkbook ledger from his case. His pen was soon upon a blank check; his hand writing a number with many zeroes.

Ignoring the number but noticing the embossed Poseidon Corporation letters on the check's header I was taken back again into unwelcome thoughts.

Caught in the path of a downhill rolling boulder with my curiosity and ego urging it along I knew I was going to do this and enjoy it too. Lindy was right: I was hopelessly engrossed in my work always leaving her second in line but neither of us had foreseen the urgency of this new mission and my orders for immediate deployment. Sharing my 'thrill of the chase' as she called it, she had often displayed the same fervor in her television reporting assignments but we had never left each other without saying goodbye and kissing for good luck. This would be the first time. Could I survive the guilt much less the danger of the mission? I had to try.

Then my guilt crept deeper. Just last month, I had promised her that we would be vacationing in Big Bear with the Briscoes in June but that plan was now on hold. *Maybe a Fourth of July holiday trip* I thought, appeasing my derelict conscience but still seeking a concrete justification. It came seconds later.

"Here's the binder, Carlos, four million dollars," Greenfield said holding out a check. "The balance will be paid on your successful completion of the contract."

With a noticeably trembling hand, Carlos took the check and called out the door.

"Suzie, come in here please."

I suspected from his reaction it was the largest lump-sum payment he had ever received. He tried to act nonchalant at the amount but failed miserably: I could see his excitement from the sweat forming on his forehead and his jittery hands.

She appeared within seconds.

"What is it, Mr. Montoya?"

"Please place this in my safe. Top shelf."

"Yes sir."

She took the check, glanced at it, and mouthed "Wow!" on the way out. Seconds later, I overheard a commotion coming from her desk: quiet cheers with muted whoops.

Abruptly the Admiral called Harper on his cell phone dropped it into his briefcase and closed it taking it from the table.

Standing he said, "I assume that completes our transaction today, Mr. Montoya. With your consent I'll be leaving now and taking Mr. Cross with me."

It was time. Precursors leading up to this point had just been talk. Now I found myself a kidnapping victim for an eight-million-dollar ransom. Against my will, I forced myself to rise and join the Admiral in the conference room doorway.

"Let me see you out. Need to hit the head before you leave?" Carlos asked looking at both of us.

"Yes think I will," Greenfield replied. "Those fighter maneuvers combat or not are hell on my bladder. Mr. Cross, your trip on the Osprey will be much shorter. Come if you'd like."

I stayed behind to thank my boss for his confidence in my work. He wished me well and stood silently waiting for the Admiral to return. I couldn't help but notice the twinkle in his eyes and broad smile that had fallen over his face since the contract was signed. For the first time in my six-year career at MBORC, I felt important and needed. I knew I would prove him right for promoting me to VP.

"Ready, Mr. Cross?"

"Yes, Admiral, but you can call me Matt."

"Fine, Matt, and you can still call me Admiral."

I laughed at his wit as we descended the steps from the entrance leaving Carlos waving alone in the doorway.

Chapter 5
Trip to Nowhere

Our emergence from the building triggered the Osprey's engines into action. Looking over at the whining turbines, I saw Harper gazing out of his cockpit window give us a thumbs-up and return to the controls. Seconds later the twin upright rotors began to spin accompanied by a low rumble from the Osprey's turbines. Then the eucalyptus trees began a frenzied cyclonic swaying surrounded by swirling dust.

Moving double-time we crossed the grassy field to the waiting aircraft in no time. There at the top of the stairway Harper motioned us in, helped us up the steps, and then slammed the door behind us with a solid kerchunk. Bending over to catch my breath I realized I needed more exercise.

"Welcome back aboard, Matt. Long time no fly huh?" he said laughing at my condition.

"Not long enough," I panted watching the Admiral buckle himself into the front jump seat of the otherwise empty cabin.

"Where are you taking me today, Bill? Back to the Trident Tine?"

"I'm still based out of there Matt but that's not where you're headed. You'll have to ask the Admiral for that information. I'll talk with you after we land."

"May I sit by you, sir?"

"Yes, young man, and please give me your cell phone," he answered holding out his hand.

I glared at him.

"What? You want my cell phone? Nobody takes that. It's my lifeline."

"Sorry, Matt. Tracking apps can give your position away. I need to seal it off in a Faraday cage until your mission is completed and you're back home. Then you'll have it back."

I looked at his hand insisting waiting for my phone.

"I won't lose any contacts in it will I?"

"No, Matt, it'll just go off the grid so to speak while you're away. No harm will come to it. Besides it won't work at a thousand meters down will it?"

He was right but turning over my phone was like cutting off an arm. Reluctantly I reached into my pocket, turned it off, and gave it to him.

"Take care of it please," I said.

Chuckling he took it and looked up at me.

"You kids are really obsessed with your phones aren't you?"

"No offense meant, sir, but I noticed the first thing you did when you landed was check the messages on *your* phone. Seems like we're all addicted to the real-time communications they afford us with the world."

Smiling he replied, "I suppose you're right, Matt. But since I keep mine locked away in a Faraday shield in my briefcase it only comes online when it's removed. And then it gives away my location so I still have to be careful when and where I use it."

I nodded agreement and realized my world was changing to one of spies, espionage, and mystery.

That made me feel a little queasy but a job was a job no matter the surroundings.

Interrupting our conversation, Harper's voice boomed over the intercom.

"Welcome aboard my ship, gentlemen. Your flight today will be smooth as we'll be traveling at ten-thousand feet through calm air with a light breeze off the ocean. Our first stop is scheduled in fifty-seven minutes. Please fasten your seat belts and acquaint yourself with our emergency procedures in your seat."

After his message ended, the Admiral smiled and nodded forward.

"You know him pretty well, Mr. Cross?"

"Yes sir, we worked together for a few weeks months ago. Why do you ask?"

Smiling he replied, "Just wondering if he's a wannabe commercial airline pilot. Sounds like it. I think he missed his calling."

His comment sparked anger in me as I remembered Harper's heroic actions: hauling two ready-to-explode nuclear warheads to the edge of international waters then dropping the last one, only minutes before it would explode.

"No sir. I think he's one of the Navy's bravest and finest fliers. If I remember right he just received the Presidential Medal of Honor for his bravery. Quite a guy."

"Oh? Sorry. Then I must get to know him better. We can always use men like that on our ops teams. What is his name again?"

"Harper, Bill Harper, Lieutenant Commander, U.S. Navy. He flies off the R/VX Trident Tine under the command of Captain Broward. You spoke of him earlier."

"Oh, but of course. He and his ship have been of great help on many of our missions. In fact some of them would have most certainly failed without his assistance."

"Is Captain Broward involved in this mission? I'd like to see him again."

"No Matt, not that he knows. He does have an ancillary function but you'll never see him or the Tine. We often use his AUVs, ROVs and other assets to assist our underwater teams but he doesn't know who he's helping; he just follows orders. Just like Harper's involvement today. He's an air-taxi because he was available and in your area."

"Too bad," I said. "I really like the Captain."

"Oh for your information he just made Rear Admiral in April. Saved our coast from a crazed terrorist in a secret undersea operation of some sort."

"Yeah, I know of that. Felt like I was there." I could have told him more but instead kept it short; we were about to take off.

While we spoke, outside our windows the rotors spun up to full speed, the turbines' rumble increased to an ear-piercing whine and we lifted off. Minutes later as we reached altitude, the rotors tilted forward and we headed south with the Pacific out our right windows. I had yet to learn my destination but I was guessing somewhere south of us about an hour away. And, knowing the Osprey's operational flying speed was three-hundred miles per hour it sounded near the NAS Point Mugu area.

But I brushed that off as highly improbable; the Point Mugu Naval Air Station had been decommissioned long ago.

There had been no further conversation between us since the Admiral opened his briefcase and started reviewing paperwork but I could see the words Operation Deep Force at the top of each page. As my eye caught a few words of the smaller print below the heading, my curiosity drew me closer wanting to read more until he caught me looking over his shoulder.

"Well, Mr. Cross, you may be better at this job than we originally thought. What did you just gain from your visual eavesdropping on my papers?"

I blushed at being discovered; I could feel it in my face. Not expecting a confrontation from my wandering gaze, I sputtered and stammered trying to give him the answer he wanted.

Then realizing it was a leading question I finally answered, "I- I didn't see much, sir, but enough to know it's time for my security briefing on what I'm about to see and hear. And you're going to give it to me now."

He backed off smiling apparently surprised and said, "Well done, Matt. You're very good. That will make it easier for me. Let's do it."

For the next fifteen minutes of my trip to nowhere, the Admiral read rules and related anecdotes and caveats from the black ops security world. I had been granted a Secret clearance a year after joining MBORC and that was adequate for the jobs I did then but this was different. I was moving into Top Secret Codeword work and the codeword was Umbra. My ultimate destination was a government facility known as Sea Station Umbra, a thousand meters below the North Pacific's surface. I was about to embark on a journey traveling on a path that didn't exist, working for people without names, and if they were ever asked about me, *I* didn't exist. In my past jobs, my wife Lindy always called me Mr. Bond, James Bond because of my love for mystery and intrigue. If only she could see me now.

"We'll be landing in a few minutes at NAS Point Mugu," he said. "Your indoctrination and update on our problem will occur there before I depart for Florida."

A cold fear washed over me.

"Naval Air Station Point Mugu?" I asked. "I thought that place was deactivated years ago."

"Matt, you're now joining that one-hundred person group on earth that knows of its existence. In a short while, you will be a member of the elite thirty-six; you'll make it thirty-seven who know the rest of the story. Remember this is the black world: nothing is as it seems."

I must have turned white as a ghost but there was no mirror available to check. His disclosure whisked me back seven years to the SeaCrawler chapter of my life. Could it be the same group still exists? Why would they need my help? At that time, they were the best divers and DSV experts in the Navy. What changed?

My thoughts were interrupted by the turbines' lowering pitch. Out my window was the familiar sight of the long Point Mugu Runway 3/21 almost touching the ocean. At the far end, a Navy F4

Phantom jet waited on the tarmac just off the taxiway.

"That must be your ride home off Runway 21," I said.

He peered out the window following my gaze.

"Yes that would be Captain Minor and his F4 waiting to fly me back to Florida. I told him I'd be ready for takeoff about one p.m. That gives us only an hour to wrap things up."

My heart raced anticipating sights that would bring fond memories of my time in the Navy back to life.

Searching the terrain below, I immediately recognized my old SeaCrawler hangout but it was dark and deserted. The parking lot adjacent to the building once filled with sports cars of all types: Corvettes, Ferraris, Porsches and Mercedes roadsters stood empty devoid of life. I remembered back when the contents of our parking lot was said to be more expensive than many buildings on base. And, in thinking back that may have been true.

We were a wild bunch that worked hard partied even harder and bought expensive sports cars living life to the fullest like there was no tomorrow. But, since nobody on base knew what we did we became known as the Ghost Squadron; we were never there but always searching under the sea for our next catch.

"If you look over there, Matt you'll see an old rundown tin-roof Quonset hut. That's where we're going."

Following his finger pointing to a building that belonged in the front of a junk yard I tried to act impressed.

"Oh that's interesting," I said. I did notice a number of strange antenna structures and dishes surrounding it but they seemed to blend in with the scrap material surrounding the building.

He laughed.

"Don't be so gullible, Matt. It looks like shit and that's the way it's supposed to look. Is that what you would expect to be the headquarters of one of the most advanced undersea endeavors in our Navy?"

Bewildered but catching on I shook my head.

"No sir. I would probably think that was an old maintenance shed or even lawnmower storage facility... except for all the antennas."

"Good. The building's cover works well. Inside is a wonderland of electronic storage and decoding equipment and some of the most powerful computers in existence. We're rather proud of it; you'll see why in a few moments. It doesn't even have a name it's just called the 'building.' Now remember this is all under the Top Secret Umbra cloak; never speak of it outside our circles."

Just then from the cockpit came Harper's voice.

"Mugu tower Osprey N0099 on approach. I'm a VTOL so I don't need much room. Please assign landing pad. Touchdown expected in two minutes."

The radio crackled a reply.

"Osprey N99, Mugu tower, please proceed to the same helipad you used this morning. No traffic expected there for two hours. Tell the Admiral a Navy Staff car will pick him up."

"Roger, tower. Just dropping him off. I'll be flying out in ten minutes. We're on final approach now. Hold onto your hats. N99 out."

Having flown on the Osprey numerous times, I was prepared for the turbines' rotation to vertical producing a weird braking sensation in midair but the Admiral wasn't. Only his second landing, he told me, he wasn't yet accustomed to flying in a 'Transformer' aircraft as he called it. Being old school, he preferred the Huey and Sikorsky fixed-rotor craft. "There is nothing stranger than riding for an hour on a plane at three-hundred miles per hour," he had said, "and then have it change shape and just stop in midair hovering on a giant cushion of air."

"I'll never get used to this," he muttered. "It's not Navy, just PFM. That's what it is."

"PFM?" I asked expecting another black world reference.

He looked at me frowning.

"You haven't heard of PFM before?"

"No sir. Can't say that I have. I'm guessing it's a highly classified acronym. True?"

Guffawing he answered.

"No it's not, Mr. Cross, although you may run across it in your new Black Ops mission with us. An important term for your vocabulary it's 'Pure Fricking Magic' and that's the R rated version. It's when some effect, action, or process is seemingly inexplicable."

I felt like an idiot not knowing that.

"Oh yeah. That PFM. Thought there might be another one."

His obvious eye roll and smirk told me that he didn't buy it.

Soon clouds of dust and debris rushed over us as we touched down and Harper killed the engines.

"Harper, let's wait inside until the dust settles," he called to the front.

"Yes sir," the voice from the cockpit answered barely audible over the rotors' spin-down.

Outside on the tarmac a dark blue sedan with a U.S. Navy insignia on the door awaited our arrival. Nearby a uniformed driver standing in the bright noonday sun waited, holding his cap with one hand and inspecting his cell phone with the other.

Moments later Harper unlatched and opened the door then dropped the steps to the tarmac.

"Ready for some fun, Mr. Cross?" Greenfield asked.

He unbuckled his harness, grabbed his briefcase, and started for the door. I was right behind him feeling like a stranger in a strange land but since it had been my home for four years, I thought I might still recognize a few landmarks.

As I exited the plane, stepping down onto the top step, I felt Harper's hand on my shoulder and stopped.

"I don't know where you're going," he said, "or what you'll be doing, Marker, but knock 'em dead. I'll be heading out now back to the Tine. Take care."

I hadn't been called that nickname since March when I had the pleasure of working with him and my old Navy diving instructor Chief Briscoe. The Chief always called me that. Must have rubbed off on Harper but since we had risked our lives together and we became brothers in arms doing so he had a right to call me that.

"Thanks for the ride, Bill," I said saluting him. Even though I wasn't in uniform or the Navy for that matter I had such great respect for him that I thought it appropriate. He must have thought the same: he returned my salute.

Greenfield waiting at the bottom of the stairs yelled back to me.

"Come on, Cross, we've got work to do. Important work." Then I saw him glance at his watch and head toward the waiting staff car.

His orders were sharp and compelling. Not sure if it was the tone of his voice or his way with words that intimidated me but I quick-stepped down the stairs and joined him just as the driver opened the doors for our entry.

He fell into the seat beside me, looked at the driver, and then barked:

"Hangar 405. Drop us in back."

I glanced over at him curious about our new destination. It was not the 'building' because I knew where 405 was: across the main drag from the 'building.' Wanting to comment on his mistake my filter finally kicked in. Instead, I sat quietly waiting to see what would happen next remembering his words: "Nothing is as it seems."

Now during my tour on the Navy Hangar 405 was a semi-active hangar, used for sheltering and maintaining the few aircraft that still used the active runways. It was a type II hangar roughly a football field wide and a hundred feet deep. Two main rail-mounted doors each eighty feet across opened in the middle yielding a gaping one-hundred-sixty-foot entryway large enough for a C-130. An average Navy hangar; there was nothing spooky going on inside to my knowledge.

The trip from our landing pad to the rear of Hangar 405 took only a few minutes but in that time I saw many familiar buildings mostly boarded up or barricaded. Exactly what I expected but depressing as hell. So was the rear of Hangar 405.

Chapter 6
Hangar 405

I found it strange that we had stopped at a small man-sized door at the rear of the hangar. A red sign on the door read: **DANGER: ELECTRICAL ROOM - KEEP OUT!**. As we stepped from the car, Greenfield motioned the driver to drive away leaving us standing alone in the dingy littered alleyway behind the hangar. He led me to the door and stopped.

Behind it was a room slightly larger than a telephone booth extending out from the hangar's rear wall. It had never caught my attention in my four years on station but then I never used the alleys for travel. Off to the side of the door at shoulder level was a gray Cutler-Hammer breaker box looking weathered by years of salt sea air exposure. My eyes went wide when Greenfield quickly surveyed our surroundings and pulled open the cover revealing a sleek black numerical keypad. Then quickly he punched in a few numbers and closed the cover. After a soft buzz from the box, he hefted open the door.

"After you," he said.

Inside, gray electrical panels surrounded us from floor to ceiling crowding us together. The warm air smelled of ozone and sintered metal. In the silence, I could hear buzzes and clicks behind the banks of breaker and relay boxes.

The Admiral carefully surveyed the panels as I watched then began counting from the rightmost panel three boxes to the left and up three from the floor. His finger landed on a panel shoulder high that mimicked the others even to the finger-hole opening latch. He pushed his finger through and pulled it open.

Rather than breaker switches inside, it had a single gray metal panel with a small speaker a numerical keypad and an optical sensor resembling a large bloodshot eyeball with a glowing red center. Suddenly I wanted to say, "Open the pod bay door, Hal" but resisted not knowing the Admiral's familiarity with that movie.

"Look into the red scanner with your right eye," he commanded reaching for the key panel.

I bent down and looked into the device expecting a bright flash or something more mysterious. Nothing happened until I felt his wrist graze my face punching numbers into the keypad.

"There," he said, "Now back off and let me get there."

He nudged me aside and stared into the sensor eye.

"Ivy, this is Admiral Sam Greenfield, ID number SSUSJG22Z. Register previous scan as authorized entry for Umbra."

A sexy and slightly robotic female voice responded from the small speaker:

"As you wish, Admiral Greenfield. Please log voice recognition entry for the previous scan."

During her response, I noticed the red eye began to dim and brighten with a slow rhythmic almost hypnotic motion. Then I noticed it was synchronized with my breathing. When I drew in air, it brightened then dimmed as I exhaled. Ivy was tracking my respiration activity.

I continued to stare in curious almost frightened amazement as the intricate login process continued not knowing what was yet to come.

"Stand here and say 'Hello, Ivy' in your normal voice," he said then moved me to the center of the panel and pressed a few more keys.

"Hello, Ivy," I said.

"Hello. Please state your full name with rank or civilian status," she requested.

I looked questioningly at the Admiral and he nodded for me to continue.

"Matthew Marker Cross, civilian," I said.

"Admiral Greenfield, what clearance level of Umbra access should I grant for Matthew Cross?"

He closed his eyes for a moment then responded, "Umbra Z."

"Understood. Matthew Marker Cross civilian rank will now have Z-access privileges to the building and Sea Station Umbra. His assigned ID is SSU-MMC-37Z. Please claim his badge at the building's main desk."

"Thank you, Ivy," he said then looked at me. "Got that, Cross? Your project ID is SSUMMC37Z. Memorize it. Do not ever write it down. That ID or your voiceprint will allow you access to anything Umbra after I'm gone."

I nodded my understanding wanting to ask questions but they could wait; I now had access to something unknown to me, an enigma in my orderly world. I could get in but into what?

Greenfield redirected his attention to the panel.

"Now unlock the passageway for two personnel: me and Mr. Cross."

"The tunnel is now unlocked, Admiral Greenfield. Please watch your step. Ivy out."

With that, he closed the ID panel turned to the next wall of breaker panels and pulled a small handle at the top. To my amazement, the entire wall pivoted out toward us like a door revealing a steep concrete stairwell into a poorly lighted space below.

"Down here," he said. "Careful. There's a handrail on your right."

Chapter 7
The 'Building'

Two minutes had passed when we exited the long dimly lit tunnel and stepped into a large busy room. Brightly lighted by rows of overhead fluorescents it was obviously below ground level because there had been no 'up' stairwell. The room was large about the size of the Quonset hut above us by my estimation. It resembled a fallout basement constructed of white-washed cinder block walls and at the far end was another stairwell apparently to the upper level of the 'building.'

My eyes had to adapt before I realized the walls were plastered with Fukushima Disaster posters: one showed a glowing trefoil radioactivity symbol centered over a map of Fukushima while another stated in large letters: JAPAN – IT'S OUR PROBLEM NOW then on yet another a green glowing cow spoke in a surrounding bubble text: "Got Radiation?" I had to stop reading before I laughed inappropriately.

On the broad wall at the end of the room was a giant map of the Pacific Ocean between Japan and the U.S. showing winding flat-colored balloon-shaped regions approaching our western shores. The posters and the lack of windows gave me an uncomfortable feeling but I had never been claustrophobic before. It must have been the cold penetrating silence of the room. I estimated twenty uniformed and street-clothed workers sitting quietly under the posters scanning data screens at computer workstations not noticing our entry.

As I followed him through the room, passing desk after desk of what appeared to be data analysts staring at screens of rapidly scrolling data, several of them looked up, acknowledged the Admiral, and then returned to their data. Approaching the stairs he motioned me upward so I followed the steps leading to the top floor.

At the top of the stairwell, a closed door awaited me. A large sign: Z ACCESS ONLY PAST THIS POINT blocked my progress.

"You know what to do now, Mr. Cross. There's Ivy."

Like a deer caught in oncoming headlights, I froze and looked back at him. He pointed to the glowing lens on the right side of the door.

"There. Look into her eye and make her swoon."

Attempting humor, I looked into the lens and said, "Hello, Ivy. You make my heart go pitty-pat."

After her mechanical laughter (and mine) died down she said, "I highly doubt that, Matt Cross, your heart rate has not changed since you topped the stairs."

The eye began to pulse faster now about once per second. It took only three cycles for me to grasp its meaning and reach my hand to my carotid artery expecting the fourth to match. It did bringing a question to mind.

"How does she do that, Admiral?" I asked.

Still standing behind me on the stoop answered, "Simple distal pulse oximetry just like the one for your fingertip but with a telescope," he answered. "She's monitoring all personnel in the building for stress or physical duress... and most importantly life signs."

Sighing impatiently, he motioned to the eye.

"Go on ask her for entry, Matt, you're cleared. Let's go."

She was still PFM to me but I tried anyway.

"Ivy, please open the door."

"As you wish, Matt Cross, but I can only unlock the door; you'll need to open it yourself," she said matter-of-factly.

Greenfield chuckled.

"There you go, Matt. The virtual assistant with an attitude."

"Is she always that sarcastic?" I asked.

"No. Sometimes she's worse," he snickered. "Push the damn door."

The new world I had entered was becoming stranger by the minute as the door swung back revealing a copper-walled room with no windows, racks and racks of large computer mainframes and ten uniformed operators each manning three video screens. They all turned toward us as the door opened and draped their monitors with black cloth-looking covers. Behind them on the longer wall was a huge map of the Pacific Ocean like the one downstairs but this map had a myriad of colored thin lines crisscrossing the ocean between The U.S. and Asia. At its top, a legend blazed Transpacific Submarine Cable Network.

"At ease, men," Greenfield chopped. "This is Matt Cross our new DSV diver on the SSU team. Cleared for Z. Ex-Navy but as good as any we have on active duty. Tomorrow he will descend to the station and attempt to solve our problem."

Smiling and nodding, they lightly applauded.

As he spoke, an ensign approached from a nearby console and handed me what appeared to be an ID badge.

"Here, Mr. Cross, you'll be needing this," he said. "Fresh off the Ivy press."

"Thank you, Ensign... Bailer," I replied reading his nametag. I glanced at my new badge and noticed it was a photo of me taken only minutes before in the electrical room; it showed me wearing the same shirt I was wearing at my introduction to Ivy.

"Much better than a driver's license photo," I said. "I'm beginning to like this Ivy gal. She's efficient and quite a good photographer too."

Smiling, the Admiral nodded to me.

"She can be an effective agent as well. Even to the point of saving your life in dangerous situations."

I smiled back at him wondering what he meant.

"How so," I asked.

"Oh you'll find out for yourself. But before we start your briefing we need the other half of Operation Deep Force: your new partner Briscoe."

"Mica Briscoe?" I asked. My heart raced at the thought of seeing him alive again. Last time I saw the Chief he had been diagnosed with a stomach tumor from eating a highly radioactive donut and I never heard the outcome.

"He's alive?"

"Yes, very much so, Mr. Cross. Headquarters recommended him to us with the highest credentials. He was once a SeaCrawler diver and instructor at this base. Close ties to the project. So we brought him in and indoctrinated him into Umbra a few days ago after waiting several weeks for his recovery from stomach surgery. They did successfully remove the tumor but we all had trouble believing his story about the radioactive donut."

"Well that really happened but where is he?" I asked scanning the room for his face.

"On his way up. He's walking through the A room right now," an ensign answered. "Ivy shows him at the bottom of the stairway starting up."

Greenfield smiling, looked at me and commented, "Biometric tracking. She does that too. You'll get used to it."

Behind us, the door opened with a loud buzz followed by Ivy's soft voice from overhead speakers.

"Mica Briscoe entering. Access authorized."

As he entered the room I noticed the same video-screen-covering activity that followed our entry and wondered why all the secrecy for already cleared individuals. I later learned that the compartmented Umbra clearance had many facets and our clearances although Z did not cover them all.

His voice rang out through the room as he approached.

"Hey, Marker, it's about time you showed up, you slacker." Grinning he rushed up ignored my extended hand and hugged me; something I didn't expect but didn't mind either. He was my lifelong mentor my surrogate father and most importantly the only other person in my life besides my wife who I considered family.

"Hey, Chief," I smiled to him, "Damn you look good. How do you feel?" I wasn't lying either. He looked much healthier than the last time I saw him ailing from that tumor.

"Marker, I feel great even though my wife and I are supposed to be relaxing by Big Bear Lake with you and Lindy right now sipping on fancy cocktails."

I looked down wanting to die. I *had* promised him that I would treat them to a weeklong vacation in Big Bear. Sadly I realized that I had just been too preoccupied to make the reservations before the Admiral snagged me into his intricate web of brewing mysteries.

"Well, Chief, look on the bright side," I said. "At least we'll be able to work together on this operation and be an awesome team as usual. Right? What could be better?"

Straight-faced he looked at me and answered, "A week in Big Bear sipping on fancy cocktails." The sly smile that punctuated his comment told me that he was as eager as I was to join forces again.

Looming behind us the Admiral put a hand on our shoulders and interrupted.

"Gentlemen, I hate to break up this reunion but if I could have a moment of your time I'd like you to join me at the reading table. I need to brief you on your mission and be off back to Florida. I've got a plane waiting."

He led us to a small four-seat table in a corner of the room by a large document vault. As the Chief and I sat, I looked around and noticed that several wall-mounted cameras surrounded us with signs below them warning: DO NOT WRITE – MEMORIZE.

"Give me a moment to pull some documents," he said walking to the vault. Covering with his left hand, he twisted with his right a combination lock various ways then pulled a handle freeing a massive door. His finger traveled over stacks of files until he found for what he searched. Quickly he pulled a folder and sat with us at the table laying it out before us. Then reading from it, he began the briefing.

Chapter 8
Briefing for Z

"This briefing is classified Top Secret Umbra Z. You have both been granted special clearance after an extensive background investigation as we delved into your pasts assuring your allegiance to your country and its allies. We found no improprieties in either of your cases. Now you will not disclose or discuss what I am about to tell you with any person not authorized for Umbra Z access.

"Extending beyond Umbra are two compartmented accesses: A and Z. You are among only thirty-seven individuals in existence today that have access to both. Seventy-five other individuals only have access to Umbra-A material and information but are unaware that a higher level exists. You may not divulge to them anything higher that their access level A."

He cleared his throat, looked at us, and continued without reference to the folder.

"Now, guys, while that may seem rather abstract without further details let me put it in more concrete terms for you. There exists off the coast of California, halfway to Hawaii, a thousand meters down, a Top Secret manned undersea laboratory named Sea Station Umbra. Twelve researchers and divers with eight support crew are stationed there on revolving six-month tours of duty. Seven of them have Umbra-A clearances, five have Umbra-Z, and the support crew has just basic Umbra. Its disclosed mission under codeword A is to monitor encroaching radiation in the Pacific Ocean from the Fukushima Daiichi Reactor disaster in 2011. The knowledge of that mission requires either the A or Z compartment access.

"Now listen very closely," he said leaning in toward us, "There is a second covert codeword Z mission of the Sea Station which requires the Z-compartmented access. That's happening is this upper room surrounding us. We support the Z-arm of the station while the room below supports the A-arm. Simple but complicated. The Z compartment is all-inclusive while the A compartment is limited to radiation collection. You may walk freely through this room and the one below us but they are not allowed up here. The radiation-collection mission is a deceptive cover for the station so that we have a respectable reason for being there.

From my left Briscoe interrupted, "Does this have anything to do with Poseidon's Palace? That place existed when I was instructing my SeaCrawler classes. We were always told to avoid the area around it."

"Yes. Poseidon's Palace was the originator: the creator of Sea Station Umbra. It was a huge deep-sea construction site where they assembled the station from modules dropped to the depths from giant ships, floating above, disguised as cable repair ships. Six years and six-hundred-thousand man hours later Discovery One was commissioned late last year."

"Wait," I interrupted trying to keep all the information straight in my mind, "Is Discovery One really Sea Station Umbra?"

"Yes, Matt, that's its unclassified nickname so dubbed by its architect David Bowman a name you may remember from the past that once commanded another fictional Discovery One."

"Kubrick's brainchild in *2001: A Space Odyssey*?" Briscoe added.

"Exactly. And it's a pretty fair analogy too. The original ship was sent forward to Jupiter to explore the depths of space and discover its secrets. The new Discovery One was created to crawl the depths of the ocean reporting back secrets passing through the transcontinental cables between the U.S. and Asia specifically those from China and Japan."

"The station crawls?" I asked not expecting that word; it was too incredulous for me to believe.

The Chief obviously also confused at this point added, "Is this the culmination of the SeaCrawler program?"

Greenfield paused and then continued.

"Yes and no. It's an offshoot of that program: the SeaCrawler divers with their DSVs are still searching for missing missiles their warheads and downed aircraft but they are not enough. We needed a permanent presence on the ocean floor that could collect more than a few hours' worth of data at a time. Thus arose Sea Station Umbra."

"What's it like? Briscoe asked, "I just can't comprehend what I'm hearing: a crawling sea station."

He pulled a spec sheet from the folder titled Sea Station Umbra (TOP SECRET SCI UMBRA-Z (NOFORN)) and held it up for us to see. [See Appendix]

"This sheet classified Umbra-Z describes the Discovery One in great detail. Visually it looks like a monstrous sea urchin without spines or a giant basalt boulder. But it's really a spherical dome camouflaged to resemble the benthic region beneath and around it. A hundred feet in diameter at its widest circumference it rests on a massive tractor base one-hundred feet long by one-hundred feet across. Twenty large geared electric motors each powering one of twenty wheels provide propulsion up to a half-mile per hour. It rides on the ocean floor like a car. Independent suspension of each wheel ensures a smooth level ride. Drives like a dream too. The technology came from the lunar rovers and Saturn-rocket crawler transporters of past space programs. Its estimated total weight is one-hundred and ninety-two tons. For power a Westinghouse AP100 nuclear reactor tucked safely away in the tractor base provides a hundred megawatts for the crawler motors and the station's needs."

He looked up from the sheet.

"Shall I go on?"

In unison, we answered, "Please."

"The dome has four decks. The larger first deck with five-thousand-plus square feet provides room for the main living and working areas, a galley and a mess hall, research workstations for fourteen scientists and air locks for the docking bays below on the tractor's mechanical floor. A second smaller deck with thirty-five-hundred square feet sleeps fourteen in ship's style quarters including two for visitors, has restrooms with showers and a rec hall with a sixty-inch DVD based entertainment center.

Unfortunately there is no cable-TV down there it's BYODVDs. The third deck bunks eight support crew with a small rec hall and two heads and the forth one nearing the top of the dome is smaller and is used mainly for storage."

"So we'll be using the two visitor bunks right?" I asked thinking ahead; I was already drowsy from the boring briefing. I was ready to dive down and start Operation Deep Force whatever that was but he had neglected to mention it.

"That's coming up, Mr. Cross," he said placing the spec sheet back into the folder.

Briscoe reached out and put his hand on the folder preventing its closure.

"Wait. What about diving equipment? Do we have DSVs? Suits?"

"Oh of course. I neglected to mention that you'll be spending much of your time away from the dome either in one of eight self-contained ADS Exosuits or one of four BenthiCraft three-person DSVs. There are also a few propeller-driven tugs for use with the Exosuits. Anything you'll need we've got you covered."

The Admiral glanced at his watch.

"Moving along it's time to get to your new mission: Operation Deep Force. That's why you're here. You're it."

Sighing he stared at us and went on.

"Some very suspicious and frightening activity occurred recently aboard Discovery One. The Ivy guardian network in the station just like the one we have here recently reported some strange almost inexplicable situations down there. Now you've already seen that she tracks the number of people on station using biometrics. In the sea station, we always expect that number to be twenty or less depending on the divers away from the dome. Everything has been hunky-dory until recently."

Stopping his story, he motioned to a nearby crewman.

"Can you please get me a coffee? My throat is parched."

"Yes sir," the young officer answered, leaving his workstation for the nearby coffee center.

"Black, sir?

"That'll be fine."

Rushing back, he placed a steaming cup by the Admiral and returned to his console. Couldn't have taken more than fifteen seconds. *This is a really tight ship* I thought.

Blowing over his cup the Admiral continued.

"Two weeks ago she alarmed an intruder alert after finding twenty-one souls in the dome including the support crew of eight but there were supposed to be only twenty; an impossible situation since there were no visitors registered or intrusion alerts noted. The staffers searched through the station on her alarm and found no extra person. That in itself was not too unusual but the fly in the ointment was on the next day she reported only nineteen persons in the station. One staff member plus the intruder had vanished. In addition following a mandatory roll call and station inspection, her dire news was verified: There were only seven Exosuits in the airlock bay where there had been eight.

"The staff took time out from their tasks in teams of two, some in Exosuits some in DSVs, searching the surrounding ocean floor for anything suspicious. After hours of searching, they found the missing Exosuit lying lifeless but powered on, ten meters out in a narrow crevasse. The interior of the suit's clear face shield was smeared with blood and a black substance so they couldn't tell who it was until they got it back inside. It also had strange hieroglyphic characters scrawled in red over the aluminum exostructure.

"Now these men are scientists, interpreters, and nuclear specialists but when they returned the suit to the airlock and opened it, they freaked out. It was nearly empty; nothing inside but a handful of moist black sand, a watch, and a pair of diving boots."

The Chief and I looked at each other. I was caught up in the mystery but when he shook his head no and frowned I felt nauseous remembering the station was our new destination; we were about to enter a chamber of manmade horrors and live there for a month. *What could possibly go wrong?* I thought. It sounded to me like one of those stories told by old divers about Davy Jones Locker but I knew better. That was just a legend.

"So what happened next," I asked.

"Nothing. But later they identified the missing crewman as Lieutenant Commander Dan Li, USN, access level Umbra-ZX. The X codeword appended to the Z is a compartmented access code meaning that he not only knows of the Z mission but can also see the intercepted data from the cables and knows its source. Interpreters all have the X appendage. Sadly, it was his first tour of duty on the station; worked there only five months. He specialized in decrypting and translating messages from the undersea cable but of course, he was thought to be a radiation encroachment specialist. We suspect that he decoded a message that someone didn't want known. His body and workbook have yet to be found."

"So what are we supposed to do down there, Admiral?" the Chief asked glancing at me as if I knew. I expected him to know; he had been here longer.

"The crew aboard Discovery One does not have time for sleuthing; they have assigned tasks that can't be interrupted by incidental happenings... unless it's a full stop emergency of course. Then we lose tons of crucial data that cannot be reconstructed. They are screaming for help with Li's unexplained disappearance. A thousand feet down is not a place to jump ship. Someone or something did that to him, and it's still down there. The crew is afraid there will be more victims but none of them have the expertise or time to become investigators."

Briscoe scoffed.

"And that's what we'll be doing? A missing person's bureau?"

"Hmm. Yes, in a way. But, you *will* have an expert witness to work with so I expect you both to become tech-savvy with Ivy's operation and methodologies. She sees everything and is aware of all activities aboard the station. That capability has to be of crucial assistance."

Being somewhat of a computer expert, I was still mystified by Ivy. She was not just about computers; she was AI.

Then wondering how we could possibly become overnight Ivy gurus I asked, "Is there an operation manual for Ivy?"

"Yes. Four-hundred-plus pages of fine print. Designed by the artificial intelligence geniuses at Google AI she is version four or Roman numeral IV: thus her name. We've yet to find fault with her intelligence or logic. The manual is unclassified but the accumulated knowledge in her memory is Umbra-Z of course. We have a copy here and you'll find another in the Discovery One. They're identical so you'll have a reference manual when you get there."

"That brings up another question," I asked trying to fill gaps in my knowledge. "Obviously you have a Z facility here and another one thousands of feet underwater. Do they communicate... and if so how?" I caught myself sounding like a College Bowl host and laughed self-consciously as I finished the question.

He must have seen it too because he chuckled and answered, "The answer is yes. The reason why: there are several ultra-high-speed laser links beamed from a floating laser buoy tethered over the station to one of our stationary KL satellites then relayed back to us here in Point Mugu. That explains all the antennas around the building."

He thought for a moment and added, "Well not all of them. Some are used for headquarters communications and others link to foreign news services. We have to stay abreast of world news to know where to send Discovery One next, what cable to tap and then inform them of the targeted-message context from the intercept. And since it can take a week or more to switch cables with travel maneuvering and re-tapping we have to get the news to Dr. Bowman as quickly as possible."

My ears perked up at hearing that name again. I knew about Clarke's 'Bowman' but deep in my early childhood memories another Bowman existed. My best friend as a kid, Jeremy Bowman. He would be roughly my age but could he have designed and then been placed at the helm of Discovery One? I had to ask.

"This Bowman guy. Is he about my age?"

"Yes he is, Mr. Cross, why would you ask?"

"Well, you called him Dave Bowman earlier but I once had a childhood friend who built majestic deep-sea-laboratory sandcastles with me, lots of them, but his name was Jeremy Bowman." Realizing how foolish that sounded I backtracked, "No that's just too much of a coincidence. Never mind."

"Well, Mr. Cross, it seems as though you may have found your long-lost friend. He goes by his middle name now but his given name is Jeremiah. Can't say that I blame him either."

"Oh my God," I whispered, "It is him. The kid who taught me to love and not fear the ocean. I guess he stayed true to his heart."

"Apparently he did." He pulled a second sheet from the folder and placed it on the table between us. Another Top Secret Umbra document it was the Sea Station Umbra crew list titled Sea Station Umbra Crew List TS SCI UMBRA-ZX (NOFORN) listing the names, ranks, clearances, and duties of the current staff. [Attached in Appendix]

I counted down to the second name and saw it there: Bowman, J. David, civilian, Umbra-ZX clearance, Station Manager. Suddenly his face and his last words came alive in my mind:

"Matt Cross, listen to me. The ocean is only dangerous if you don't love and respect it like a wild animal in captivity. There is nothing to fear." I loved him for that advice. It changed my life and put me where I am today living my dream.

Greenfield took the list and slid it to Briscoe.

"See any friends there you recognize, Mr. Briscoe?"

He pulled it closer for reading studied it a few seconds then slid it back.

"Nah. I got all I can handle sitting next to me."

"Well then, I'll leave you in good company, Mr. Briscoe."

Greenfield checked his watch again.

"I must be going now. There will be a CH-60 Seahawk helicopter waiting for you on the helipad at 2100 hours tomorrow night. Be there in wet suits with your personals in a small waterproof bag and wear your watches. Nothing else and no flashlights. You'll be well provided for once you reach the station."

I panicked realizing that wet suit diving could only take us to thirty meters or about one-hundred feet down. We would need to travel much deeper to ten times that depth to reach the station, an impossible task without assistance especially in the dark.

"Wait. Am I missing something? We can't make that dive with wet suits much less in the dark."

Smiling, the Admiral said, "Let me finish."

He sighed and continued, "At a predetermined point over the Pacific about two-hours out you will be dropped into the water under the cover of darkness. That should be no later than midnight. You'll carry a small low-power sonar pinger provided to you. Using your life vests, you will float awaiting a pickup from a surfacing three-man BenthiCraft mini-sub sent from the station below. The transfer has to be quick to evade foreign satellite photo-reconnaissance but your profiles will be smaller than the surrounding waves so you'll be invisible from space considering the lack of light."

"Oh that's a comforting thought," said the Chief. "I don't like waves bigger than me especially at midnight."

"Not to worry sir. It will be a precisely timed transfer. You shouldn't be in the water for more than ten minutes."

"Ten long cold sickening minutes in waves bigger than me," he groaned. "What could possibly go wrong?"

Laughing, I noticed him looking sickly. My hero diving instructor, my life's mentor had always been prone to seasickness and he had no qualms admitting it. But once he was under the waves he was one of the best divers in the Navy. It was just those few minutes going from the surface to ten feet under that bothered him.

Off to my side the Admiral was packing up the folder tidying the pages and readying it for the vault.

"Well, gentlemen, my time with you is done. I'll alert Bowman to your arrival tomorrow. Remember 2100 hours sharp at the helipad. Your CH-60 pilot and crew will be informed that you are part of a search and rescue training mission, that you will be safely found and the bird must disappear as quickly as possible after the drop to avoid disclosing your location. Got it?"

"Yes sir. We shall be there," I answered comforted by the Chief's confirming nod.

Standing at the vault Greenfield stashed the folder and locked it. Then he turned to us with an extended hand.

"Welcome aboard Operation Deep Force. I certainly hope you can find out what in the hell's going on down there and fix it. The station's bordering on chaos right now but that won't last long. Soon it will be a full-blown mutiny if we let it continue. We're counting on you. Carry on."

With that, he turned and left the room.

Sitting with the Chief in silence, I gathered my thoughts. It had been only six short hours since I reported for my normal workaday life at MBORC and I was exhausted. In that time, my comfortable structured existence was shattered. Now homeless again with nowhere to go and no place to sleep I felt alone, abandoned. I was a kid again looking forward to another day at the beach with Jeremy.

"Where you staying, Chief? Got room for another?" I asked. I knew he had been on base a few days and with his resourcefulness would have settled in.

Smiling he answered, "Yes, I'll always have room for you, Marker. It's a little hole-in-the-wall motel across the street but it has soft beds a TV and a pretty good coffee shop. I asked for twin beds thinking you might be as lost when you arrived as I was. The town has really changed since we were here last. Let's go. I'll show you around."

After a quick blue-plate-special lunch and two large slices of warm apple pie for dessert, we wandered the town skipping the girlie places (we were too old and too married for that) and found a movie theater back on base aptly named the Station Theater. It was dark and empty but it kept our minds occupied for the better part of two hours with an encore showing of, of all things *The Abyss*. Just what we needed to take our thoughts off our upcoming mission. The Chief left several times during the movie to visit the head claiming he had too much coffee but I believed he was throwing up; he came back each time wiping his mouth with a tissue. Several times, I wanted to join him but thinking that might look funny I just threw up in my mouth.

After the movie when we returned to the Chief's room, there was a note about a package waiting in the lobby.

"That'd be our wet suits," he said bluntly.

Turns out, he was right. Wet suits plus two small watertight bags filled with toiletries, special slots for our ID badges and two small belt-clip sonar beacons. Digging deeper we laughed as each of us pulled out a black business card with bold white lettering. Welcome to Discovery One it read. Then J. David Bowman, Station Manager. Somehow, that simple card eased my anxieties and lessened my fears. Not sure why but it did.

"Looks like a DV kit for distinguished visitors," I mused. "Wonder how many of these he gives out a year and I wonder if we really *are* welcome."

"We'll have to tread carefully at first to see his mood. In my opinion, no one on station is above suspicion. Sounds pretty spooky down there to me."

"Agreed," I said. "I just can't imagine that story about the empty dive suit and missing diver. Must be more to that story than we heard."

"Yeah," he said glancing up from the card, "I know I'm going to dream about *that* tonight."

"And probably for the next month too," I added.

"Hey I'm going to hit the shower or do you want to go first?"

I grabbed the TV remote from the dresser and flipped to an old movie.

"No. I'll be fine with this if it doesn't put me to sleep. Took one this morning. Oh and don't steam it up too much in there. I'm already sweating. Wish the AC had a little more oomph."

Entering the bathroom, he glanced back and said, "Hey, Marker, beggars can't be choosers," and shut the door behind him.

Chapter 9
Discovery One

T wo hours into the flight, our pilot informed us we were nearing the drop point. Through turbulent winds, we had flown over black nothingness since our departure and Briscoe sitting in the jump seat next to me complained the whole way. He hated the instability of helicopters and their tendency to slide sideways bringing his stomach into his throat (which had happened more than a few times). Only thirty more minutes and the rescue drop-line crewman would open the side door and shove us out if we didn't go willingly, he joked. No drop line for us though. The crewman explained that during the fast-drop procedure they were instructed to use the chopper would stop in mid-flight only ten feet above the waves, hover for five seconds while we jumped and then speed back to home port.

With only minutes to spare the Chief pulled what looked like a checklist from a sleeve pocket and read from it.

"Life vest?"

"Check," I said.

He patted his.

"Sonar pinger clipped on belt?"

"Check."

"Kitbag clipped on belt?"

"Check."

"ID card in kitbag?"

"Check."

"Watch? Time?"

"Check. 2325 hours."

"I also have 2325 hours. Should be dropping soon," he confirmed then wadded the list and threw it to the floor.

No sooner had he spoken those words than the crewman slid the side door open. The sound of the rotors' roar with waves crashing a few meters below us was deafening. A cold humid wind rushed through the cabin telling me the time was now. Briscoe stood, approached the door, and grabbed a hanging hand strap.

"C'mon, Marker," he screamed barely audible over the thunderous clamor.

The crewman nodded and motioned me over to join the Chief then mouthed my fate.

"Here's your stop."

Waiting for his signal, we stood hanging from the hand straps with our toes over the open door's slide rail ready to jump. There were no lights under our feet; only a brief green or red flash reflecting from the waves when the navigation lights on the tail blinked. I can't say I wasn't scared.

The Chief had once said to me, "My life is under the surface of the ocean not on it," and I agreed. I was not happy, about to jump feet first into a thousand-meter-deep unknown mystery. He had also said, "The first step is the hardest," and I was feeling that now.

"Go! Go! Go!" the crewman yelled curling his arm around us from the rear. I couldn't have stopped if I wanted to. Leaving my side the Chief yelled, "Aw shiiiiit," as he disappeared into the pitch-blackness of the waves.

I was right behind him and screamed something too but can't remember what. Before I could close my mouth a wave filled it with salt water then tried to invade my nose. *This is not supposed to happen* I thought. That one-second free fall into the cold dark Pacific Ocean must have taken years from my life. I vowed never to do that again.

When I finally popped to the surface, over the receding helicopter's flutter I heard Briscoe screaming from some distance away.

"Are you okay, Marker?" I also heard a chill in his voice that reminded me how cold I was.

"Fine, Chief, over here," I yelled hoping he could hear me. Then there was silence except for the clapping waves topping out over me. Worried looking around I saw nothing but darkness and a sky full of sparkling stars with not even a glimmer of moonlight to help my vision.

I flinched, startled at the nearby voice from the waves:

"Got your beacon on?"

"Yes I do but how the hell did you find me, Chief?"

"I just followed your whimpers when the waves crested over you. Simple."

"I don't whimper," I argued.

"Well how *did* I find you then? Sonar?"

I had to laugh at his strange logic then he began to laugh too. Suddenly the surrealism surrounding us hit me: we were two humans laughing, floating helplessly at sea, hundreds of miles from the closest shore. Two lost rudderless ships meeting in the dark. This was definitely not our normal mode of diving.

69

"Hey, did you bring any shark repellant?" I asked fending off another wave.

Even through the darkness, I felt his face flush.

"No. That wasn't on my checklist. Did you?"

"No, but maybe they're sleeping. They won't bother us."

"Oh sure and I have some swampland in Florida I'll sell you too."

I can't tell what it was, maybe fear or brainless camaraderie, but we laughed together for what seemed like hours waiting for our ride to show up. Neither of us had ever heard of a BenthiCraft mini-sub so we didn't know what to expect other than a small sub with three seats: one for the pilot, one for me and one for him.

Then something appeared. A dim light from below illuminated the waves with an eerie blue cast. Gradually a huge lighted bubble pierced the waves like a UFO rising from the depths. As it surfaced not far from us I searched for a hatch and noticed a hatch cover, a sizable drain-plug-like object, a cork so to speak seated in a large hole at the top of its dome. Attached to it was a reinforced curved arm reaching down with some form of lifting hinge at the hull. The whole bubble couldn't have been more than eight feet in diameter and the hatch looked only a few feet across.

"See that, Chief?" I asked pointing forward trying to stay upright in the waves. "There's a hatch on top. Think you can fit through that with all the donuts you've eaten?"

"Hey easy, Marker. Don't make me think about donuts right now I might throw up."

As I watched, the hatch cover lifted mechanically and slowly pivoted back with the arm leaving a gaping hole for our entry in the thick dome.

"Yeah I can fit through that. Let's go, Marker," Briscoe said swimming toward the light struggling against the waves.

"Right behind you, Chief," I called out.

Suddenly a motion in the sub, something standing from a seat preceded a body shape rising through the hatch. Expecting a male crewman I heard a female voice greet us.

"Come on, fellas, can't wait all night. We've got a hot date down below."

As I bobbed paddling toward the craft, I had to look twice; I thought I was seeing Charlize Theron standing there smiling, a mirage of loveliness rocking with the waves motioning us toward her like a mermaid from the sea.

"See her, Chief?" I asked rubbing water from my eyes trying to clear them.

"No way. They wouldn't do that. Would they?" he said coughing almost choking.

"Looks like they did. Things just got more interesting."

"Okay guys cut the small talk. Somebody climb on the hull and give your hand before I get sick. Let's get underway," ordered the voice.

I unclipped my kitbag and beacon from my belt pitched them in then slid through the hatch and sat. Seconds later Briscoe threw in his bag and beacon and followed still coughing. Although he claimed he was fit he struggled through the opening then slammed into a seat across the pilot's from me with a loud grunt, panting and wheezing.

"Swallowed some saltwater," he coughed.

She ducked down and sat between us then forcefully slapped him on the back.

"Cough it up," she said. "By the way I'm Lt. JG Susan Williams at your service. Welcome aboard SeaPod 2."

Situating himself in his seat the Chief stopped sputtering and stared at her, squinting.

"Does that mean you have pod bay doors on Discovery One? That's pretty corny."

"Oh yes of course Mr. ---? Sorry I didn't catch your name but I was told the older one was Briscoe. Is that you?"

Briscoe had always been sensitive about his age. I knew that from way back when I had once called him an 'old man' in jest and he nearly took me down over my comment. His years had given him wisdom and smarts rather than age he told me and I almost agreed.

"Yes, ma'am," he answered. "But young for my age I assure you. I once was the Navy's best diver."

"As I was saying our architect, Chief Scientist and Station Manager, Dr. David Bowman is quite attached to the allegorical nature of his name and Kubrick's 2001 if you know of that movie."

"Certainly. Who doesn't know of Hal?" he said.

"So we call her Ivy down there the same as back at HQ in Point Mugu. He tried to change her name to Hal but couldn't override Ivy. He's very egocentric. You'll see."

"Oh really?" I said, "I once knew him as a youth and he was my best friend. Of course we were only

72

ten but he seemed like every other normal kid except he *was* obsessed with sandcastles."

"He must have changed then," she said, "Now he won't even consider letting anyone else named Dave work in the station. In time, you will learn from him as everyone has that he was a Navy brat and child prodigy. He designed and mentored the construction of a unique undersea missile storage facility for the Navy by the time he was fourteen. After that, his parents put him in Annapolis with a special dispensation at age fifteen. He graduated by seventeen, got his PhD by nineteen, then left the Navy and formed his own company by twenty, designing and building subterranean and submersible structures. Truly, a fast-track wonder. His most recent creation was Discovery One and he's understandably quite proud of it."

Hearing of his good fortune disturbed me. I should have been proud of him but I was jealous; I could have matched his achievements but my parents---.

"Hatch closing," she called interrupting my thought.

Glancing around the cabin, she pulled a lever on the small streamlined control panel the likes of which I had never seen. Sleeker and simpler than the Canyon Glider's it put the controls of my old mini-sub to shame: a Ferrari style sub compared to my militarized Jeep version.

Behind my seat, a motor whined as the hatch-cover arm dropped down over us and seated itself into the hatch with a loud clunk causing my ears to pop. Heated air began to wash through the cockpit bringing the first warmth I had felt in hours. What surprised me the most was the air had a 'new car' smell. I loved that smell.

Quickly she reached overhead and twirled the hatch lock sealing us into the large Plexiglas bubble probably six inches thick and not more than eight feet across sitting on a sturdy yellow motorized propulsion hull. I could hardly wait to see and inspect it in full lighting and marvel at its beauty. Still as I looked around the interior with its subdued blue-white led lighting it impressed me; it was like a showroom ad: a simple and magnificent machine.

"Ready to dive?" she asked.

"Always," said Briscoe looking behind his seat, "Especially in this chop. Git 'er down, Lieutenant."

I glanced back to see what he was looking at and saw meters, indicator lights and pressure gauges on a large panel. In front of her, small flat screen displays covered the space I expected to be the sub's dashboard. Digital meters, status icons, and moving bar graphs glowed in sectioned regions filling the panes requesting her attention. As I watched mesmerized by the new science, she touched a few buttons and then propulsion motors rumbled and vibrated the cockpit. Then sounds of water rushing into ballasts roared below us. All familiar sounds I recognized from my sub; at least *they* weren't changed by new technology.

Reaching forward with a gentle twisting pushing motion she moved the joystick and we headed downward.

"We're diving at the SeaPod's maximum speed of three knots," she said. "The Discovery One currently rests on the floor below us at 985 meters.

That puts our ETA roughly twenty-five minutes from now."

As we dove, I tried to look out through the bubble but my efforts were futile. All I could see were our distorted reflections like those from a funhouse mirror.

"Does this have forward floods?" I asked.

"Of course, Mr. Cross, but they won't activate until we're ten meters down. Can't see them from the surface then. Remember, visual stealth above all else."

I had to keep reminding myself at these moments that we didn't exist so any visual or physical cues to our presence were verboten. My introduction to the extreme secrecy of the black world was slowly sinking in.

I checked the second hand on my watch expecting the floods to illuminate in six seconds at our three-knot or 1.6 meter-per-second descent rate. We had a huge almost 360-degree view through the bubble but it was a bit disconcerting to see nothing out there but reflections.

Seven eight nine... ten.

The submarine environment blazed to life around us. Multi-hued fish wandered up toward us searching for food as we passed through them; plankton, anchovies and other tiny wiggling sea creatures reflected our lights: a moving living fog of existence in otherwise crystal-clear waters.

"Sure beats our tiny DSV viewports doesn't it, Marker?" said Briscoe open-mouthed looking around.

"Uh yeah," I said. "It's like a 3D wraparound aquarium. Not at all what I would have expected."

Lt. Williams diverted her attention from the controls to our surroundings.

"Yes, it is beautiful up here. Down where we live, not so much beauty except for a few benthic-zone species trying to thrive in the great pressures of the ocean floor. This is the ocean's rainforest; we live in its desert."

I had never thought of it that way before but she was right. The earth's more or less constant-temperature oceans varying less than twenty degrees Centigrade from top to bottom could support most forms of sea life so depth rather than temperature was the defining obstacle for life. For example, an ocean's pressure ranges from around 14.7 PSI at the surface to one hundred times that or 1,472 PSI at a thousand meters down.

We would be living and working in that. And, figuring an average human body's surface area of 2,700 square inches at a pressure of 1,472 pounds per square inch, it meant that if we lost protection down there we would be subjected to 1,472 X 2,700 = 3,974,400 pounds, almost four million pounds of pressure, squeezing the life from us. I closed my eyes imagining a squished tube of screaming toothpaste with arms and legs. Not a pretty picture.

I was accustomed to working in those pressures oftentimes even greater but in a sturdy Abrams Tank of a military submarine rather than the comparatively flimsy but quite sporty SeaPod I was trusting with my life.

"Hey, Marker," he said dragging me from my trance. "You've missed a lot. Are you asleep over there?"

I almost was and I was glad he roused me back just in time to see a huge dark bulbous structure looming below us growing larger looking exactly as Greenfield had described. No details were visible but the absence of the surrounding ocean floor gave it away since it was noticeably darker than its background in our floods. Then as we moved deeper down past the top of the dome, it disappeared against the deep-water environment. Then a small rectangular blue light appeared far away toward the bottom of the shape.

"There! That's our docking port," Lt. Williams said pointing forward.

We had veered onto a horizontal path approaching the station from the side so I expected to see the outline of something, anything other than a huge darkened mass ahead with a tiny blue-white light at its base, and a few specks of moving lights below us.

"What are those lights down there? They appear to be moving across the floor," I asked out of curiosity.

"Oh those are a few of our divers in ADS Exosuits probably resetting our sensor probes. They foul with sea life excrement and silt on a regular basis. Isotope collectors are notoriously temperamental."

"Here let's listen in," she said touching another icon on her screen.

Nothing happened for a few seconds then voices crackled through the speaker behind us.

"... looking. Alvarado here it is. It's the strontium-90 probe. There's silt caked over it. Looks like it took the fluke-wash from a sperm whale or big fish. Bring that vacuum over here and I'll get it."

"Hey, Norris, didn't we just clean that sensor a few days ago? Something attractive about it?"

"Not that I can see but until I get the vacuum I can't tell. Hurry up move that suit!"

"Running fast as I can but I've got a sticky joint. Got any WD-40?"

She clicked off the intercom and smiled.

"Wonderful divers, Alvarado and Norris. They keep us in stitches with their antics."

Briscoe alerted by their conversation added, "I love those Exosuits. Used my first one a few months ago. Worked like a charm. At least until I damaged a joint on a coral reef but the techs fixed it right away. Nothing better that an atmospheric diving suit. No decompression, no worries. How are they working out for you guys? Like them?"

She hesitated before answering.

"They're great until you find one empty, defaced and missing its diver. Then they're just plain spooky."

"Your divers all work in teams like those guys?" I asked.

"Always."

Knowing that buddy system diving was usually observed by professional divers I couldn't help but wonder how a single diver had made out without a partner. I put that on my mental list to check out later.

"Any new information on that incident Lieutenant?"

"No, nothing more but we've had some rather eerie banging and scraping on the station's outer shell in the past few days like someone's trying to get in, but all personnel were accounted for; they were in the station."

Quickly I realized this information was connected to our mission and possibly a clue for us to start working from.

"How many of the crew heard the noises?" I asked.

"All of them. The sounds echoed throughout the dome for seconds leaving some very terrified divers and staff including me. In fact the incident brought back the fear of the Davy Jones Locker superstition in some."

Silently, on Lt. William's sonar screen, a red blinking dot appeared growing larger as we neared the lighted rectangle but seeming no larger than a matchbox through the bubble.

Being a backseat diver (yes that's what we called ourselves sometimes) I had to ask, "How big is that port? Looks too small. Does this thing really fit in there?"

Scoffing she glared at me.

"Now that truly is a man's question but yes it does after I push the AutoDock function. Our breadth is twelve feet, our height is nine feet, and the bay is twenty feet wide by twelve feet high. Size does matter in this case. We have plenty of room even when our hatch opens inside the bay."

Looking at the Chief I asked, "What do you think? Easy peasy docking?"

"AutoDock huh?" he said. "I'll take that. But does it work?"

"Okay watch," she said touching a dimmed icon on her panel. As it brightened additional motor whines joined the main propulsion motors sounds. Assuming they were from horizontal and vertical thrusters, I must have been right because we began to slide sideways in the water centering ourselves on the growing matchbox.

I examined her face checking for any sign of stress, which would suggest something amiss but she stayed relaxed smiling enjoying the ride with us watching the docking port approach.

All of a sudden from a speaker behind our heads came a voice, a woman's soft voice, crisp and slightly mechanical.

"SeaPod 2, you're on course for a perfect docking into Pod Bay 2. Reduce speed to one-half knot."

"That was Ivy over the SeaCom our sea intercom," Lt. Williams said pulling the joystick slightly. "She functions as our control tower when we near the docking bay."

"Does she control our approach remotely?" Briscoe asked.

"No, that can be too risky with random interference from whales in the area. She just advises us of our approach as an air traffic controller would. For example she just requested we drop our speed to less than a foot per second."

"Are we still on AutoDock," I asked noticing our course drifting downward off dead center.

"Yes until I cancel after docking."

"Then why are we drifting downward off course?" I asked suspecting otherwise.

She jerked her attention to the sonar display then looked forward and shouted.

"Holy shit! Something's wrong. We're going off course. This can't be happening!"

"Pull up! Pull up!" Ivy squawked rattling the intercom speaker with her volume.

Wide eyed, Briscoe shouted, "Is there a manual override?"

She pushed the AutoDock icon turning it off. We still drifted downward now only twenty meters from the docking bay with its bright xenon lights beaming through the water awaiting our entry. I quickly calculated we had about a minute to impact but at our foot-per-second speed, I didn't expect a disaster.

"That didn't help," she screamed.

"Pull up! Pull up!" Ivy blasted.

"Guys? Ideas? I need help here," Lt. Williams pleaded.

"Reverse thrust!" Briscoe shouted with a fear showing in his face I had never seen before.

She pulled back on the joystick.

"Not helping," she screamed.

In my mind amid the chaos, I envisioned the control circuitry of the SeaPod and saw the answer. I'm not sure how I did it but suddenly the solution became clear to me.

"Where are the power breakers? The breaker panel?" I asked.

"Behind your seat near the floor. But don't kill our power we'll be helpless and blind as a bat out here without lights."

Turning rotating in my seat, I reached for the panel. Looking down I opened the cover and felt for the largest breaker switch. The sub's designers had neglected to put lighting in the panel so I was grasping in the dark. Then I found it.

"Here goes nothing," I said switching off what I guessed to be the main breaker.

In total darkness with the SeaPod's motors grinding to a halt I counted to ten, ignoring William's warning and Briscoe's cursing. Then I flipped it back on.

The SeaPod returned to life slowly as we drifted forward; our inside lights and exterior floods flickered then brightened to full on as the computer panel flashed with a BenthiCraft boot-up splash screen. Seconds later came the message: Restarting Please Wait.

Out the bubble with floods reactivated, I could see we were less than five meters from the station's hull and still falling away from the docking bay.

"Ten seconds to impact," I estimated.

Precious seconds passed as the blue 'Loading' bar crept across the screen. I wanted to push it faster.

"Wait!" Williams said. "I've got control back! Halleluiah!"

Breathing a sigh of relief, I saw Briscoe with his hands clasped in front of him whispering words. I thought it wise to whisper a few words of thanks myself so I did.

"Pull back now! Pull back now! Pull back now! Impact imminent!" Ivy announced her voice insistent.

The roar of the thruster motors and the backward push throwing me forward in my seat brought a lump to my throat. How could I have known to do that? Then I remembered my old maxim: When in doubt reboot. That's all I did.

Briscoe opened his eyes at the reverse acceleration and looked at me. Then he raised his hand for a high-five.

"My God, Marker, that was pure genius," he said. "You saved our lives."

Backing us off from the station's hull Lt. Williams glanced over and smiled.

"Yeah, Marker, if I can call you that, I agree. I thank you with all my heart. Now I know why you're here... and Mr. Briscoe said *he*'s the Navy's best diver. That makes you better than the best."

"Well thank you both," I told them. "And yes, Lieutenant, you're on the short list of those who know my middle name. Use it wisely. And, as far as what I just did it's just called self preservation and you happened to be with me when it happened."

"Course corrected." Ivy announced. "Docking expected in twenty seconds. Proceed at one-half meter per second."

The Lieutenant back in control keeping her cool adjusted the joystick.

"That's never happened to me before. I'm so sorry. I almost killed us. Wonder what went wrong."

Chief Briscoe looking over her shoulder at the screen suggested, "Maybe someone doesn't want us here. Ever thought of that, Marker?"

I had not and it sent chills up my spine. My mind was already reeling from being sent into what seemed like a deep-sea death trap and his words confirmed my fears. Only time would tell.

Nearing the pod bay, only a few meters out we saw the brilliantly lighted room come into focus ready for our entry. As we slowly drifted inward, the docking chamber appeared as a cavernous swimming pool turned on its side with a ladder climbing the wall at the back. She pulled back on the joystick bringing us to a slow halt.

"You're about to experience a sharp bump as we land on the docking pad and are gripped by a strong electromagnet locking us down. Then the pod bay door will close and seal behind us as we wait for pumps to force the water out and fill the bay with air. We're basically in an open ballast tank with a sea-proof door called a pod docking bay. Once we're in dry dock we'll pressurize, open the hatch, and exit the SeaPod."

It happened just as she described although it took almost ten minutes to pump the bay empty; it was a painfully slow process but then I had never been on the inside of a huge purging ballast before: it was quite a unique experience.

When the large indicator on the bay's back wall changed from red to green an icon illuminated on the SeaPod's control panel. Then my ears popped as a slight overpressure filled our cockpit from a pump below my feet. Williams reached up, spun the hatch lock open, and touched the icon starting the hatch cover into motion. Like compressed gas, escaping from a soda pop bottle air hissed past the cover as it drew back from the hatch.

"Now we wait," she said.

"For what?" asked Briscoe, standing glancing around the empty bay.

"Well you can go now if you don't mind risking a broken or sprained ankle jumping down from the hatch over a very slick sphere onto a wet very slippery floor. Otherwise we wait for one of our crew to roll that stairway up the hatch so we can exit gracefully... and safely."

He sat back and sighed.

"Not knowing if you have a doctor on staff or even a sickbay I'll just sit here be safe and wait."

"Oh we have a lot of doctors on staff but none of them are MDs, just PhDs. And there *is* a sickbay but the best treatment you'll get is from those of our crew who have served as wartime medics."

As she spoke a ceiling hatch dropped down at the top of the rear ladder. Feet, legs, then the body of a crewman appeared in a blue jumpsuit. With his feet grasping the ladder's rails he slid down to the floor walked to the stairway and unlatched it from the wall, then rolled it up to our bubble's hatch. Soon a hand followed by a head dropped through the hatch welcoming us.

"Hi guys I'm Captain Bill Edwards U.S. Navy. Welcome aboard Discovery One. Can I give anyone a hand jumping ship? Take your bags?"

Laughing, Briscoe said, "Hi. I'm Mica Briscoe. After that wild ride I thought about it Captain but ladies first."

Williams glared at him.

"We don't do that here, Mr. Briscoe. I'm an equal to every crewman on board. No better no worse and I'll be the last to leave my ship."

Watching him blush I felt his embarrassment even though he was just being chivalrous: a trait appreciated in the civilian world in which he worked. Not every ex-Navy California Highway Patrolman would have even offered.

"I'll go, Captain," I said grabbing his hand as he helped me stand from my seat. Then dropping my bag out I wiggled through the hatch to a platform at the top of the steps large enough for several people to stand.

"Mr. Briscoe, you're next."

He stood through the hatch, dropped his bag on the platform, and took the Captain's hand.

"Now, Marker here says I'm a tight fit through there---too many donuts. Think I can make it, Captain?"

"Well if not, Mr. Briscoe, I'll just have to get our hatch stretcher." He grinned broadly after his comment and pulled.

Tugging his hand Edwards brought him easily through the hatch eliciting a quiet applause from Lt. Williams.

"Enough of that, Lieutenant," Briscoe chided. "We're equals remember? Except for a few inches around our waists, maybe."

As Briscoe and I took our kitbags and stepped down to deck level Williams hopped through the hatch and quickstepped down the stairs with the Captain and joined us.

"Captain Edwards is the second team's leader," she said turning to him, saluting. "He'll prep the SeaPod for the next dive. Now please follow me."

She started off and then looked back.

"Oh, Captain, would you please check the AutoDock function on that SeaPod. It went off course and almost killed us. Mr. Cross had to reboot the system to regain control. Never happened before; hope it never happens again."

He nodded and frowned back at the SeaPod then went about his prepping.

"Wait. I'm confused, Lieutenant," I said stopping her. "I've heard the people on station called the crew in one sentence and staff in the next. Which one is it?"

"Both," she said. "When I'm talking about us operating in the maritime environment we're the crew. When I speak of us acting as scientists collecting and analyzing data we're staff. Then we also have the support crew. Everyone wears two hats, some three, some four. That's the way I see it."

Briscoe shrugged his shoulders.

"Same difference to me. Six of one half dozen of the other but which hat do we wear?"

Smiling slyly, she said, "I guess you're the MPs. Yet another hat."

"I like peacekeepers better," I said. "Maybe even investigators. MP just sounds too harsh and we're not even military. Right, Chief?"

"Just call me Chief... and when the Mess Hall opens. I'm here to solve problems nothing more."

"Then let's go do it," she said. Then she smiled turned and raced up the ladder two rungs at a time through the hatch.

Briscoe followed her up easily matching her pace.

By this time of night, I was dragging a bit, but made it up as well.

Soon we stood in an engineering marvel. Williams had closed the pod bay hatch behind us as we topped the ladder and suggested a brief tour before she released us to our quarters. I reminded her it was approaching 0130 hours and it had been an exhausting day. *Brief* was the operative word.

The deck we entered Deck 1 – Quad 2 from a large sign on the wall reminded me of the entryway to one of Jeremy's better sandcastles he and I created when we were kids. That design was a pie-shaped deck cut into four slices with a large circular center section accessible from each slice through one of four watertight bulkhead doors. I called that a submarine core because it resembled a sub hull turned on end.

I remember him telling me that it was a good idea because the rounded convex bulkhead walls of the central core provided better protection against quadrant flooding pressures. It was all too complicated for me back then but I went along with him and pretended that he knew what he was talking about. Now looking back it all made pretty good sense.

The stark white surroundings reflecting the intense overhead lights blinded my eyes so I couldn't see all the details but they were adjusting slowly. Briscoe standing beside me must have been affected the same way, he shielded his eyes waiting for them to adapt.

Several of the staff in blue jump suits walked hurriedly through the room ignoring us carrying empty coffee mugs to a coffee pot somewhere. Briscoe eyed them curiously until they disappeared behind a wall.

"Now this is the main level Deck 1. Decks 2, 3 and 4 are above us," she said sweeping her hand across the room giving us a tour she'd obviously given before.

"We're in quadrant two... Q2 with Q1 to our left, Q3 to our right and Q4 opposite the central core. Remember they increase going clockwise when looking down from above. Past that bulkhead door at the end of this room a central core chamber twenty feet in diameter, matching our deck height, joins all four quadrants through watertight bulkhead doors. Above it are more core rooms surrounding an elevator rising to the top of the dome. The top core room we call the panic room is a safe haven for us. The last room to be flooded in a dire emergency. Attached---"

"Wait a minute," I asked, "So if we have a pressure breach and water rushes in, we race up the core trying to beat the rising water to the panic room at the top of the dome. Is that right?"

"Basically, yes."

"Then what from there? We kiss our ass goodbye?"

Chuckling, she patiently explained:

"No, Marker, the panic room is attached to a thirty-man pressurized escape pod bathysphere we affectionately call the EPod. It can separate from the dome and float to the surface buoyantly: a lifeboat of absolute last resort. Why? If we ever use it, it will inundate the station with seawater leaving it forever unusable. That escape pod also serves as our scuttle mechanism if an enemy force ever commits an unauthorized entry. Then sixteen hundred pounds of strategically placed C4 explosives will obliterate the station. Does that answer your question?"

I gulped loudly.

"Er... yes, Lieutenant. Thank you. Please proceed."

Walking us through the room toward the narrow end, she continued:

"Each of the quadrants on this deck has almost two-thousand square feet and only two passages in or out: the pod bay hatch we just used and the bulkhead core room door we're approaching. If we ever have a dome rupture or docking bay accident God forbid then we can seal off each quadrant independently from the core for flood control."

"Yes, God forbid. What's behind that wall over there? I smell fresh coffee," Briscoe added preoccupied looking over a bank of workstation consoles with several seated workers scrutinizing large video screens.

"Oh, that's the coffee bar for this quadrant, want some?" she replied. "I could use a cup myself."

"Well does a whale poop in the ocean Lieutenant? I thought you'd never ask."

90

Fortunately, that broke our red-eye tour. I mean it was interesting and everything but I was so tired her words were bouncing off my brain; it was so overloaded with new information it couldn't accept more. Besides, I had started worrying about Lindy wondering if she had been told of my disappearance, what her reaction would be and if she'd hate me forever for this.

When I finally voiced my concern to Lt. Williams as we sat with our coffee at a small reading table, she suggested, "Ask Ivy. She'll know."

"Really?"

Surveying the surrounding area filled with bookshelves and a black vault like the one that Greenfield opened at HQ, I asked, "Where is she? Where's her eye on the wall?"

"She has four sensors in each quadrant one on each bulkhead wall. The closest one is right by the coffee pot over there. Many of our staff use her for retrieving information as they sip their caffeine trying to find answers to their problems. Ivy has a great scientific mind, is an expert educator and logician. and does pretty well at answering medical and psychological questions too. She can even send email for you but security filtered. Ever use Google?"

"Of course." I answered.

"Well since you have no laptop or smart phone down here you'll still have unanswered questions for Googling and a need for external contacts as we all do. Just ask her. She's your verbal link into that ginormous database they keep plus more from our station's files."

"Mind if I try?"

"No knock yourself out."

Taking my cup to Ivy's panel, I stood and read a few brief instructions.

"Ivy, Matt Cross here. I have a request."

The dark reddish center brightened and began to pulsate with my heartbeat.

"I know who you are, Matt Cross. Welcome to Discovery One. What is your request?"

Her soft voice was eerie but soothing like a voice from my conscience, a guardian angel, a close friend. It drew my confidence and trust.

"Has my wife Lindy Cross been told of my sudden disappearance? Is she worried or mad?"

Her lens pulsed faster reading my anticipation of an answer. I didn't notice my increased heart rate but she did.

"One moment," she said. A soft mechanical purring filled the silence for seconds before I heard the sound of a telephone line ringing.

"Hello this is Lindy."

"Hello, Ms. Cross. I called your husband from Florida early this morning and spoke with him. Do you remember the call?"

"Yes sir, oh-dark-thirty about some new mission I believe."

"That's correct, Lindy. An emergency mission to save a U.S. deep-sea asset and its workers from their demise. We had no choice but to deploy him immediately."

"Deploy him immediately? Oh my God! He won't be coming home today?"

"No, ma'am. Not today or tomorrow. I'm sorry. He's working with us now. You can expect him to be gone up to a month."

"Who's *us*? Where is he?"

"Ma'am, I can't tell you that but if you need more information please contact his boss Carlos Montoya at MBORC. Do you have that number?"

"Why yes of course b-b-but---"

"I'm sorry, Ms. Cross, but that is all I can say. Have a good day."

A dial tone replaced the conversation over Ivy's speaker.

"Yes, she has been notified, Matt Cross. Does that answer your concern?"

"Sure but how did you do that? That *was* her voice."

"You would be quite surprised at my intercept resources, Matt Cross."

"Well thank you, Ivy. That comforted me somewhat," I said worried at the trembling in Lindy's voice at the end of her conversation.

"Oh, Matt Cross," Ivy said as I turned to leave, "I previously printed an ID badge for you and Mica Briscoe. Please wear them at all times on station to insure your identity. I see that neither of you is wearing one."

"Understood, Ivy. Mine's in my kitbag; I'll put it on immediately. I'll tell Briscoe to wear his too."

"Thank you, Matt Cross. Ivy out."

Back at the table I found the Lieutenant's instruction continuing. I sat, pulled the ID from my kitbag and clipped it to my drying wetsuit's collar, then nodded for Briscoe to do the same.

Although I was interested in learning everything about my new residence and its wonders, I could hardly keep my eyes open and my wetsuit was beginning to bother me. I needed sleep, dry clothes, and another cup of coffee. Luckily, I had just refilled it while talking with Ivy.

"The station operates in three eight-hour shifts," she continued, "graveyard, early, and late. That's 0000 hours to 0800 hours for graveyard, 0800 to 1600 hours for early, and 1600 to 2400 hours for late. Now since you're both on non-essential duty and you need to interact with all the personnel you can work whenever you want. Because there's no day or night down here we work around the clock but we keep the first and second team separated. And their shifts will vary depending on task urgency."

She looked around lowered her voice and continued:

"The first team is concerned with the A-mission of radiation monitoring while the second's concern is the signal intercept Z-mission. Got that? You can tell which team you're interacting with by looking at their ID badges. The A-team has a small notch cut from the right corner of the badge while the Z team has a full top margin. Almost undetectable for the unknowing it's there if you look closely. Now a crucial warning: never refer to anything Z unless you're in the walk-in vault in Quadrant 4. I shouldn't be telling you this here but I know this week's graveyard shift includes only Z staff so we're secure here. You'll learn more about that over time but consider that information under your clearance Umbra Z."

"What about Ivy? She can probably hear," I asked, remembering she was just over my shoulder.

"She's cleared way above everything on this station so no worries. Just be careful because she can tell if you're discussing Z-information with A-cleared staff. That's a no-no and you'll be quickly flagged with a security violation isn't that right Ivy?"

From the wall, she answered:

"Correct, Susan Williams, and you're correct there are no A staff in your vicinity at this time but you should be in the vault for this conversation. Minor violation but good test."

She backed her chair from the table, stood and looked at us.

"You guys done with coffee?"

We nodded together and stood. I dreaded the thought of more touring and fortunately, she must have read my mind.

"Let's save the rest of the tour for later today after you catch some z's. I know you both must be exhausted so why don't you head off to your quarters and hit it. There's no reveille in the station so don't worry about being awakened by a bugle or ship's 1MC or anything like that. Just tell Ivy your desired wake up time and she'll awaken you pleasantly."

Turning to leave with Briscoe, I spun back.

"Wait, where are our quarters?"

"Oh I'm so sorry. I forgot. The time must be getting to me too. Follow me and I'll show you."

She wound us around unused workstations to the front of the room then through the convex bulkhead door into the core chamber. There a cylindrical elevator awaited us its curved door open.

"Please push Deck 2," she said nodding to the Chief.

The door slid shut and swiftly we rose sucked up like a money carrier in a bank's pneumatic tube. The Deck 2 light illuminated immediately followed by the whishing of the opening door.

"Pneumatic elevator, huh?" Briscoe said.

"No. Hydraulic elevator," she answered, "Uses external water pressure to push it up and down. Another Bowman invention."

"Of course," I said rolling my eyes.

Through the elevator's open door, she led us around a circular hallway I estimated to be ten feet wide, its inner wall surrounding the core chamber. Above each outer wall door (I counted seventeen) was a crew member's name, his rank and military affiliation except for the last six. All affiliations were U.S. Navy except three: J. David Bowman – PhD, DV#1 and DV#2. Three more door titles extended down the hall beyond those: Head 1, Head 2 and Rec Hall. *These last six must be suites* I thought: they're twice the width of the others. Must be my lucky day.

"Pick your poison," she smiled returning us to the Distinguished Visitor rooms. Then pointing past them she added, "There are unisex heads down there so knock before entering and use the Rec Hall freely when you need a break, coffee, or snacks."

I hated when the Chief and I had to choose between anything. I always deferred to him and he always threw it back to me usually winning.

"You take DV#1," I said, "You're older and wiser. Suits you better."

Snickering he bantered, "No, Marker, you just want to be nearer the bathrooms. If I'm older and wiser as you said then *I* need to be closer to the bathrooms. Admit it."

Agreeing I pushed open the door to DV#1 and glanced inside.

Briscoe did the same with DV#2 and exclaimed, "Wow there's a lotta room in here, but it's kinda like a wacky-house bowling alley."

"You should see mine," Williams said. "It's not one of these suites but it's really quite comfortable. They do take a little getting used to but they grow on you especially with the rocking of the deep-water currents at night."

She turned to leave and looked back.

"Oh, you'll find a dresser with a stock of one-size-fits-most jumpsuits, shirts, socks, underwear and as for shoes we recommend always wearing dive boots because the decks are often slippery. Ivy is on the wall at the head of your bunks; you can't miss her glowing eye. So good night gentlemen. See you around 1000 hours in the Mess on Deck 1. Okay?"

We both poked out our heads from our rooms and watched her walk to her room six doors down shaking her head.

As her door closed, I looked back at him. "I gotta hit the head before I bed down, Chief. See you in the morning."

"Number one or number two?" he asked.

"Hey, Chief, that's none of your business," I answered wondering why he'd ask.

Snickering, he answered, "No dummy I meant head number one or two. I'll use the other one."

"Oh," I laughed, "I'll take one you take two."

"Roger that, Marker. Right behind you. Too much coffee. I'll be rising around nine; still not comfortable with going back on military time."

"But you'll get used to it," I added, chuckling down the hall.

Not long after that I returned and settled into my pie-slice of a room. It was eight feet across at the door thirty feet deep and the far wall, I stepped off at about twenty feet across. After confirming my measurements, Ivy assured me that everything was okay in the station and that the incident with Li was just an anomaly caused by human error. It appeared that we might be going home early.

Sleep soon overtook my curiosity ending my day... then from outside a loud booming thunderclap and rumbling shook me from my bunk.

Chapter 10
The Midnight Zone

The last time a bone-chilling fear of the ocean affected me like this was when I was ten on the beach with Jeremy and he challenged me to enter the water. Thinking back to that time my panic probably wasn't justified. The water had taken my little brother and in my young mind, I blamed it. Now Jeremy was in my mind again surrounding me with his creation: a giant half gumball machine teetering on the bottom of the Pacific. Informed that it was an engineering temple of safety, I expected it to be just that, not the spook house I was experiencing. Dealing with the unknowns of a failed promise was far worse.

Rushing from my quarters, I ran into Briscoe exiting from next door wide-eyed and searching the hallway. All at once, doors down the hall crashed opened and seven crewmen flew into hallway appearing startled and confused.

"What in the hell was that?" one asked. Another mentioned that the jolt threw him from his bunk. A brief chaos ensued as the hallway filled with questions mostly about Bowman's whereabouts.

One specific question caught my ear, "Where's the Captain? Edwards? He's not here either."

Lt. Williams in camouflage pajamas scanned the small group and remembered.

"Last I saw of him he was prepping SeaPod 2 for today's dives and intending to repair its AutoDocker."

Her eyes widened.

"Oh my God I wonder if he's okay."

Across the hallway on the core wall, the Ivy panel brightened and glowed steadily with the answer.

"No. I am sorry, Susan Williams, he is not. He took SeaPod 2 out of the bay an hour ago saying he was testing the AutoDocker but never came back. I warned him against diving alone but he insisted it was safe. I have analyzed the frequencies and source of the vibrations that rocked the dome with two conclusions. Either the dome just had a direct hit from a wandering sperm whale or a SeaPod impact just below Q1 on the crawler base. I have no other information. However I do not find the Captain's biometric signals registering anywhere in the station so he must still be away on the outside."

She ran to Ivy's wall console.

"Did you try to SeaCom him?"

"Yes of course. He did not respond but it is possible that he was out of range."

"What about sonar? See anything?"

"No. My sonar was in the passive mode. There were no sounds other than the SeaPod's motors and some echolocation clangs from nearby sperm whales. They seem to be very active near Discovery One lately."

"Ivy, heat and prep two Exosuits in Pod Bay 1 for an immediate dive," Williams said, "Unlike Edwards I insist on going out with a diving buddy. His action was rather careless."

The Lieutenant glanced back at our group.

"Who wants to go with me?"

Briscoe held up his hand.

"Count me in. Where do I start?"

He stared at me questioningly, but I shook my head no. I wanted to volunteer but I had never been in an Exosuit and now was not the time to learn. I bowed to him and smiled my approval.

"Good," she said, "Get into your jumpsuit and dive boots and meet me in Pod Bay 1 in five minutes. Marker, you're up next time but you can help us load."

Off the elevator onto Deck 1, Briscoe and I found the door leading from the core chamber into Quad 1 by its large overhead letters. Entering the room, passing banks and banks of large electronics racks with indicator lights flashing wildly, I immediately knew it was the computing quadrant. It was warmer than Quad 2, hummed with whirring fans, and smelled of electronics.

On the rear wall a stenciled sign over a downward pointing red arrow read Pod Bay 1 Hatch. It caught Briscoe's eyes and he veered off toward the arrow looking at his watch. My watch said six minutes had passed since Lt. Williams told us to meet her and she was nowhere around. Suddenly Williams' head poked up through the hatch; an eerie sight appearing to be a separated cropped-blond-haired head resting on the floor.

"Hurry your asses up," she squawked. "Dr. Bowman and I are waiting."

Briscoe followed her straight down but I hesitated leery of meeting Jeremy after almost twenty years. *Would he recognize me? What would he be like? Was he really the tyrant they claimed he was?*

I took a deep breath and started down the ladder.

Before my foot could hit the last rung, a somewhat familiar voice rang out through the bay.

"Well if I didn't see this I wouldn't believe it. I saw the name Matt Cross on the DV boarding list but never in a million years would I have expected it to be you my aquaphobic friend and sandcastle apprentice from long ago. How in the hell are you Matt? Long time no see."

I smiled, pleasantly surprised at his warm greeting, and held out my hand for a handshake. Instead he rushed over, ignored my hand, and hugged me.

"Hello, old friend," I smiled. "It looks like you've done quite well for yourself Jeremy."

I'm not sure if I would have recognized him had I not known it was him. He had shot up in height now reaching two inches over me (and I'm six feet tall) lost some weight to the point of almost being skinny and wore Ben Franklin frameless round glasses on the tip of his nose. With his short graying hair, black turtleneck, and faded jeans, he reminded me of someone but I couldn't quite put my finger on who. I glanced away shaking the familiar but unidentifiable image from my mind.

"This is some sandcastle you built."

"Thank you, Matt, but I go by Dave now. Jeremy just brings back too many bad juvenile memories."

"Well then Dave it is. You do realize that you're the reason I'm here don't you?"

"And, Matt, you're one reason Discovery One is here. Many of your additions and suggestions for my sandcastles were incorporated into my design of this station; you should notice them as you tour it."

"Like the submarine core?" I asked.

"Exactly. But how did I influence you?"

"That day on the beach before you left. Remember what you said?"

"Something about not fearing the water like a wild animal I'm sure. I wasn't smart enough to create that maxim myself. I learned it from my dad. Except he continued on with words that I never told you. He always added 'Learn from it. Live by it. Shape it. Make it your world.'"

"Ahem," Williams interrupted, "I hate to break up this old home week, but in case you've forgotten we're supposed to be diving right now. Briscoe's already suited up and I need help getting into mine. Marker can you assist me while Dr. Bowman fires up SeaPod 1?"

"Sure, where do I start?"

Having sealed her in the Exosuit, I rolled the hatch stairs back from SeaPod 1 and followed her instructions. After climbing the ladder, I closed and locked the hatch then pulled a microphone off the wall.

"Ready. Now what?"

"You're now communicating with us on the bay intercom," Williams answered. "See the green Flood Pod Bay button to your left?"

"Yeah, got it."

"Push it. It'll turn yellow as the bay fills then red about five minutes later when you can push the Open Pod Bay Door button. If you forget my instructions Ivy will do it automatically so don't worry too much but never try to open the hatch lock with a red light. A tiny stream of seawater at this pressure can cut you in half. We call it a water knife. Norris lost part of his hand to one."

"Roger that," I said.

"The hatch does have a safety interlock that prevents its opening with a flooded bay but things around here have been so strange lately I wouldn't trust it. Just remember: green – bay is clean, red – open you're dead. Same for when we return; wait for the green to open the hatch. Got that?"

"Well, I certainly hope so but what if the light fails goes dark? Then what?"

"Then SeaCom us. We'll let you know when it's safe."

"All right. Ready for flooding?"

"Briscoe's got a pincer up, Bowman's got thumbs up in the SeaPod, and I'm ready so go!"

It was all new to me but very logical and mostly aligned with my prior diving experience. I had rarely used a floodable diving bay but it seemed safe enough so I was comfortable with pushing the Flood button.

"It's a go," I said.

Five minutes passed before the yellow light on the wall changed to red. During that time, the floor under my feet had vibrated with the flooding water's flow but stopped abruptly when the red light illuminated.

"Opening pod bay door," I said into the microphone.

Slowly and cautiously, I reached up and flipped open the switch's safety cover and pushed the button.

"We're out, yippee," said Briscoe sounding euphoric. The last time I heard him that happy he was wearing the same type suit about to be accidentally dislodged from the hull of my mini-sub only to float lost at sea for twelve suspenseful hours. Nevertheless, he loved that life.

"SeaPod 1 leaving the bay," Bowman said. A motor rumbled below me then whirred away into the distance.

The silence for the next few minutes was deafening. I expected something, anything from the SeaCom and then it came.

"Oh my God! I found the SeaPod. Wrecked down on the base of the crawler platform. Broken into pieces. Tangled in one of our tractor wheels," said Bowman. "Divers get over here and help me find Edwards. I don't see him."

"Be right there, Dave," Lt. Williams said. "Briscoe where are you?"

"Right behind you, Lieutenant, coming up fast."

"Yeah now I see your floods. Follow me. I've got the SeaPod in sight. Heading down."

More silence.

"The hatch cover is open bent backward. Edwards is not inside. The cockpit is flooded empty of life," Williams screamed distorting the SeaCom. "Dave, can you point your floods down at me?"

"Just a minute, Lieutenant. Maneuvering around."

"I see the point of impact on the crawler base right below the bridge's viewport," she yelled. "A few feet higher and it would have taken out our helm."

That was the first time I had heard the bridge mentioned. I knew it had to exist but had no idea where it was located in the station. It resided in the crawler base a logical place for the driver near the ocean floor with a full view of the seafloor ahead.

"Ivy, activate the bridge's forward floods," Bowman's voice crackled.

"Wow!" said Briscoe.

"What a mess. I don't see the Captain but we're not going anywhere until we pull this wreckage from these forward wheels."

"Briscoe, can you move anything with your claws?" Williams asked.

"Unh. Argh! Damn!"

"No. It's locked in tight. Looks like it's going to take a bigger force than I've got and my power level is dropping."

"Back off guys and let me grab it with my claw arms. I can try pulling it with my reverse thrusters. Maybe that'll work."

Seconds went by.

"We're clear, Dave. Move in."

"Got it in my grippers. Careful of my prop wash divers. Don't want to blow you guys around."

"See anything to grab onto, Briscoe?" Williams asked.

"Yeah. Got a handgrip bar in my pincers. You?"

"I'm hanging on to another one. You're okay to go, Dave."

Moments later, the intercom crackled with Briscoe's voice.

"Whoa whoa whoa! Stop, Dave. You're about to pull the tractor wheel off its axle. It's tangled in the SeaPod's cables. Looks like it's gonna take a cutting torch to break it loose."

"Yeah, I was afraid of that," Bowman sighed, "My SeaPod's starting to act up so I'm breaking off and heading back to the bay. You divers take one last look, make some mental notes of what you see and the follow me in. I'll inform you when I dock and the turbulence settles."

"Roger that, Dave. Give us five," Williams replied.

Even though I had no visuals of the action outside I could see them in my mind through their intercom conversation. I knew Bowman was motoring back to the bay and Briscoe and Williams were inspecting the crash site in Exosuits looking like storm troopers probing a crash site but I needed more information to follow their discoveries. It soon came just as I wished.

"What's that on the SeaPod's hull, Briscoe? See it? Right below the big crack."

"Yeah. Looks like some form of writing maybe with a red grease marker. Symbols look Egyptian like stylistic hieroglyphics."

"We'll take a look at them when we get the pod back in the bay later today. Now for some reason my suit is prematurely losing power. I need to go in and check it. Ready to head back?" she asked.

"You bet. My suit's getting cold. I'm gonna need a whole pot of hot coffee to take this chill from my bones. After you."

"I'm buying," she said.

Their return to the pod bay mirrored their departure quick and silent. I guess I must have nodded off sitting there by the floor hatch waiting for them. Only when a voice over the intercom shouted, "Hey open up in there," did I jolt awake with a green Flood Pod Bay button blinding my eyes.

"Sorry guys. Coming."

After securing the SeaPod and Exosuits in their racks then clearing the pod bay, we followed Bowman to a large table in the Quad 3 Mess Hall. Across the back wall recessed behind a cafeteria style serving line appeared to be a kitchen of sorts but it was closed and dark. On left end of the tray-slide railings, a steaming urn of perking coffee invited us to partake and nobody refused.

Bowman sat centered on one of many long dining tables visually searching the room for something. Occasionally he would sip from his coffee then look back at his tablet and type into its keyboard. Briscoe and Williams sat at the table's end with me relating details of their dive. Nothing stood out as unusual other than the strange markings on the hull but after some discussion Lt. Williams remembered that they were the same as the hieroglyphs she saw on Lt. Dan Li's empty Exosuit.

The SeaPod had broken into three pieces: the central bubble and the port and starboard hulls held together by wiring and cables as if something had split it down the middle. Briscoe assured me that from the looks of the damage to the tractor base it was the impact that did it but Williams wasn't so sure: Edwards was an expert SeaPod pilot and wouldn't have made such a fatal error.

She referred to the nearby Ivy console.

"Ivy, how much time has Edwards logged in SeaPods?"

"As a passenger or driver?" Ivy asked.

"Driver."

"One moment, Susan Williams."

A soft purring sound, which I now related to her computation mode, filled the silence.

"Over his five month tour of duty on station Captain Edwards has logged 304 hours in SeaPod 1, 396 hours in SeaPod 2, 105 hours in SeaPod 3 and 95 hours in SeaPod 4 for a total of 900 hours at the joystick. That averages to 5.96 hours per day over his tour. The highest of any driver on the second team. Does that answer your question, Susan Williams?"

"Yes. Thank you, Ivy."

"Why so many more hours logged in SeaPod 1 and 2?" I asked.

"Oh, those are located in the front-facing bays on our bow. They're simply closer to the work area when we stop at a new location. The rear-facing aft bays are used mainly when obstructions or malfunctions block the main ones."

She wrote something on a small notepad and then looked at us.

"So see? I highly doubt that with his experience he would nosedive a SeaPod into the crawler base."

"You mean like you almost did, Lieutenant?" Briscoe asked grinning.

Blushing, she took a swig of coffee and glared back at him.

"Yes, Mr. Briscoe, like I almost did, but I didn't say his crash wasn't caused by a defective AutoDocker. He may not have known how to fix the problem like Marker did. I should have explained the fix to him before he took the pod out." She dropped her head, sniffled, and wiped her eyes.

Trying to break her mood I whispered, "Hey, Lieutenant. what's Bowman working on so intently?"

She glanced his way then back at me and softly replied, "Probably today's POD, our plan of the day. He posts it early every morning before the vault meeting at 1100 hours. It'll be out in a few hours. Tells everyone their tasks for the day."

"Yep," the Chief said, "Seen lots of 'em. Never good news."

"Well I'm sure this one will focus on Edwards's accident and its cause. And since we're rather hard to reach by the NTSB and they don't even know of our existence, Bowman will name a Go Team as they do and send them out. In this case, I expect your names will be on his short list. That's why you're here isn't it?"

"According to Admiral Greenfield, yes," I answered, "But I should first learn the Exosuit before I go out don't you think?"

"No better time than the present," Briscoe said rising from the table, his chair screeching over the floor. "Drink up your coffee and follow me back to Pod Bay 1."

As I stood to follow him, Bowman looked up from his tablet and over at us.

"Where are you gents headed? Up to your racks?"

"No, but I wish," Briscoe said, "I'm taking Marker down to the Exosuits and give him a ten-minute crash course on their use."

He chuckled.

"Well, Mr. Briscoe, you could have chosen a better word to describe your intensive course but it's good that you're training him. You'll both be going out at 1200 hours to survey, assess and recover the wreckage. Bring it back to Pod Bay 2. I'll want to inspect it there."

Pausing he added, "Oh, you'll need a cutting torch; I'll have that ready and waiting in the docking bay for your departure. Now Lt. Williams will track you in a SeaPod for your recovery needs like towing, lifting, or moving big things around. It's all in this POD."

I looked at my watch for the first time since they found the wreck and saw it was six-fifteen a.m. civilian time. A half-mile over our heads the sun would soon be rising above the eastern horizon, a sight I knew I couldn't enjoy for another month.

I hadn't slept more than an hour in almost a day but this was what I expected: either balls-to-the-wall busy or twiddling-your-thumbs idle with no in-between. I knew I could sleep later and enjoy it better.

"Let's go, Chief," I said.

His 'ten-minute crash course' lasted most of three hours but in that time I had been locked in the suit twice almost gagging on the neoprene-permeated airflow, walked through the unflooded bay once and then spent thirty minutes floating and propelling around the flooded bay testing all the joints and seals. He never trusted me enough to open the bay door to the ocean fearing another accident but dousing the bay lights perfectly simulated the outside midnight zone. And as I expected in that simulation I found the suit's forward floods crucial to seeing and finding anything; but just like driving a car at night with its headlights on I had to point myself toward where I wanted to see or go. I passed the course with 'driving colors' as he put it.

We entered the Mess at 0930 hours to a half-empty room but the kitchen was still lighted and open. Aromas of eggs frying and bacon broiling lingered in the air. On the way to the serving line we passed a group of four crew members sitting together at one of a long table finishing their meals and another lone crew member sitting by herself at a smaller four-top table. Her nametag read DEASON, JILL and her ID tag had a notch telling me she was part of the nuclear assessment team. Her flowing red hair, a cute freckled face, and a tight-fitting blue jumpsuit must have attracted Briscoe. He stopped at her table, pointed toward the tray line and asked:
"Is that where we order?"
I tried to suppress a snicker but couldn't. I just hoped that she didn't see through his ruse as I did. Shortly I learned that he was just being social hating to see anybody eating alone and it worked.

"Yes it is," she answered smiling. She dropped her fork and swept her hand over the empty chairs.

"Please join me with your trays. It's always good to see new faces around here. We see so few."

"Interesting lady," said Briscoe grabbing a tray, entering the line. "Everyone seems so alone down here. Must be the tight security. Always watching over your shoulder. Two eggs over easy, two donuts, and four sausages, please."

"Or maybe a fear of the strange occurrences lately." I said placing my tray behind his. "If someone's creating them they're still down here mingling with the staff. Who knows who will be next? A short stack of pancakes, lots of butter and two slices bacon. No eggs."

"Welcome to my mess hall, gentlemen," said the culinary specialist, a tall heavyset older man dressed in a blue chef's coat and toque.

He glanced at our ID badges then continued, "My name's Chef Bill Saunders and I'll be your chef while you're at the station." Pulling our orders from steam trays, he plated them and slid them to us under the sneeze guard.

"It's your day today. It's bagless day."

"What's that mean Chef," Briscoe asked grabbing utensils for his plate.

"One day a week I cook all your meals in the kitchen. The other six... see those microwaves over there... I give you MREs in bags and you heat them up yourselves. Pretty good food and just as nutritious, but much easier on the pantry... and me."

"Oh? How big is your kitchen staff, Chef," I asked.

113

"You're looking at 'em, Mr. Cross. It's a pretty simple job except for bagless days when we run out of MREs and some damn Pacific storm hovers over us preventing a timely food drop. Then I have to make do with powdered foods and you don't want to wish those on anyone... but they're still nutritious."

"Thanks, Chef," I said filling my cup from the coffee urn. "Hope I don't have to stay that long."

I turned back, saw Briscoe seating himself at Deason's table, and joined them.

"So are you guys the troubleshooters that HQ sent down to calm our fears?" she asked as I sat.

"That's what they told us," Briscoe answered forking a piece of yolky egg white into his mouth, "but we may have trouble keeping up with the boogie man; he's already struck twice since we arrived last night."

"Yeah, that's what I heard and I hate it when things go bump in the night."

She took a small bite of toast and continued, "That really shook me up. Sometimes I wish I'd taken a desk job pushing a pencil in some nuclear lab on shore."

"What's your specialty, Ensign Deason? I see from your ID badge that you're Navy."

"I've got one doctorate in nuclear physics and another in chemical oceanography. Seems to fit well with our mission. Basically I keep the nuclear sensors calibrated and honest ensuring that the data they report is really encroachment radiation from Fukushima and not spurious radiation from other sources."

"Like what?" Briscoe asked taking another bite.

"Well, for example, when nuclear subs pass nearby or nuclear warheads are tested at sea; we occasionally find false positives in our data and must differentiate between them and our targeted data."

With my curiosity tweaked I asked, "How do you distinguish between the radiations?"

"Isotopes. From the reactors at the Fukushima Daiichi nuclear power plant. That meltdown released iodine-131, cesium-134 and cesium-137 into the Pacific. Cesium-134 is unique to the Daiichi incident while cesium-137 is produced by nuclear power plant effluents and underwater nuclear weapons testing."

Briscoe winked at me and asked, "Did you notice any unusual radiation activity during the end of March of this year?"

She thought back twirling her hair in her finger.

"Oh, hell yes. I remember now. We had the strangest event. The news said it was an underwater volcanic eruption several hundred miles south of us but it spewed out cesium-137 like crazy. Also shook the lab like a bell and disrupted our operations for days. How would you know of that?"

"Oh, a little bird told us," Briscoe answered, "but we're not talking."

"More like a big bird: an osprey," I winked back at him.

Deason looked confused then smiled.

"Well that's obviously a private joke so I won't pursue it further."

"So do we call you Dr. Deason or Ensign Deason? Which do you prefer?" I asked.

"I prefer Jill. Now if you will excuse me," she said referencing her POD, "I have to recalibrate the strontium-90 sensor, another of the Daiichi isotope probes. Took on a mound of whale dung last night from a cetacean passing overhead. Probably another damn sperm whale. Never a dull moment around here."

She stood and smiled at us.

"Welcome aboard Discovery One, gentlemen. I hope you discover what's happening down here before I have to ask for a transfer." With that, she took her tray to the wash rack and left the room.

"Hey she forgot her POD," said the Chief.

He picked it up and glanced at it then looked at his watch.

"Holy shit, Marker, we're supposed to be diving in two hours. It's on the POD."

I took it from him wanting to see for myself; knowing my memory was better with visuals than words.

"And we're supposed to be in a Vault meeting in an hour in Quad 4. Better chow down on those donuts, Chief. Clock's ticking."

Abruptly he stood and grabbed his mug.

"Want another cup?"

"Sure might as well decrease my buoyancy a little."

Returning he handed me mine, sat and then sipped from his.

"Love this coffee," he said, "At least I'm not condemned to hell with bad coffee."

"Spoken like a true CHP patrolman," I retorted laughing at his comment.

After a slug, he looked around the room then hunched over the table toward me and in a hushed tone asked, "So what do you think so far Marker? See anything we can fix?"

"Not yet but if I did I'm not sure how we could fix it. Make some voodoo dolls and stick pins in them?"

"Have you dug to the bottom of your kitbag since we got here? I mean to the bottom bottom?"

"Not yet, Chief. Haven't had time. Found a toothbrush and toothpaste but there was still something heavy further down. Know what it is?"

"Yeah. I assume you got one too. It's a tiny Smith and Wesson nine-millimeter Shield pistol. Really nice sidearm. Weighs about a pound in my hand, fits in my pocket, and holds eight rounds which are already in the clip ready to fire."

"Wow! Think we're going to need them? What if we miss and hit the dome? That could end us all."

"They supplied them with laser sights Marker so you'd have to be blind to hit the dome. Beats anything I ever carried on the force. They're easily concealable and small; we should probably start carrying them with us."

"But why? Nobody's after us."

"Yet," he said, "But what about the AutoDock failure? That could have been us if you hadn't reset the controller."

"Possibly. We'll have to examine the control unit and see if it's been sabotaged. Someone down here should know how to tell."

"Unless it was Edwards. Then we'll have to learn how ourselves. Think you can do it, Marker?"

"Uh yeah, probably with Ivy's help."

As we sat finishing our coffee, we felt a sharp bump. Not strong enough to spill our cups, but more like driving over a hump in the road; yet we were not moving.

"What in the hell was that?" I asked reflecting Briscoe's widened eyes.

"Oh, probably ran over an armadillo or something," he said with a snicker.

Not laughing. I called out.

"Chef Saunders did you feel that? What was it?"

From the kitchen came his answer.

"Don't worry; we get those bumps quite often down here. Whales diving this deep love to rub against things larger than them. Knocks off the whale lice and barnacles. That was probably one of them. Smaller one at that. Maybe a calf. The big ones often knock over the tray stack and rearrange the chairs."

"Thanks, Chef, for that comforting information," said the Chief.

I glanced at my watch and saw we had twenty minutes to find the vault room before the meeting started.

"We better get on the road, Chief."

He upended his mug and exhaled deeply.

"Ready as I'll ever be. I'm following you."

Chapter 11
The Vault

I had found navigating through Discovery One to be very intuitive thanks to Bowman's design. First, we headed out of the mess toward the narrow part of the quad, stepped through the hatch door into the core chamber, then circled until we found the Quad 4 entry door. Each quad had a unique entrance and Quad 4 was no different. Its entry hall was a severely truncated wedge of a room with two large blank video screens on opposing walls, a heavy gleaming vault door in the far wall about ten feet across, and an Ivy console beside the door. Six small chairs were distributed around the walls. To the right of Ivy was a rack of fourteen lockers with cipher locks and names on the doors. Wondering why they were there, I noticed a sign above the lockers: PLACE ALL PERSONALS IN YOUR LOCKER BEFORE ENTERING.

Briscoe was already standing in front of one labeled BRISCOE when I heard the keys beeping.

"What are you entering?" I asked.

"It says to enter your ID#. Mine's SSUMJB36Z. I'm entering it."

"Shh... don't tell *me*, Chief, just enter it. What are you going to put in there anyway?"

"Nothing. Just want to see if there's anything in there for me."

He pulled open the locker and poked his head in.

"Well see anything?"

"Two sheets of paper. One's an unclassified crew listing and the other's a Discovery One map."

He drew then out and studied them.

"Only ten of the original crew are left on this list. Li and Edwards are marked through."

"Let's hope that doesn't change. We have enough problems as it is."

Briscoe checked his watch.

"It's a quarter till. Think we should go in?"

"Nah. I suggest we wait for someone to arrive and show us the entry protocol. Could be tricky. We don't want to set off any alarms."

"Agreed."

Sighing, he sat in a chair by the lockers.

Several minutes had passed when a short stocky Asian-looking crewman entered the room, went to Ivy's panel and hesitated. He swiveled back to us revealing his badge: his name was Yung Ching and then in perfect English he said:

"May I help you, gentlemen? I see from your badges that you *are* cleared for this meeting. Are you waiting for someone in particular?"

"N-no. We just don't know how to get in," I answered embarrassed at my ignorance.

"Ni hao," he said pushing his right hand toward me.

I shook with a smile not knowing the proper Asian greeting etiquette.

"Ni hao. Don't believe we've met. My name is Matt Cross. But what does 'ni hao' mean?"

"Oh 'hello' in Mandarin. Sorry. I'm Yung Ching. Dan Li and I were trying to teach bits of Mandarin to the staff to better cope in the new Asian-American culture."

Shortly, another crewman of Asian descent joined us.

"Konnichiwa Yung."

"Ni hao Umi Shin. Did you get that message I sent you?"

"We'll talk inside," Shin answered.

Then from the hatch door came another voice, a female one:

"Well, fellas, you think you can fit a few more in here. What? Is Ivy broken again?"

Lt. Williams laughing edged into our group of four cramped together waiting to enter the vault.

Briscoe quiet until now spoke up.

"We didn't intend it this way Lieutenant; we just wanted someone to show us how to get in. Can you do it? We're gonna be late."

Smiling she nodded to Umi and Yung then walked to Ivy's eye.

"Ivy, this is Susan Pamela Williams. Requesting entry please."

Ivy's eye began to pulsate at about a beat per second.

"Greetings, Susan Williams. Please allow iris scan."

Williams placed her eye to the glowing sensor and waited.

"Thank you, Susan Williams. Now please repeat after me 'Thick rain falls through verdant rainforest zoos.'"

She repeated the phrase and looked at us.

"That's an Ivy Captcha phrase. Different for each entry. Just repeat it back to her. Assures you're not a prerecorded voice."

After a second of purring Ivy spoke:

"You alone may enter, Susan Williams. Others with you must individually log through."

I turned from Briscoe as the vault door unlocked and opened. Williams entered a small chamber with criss-crossed laser beams then passed through into a larger room. Behind her, the heavy door slammed shut.

"We should have arrived earlier," I said.

"Next?" Ivy called.

Umi, Yung and Briscoe entered the vault before me so I was the fourth and final one through. Having never been in a top-secret meeting vault before, I marveled at the security gadgets surrounding the room and the anechoic foam wedge tiles covering the walls and ceiling. On the distant wall was another hatch door covered with foam wedges, leading to somewhere. Like a sound recording studio, it was dead quiet and the eerie lack of echoes really spooked me. I guess it was to keep our conversation from being overheard by unwanted ears but I thought it was a definite overkill. As I slid into my awaiting chair, Bowman began the meeting.

"First I am required to say if any of you are not currently cleared to receive Top Secret SCI Umbra Z information you must leave the vault now under penalty of existing DOD espionage laws punishable by incarceration for life."

Pausing to scan our badges, he continued:

"No? Then I'll begin." He pulled a folder from his briefcase, opened it, and placed it in front of him by his tablet.

"First of all I'd like to welcome Mica Briscoe and Matthew Cross to our group. Sent down by HQ from Point Mugu they are top-notch divers and as they have recently shown excellent crime solvers too. They are here to investigate the strange disappearance of your friend and crewmate Dan Li. Their mission here is code-named Operation Deep Force but I'll refer to it as ODF in public.

"As you may know we've just had another accident here in Discovery One and Capt. Bill Edwards is missing. I will not yet call that an attack until we can prove it wasn't from a random failure. Now what I cannot overlook is the fact that both men are part of the TPCI group, our Transpacific Cable Intercept team. Within the next hour Cross, Briscoe and Williams will venture outside to the wreck, recover it, and bring the SeaPod's debris back to Pod Bay 2.

"Now Shin and Ching your workload has doubled with the loss of Li and Edwards so you'll be busy completing the translations from our current cable attachment but you must hasten through them; headquarters has just issued us orders to change cables starting tomorrow."

Their eyes widened with their gasps.

"Tomorrow?" Ching shouted frowning looking at Shin. "But we still have ten terabytes of data to process from Unity. Even with the TrueNorth translators helping us that could take days."

"Do what you can now then save it for later," Bowman said. "We're relocating eighty miles north to the CHUS cable, the China-US Cable Network, for a top-priority intercept. You'll have a week's time to resolve your current data before we attach to CHUS and begin data collection. Now that deadline is not flexible; several suspected Chinese national spies on the U.S. West Coast will be seeded with code-word disinformation at a DOD defense briefing on June 24. By then, we'll need to be connected and scanning for those keywords and their internet addresses through the CHUS. There's no leeway or we will miss the messages. NSA, the DIA and the CIA will all be waiting for our results so if we don't collect them all hell will break loose. They told me that they've been searching for these spies for years and this new sting may work. In fact, we have to make it work. That's why were down here. Discovery One may be decommissioned if we fail."

Lt. Williams fidgeting with her pencil, glanced at her watch.

"We'll have to retrieve the isotope collectors as well as the cable tap before then right?"

"Of course, Lieutenant," Bowman said, "as we've done before. You and Castro will attend to the Z disconnect while Norris, Alvarado and Turnbull will collect the isotope sensors. Just make sure you don't accidentally bump into each other. But if that happens remember you're removing a new experimental isotope sensor still under test."

"As we've done before," she replied.

"Correct. Now changing gears: As for progress on our Fukushima mission, I'm sad to report that our isotope sensors indicate the radioactive plume is growing, increasing in strength and moving faster than expected toward the California coast. Our instruments most recently produced readings of 7.1 becquerels per cubic meter for the Cs-137 isotope and 1.9 becquerels per cubic meter for Cs-134. Once these levels reach the beaches they could pose significant health risks for Californians. Because of this rather alarming data, we've notified the CDC and EPA to issue appropriate beach warnings. We'll have a chance to collect new data as we move the station and sample a new part of the ocean.

"The TPCI mission has been successful in collecting the requested data from the Unity cable and is the process of translation from Mandarin and Japanese to English. That resolved data will be transmitted back to Point Mugu HQ before we pull anchor tomorrow."

Forty minutes into the meeting as Bowman talked Williams checked her watch again. Bowman, running through the cable disengagement procedure for the divers noticed and stopped in midsentence.

"Got a train to catch, Lt. Williams?"

"Well no, Dr. Bowman, but we do have a SeaPod to retrieve. Your POD says we start at 1200 hours. We should be starting our pre-dive activities any time now."

"Very well then," he quipped, "Be on your way and message me through Ivy when you return."

"Yes sir, will do."

"Wait. Before you leave I want to show our guests the Z-room. Follow me, gentlemen."

He stood and walked to the back hatch door, punched a few numbers into a keypad, and pulled the handle, opening the door to a room that I would call a computer geek's dream.

Six ultramodern workstations occupied the room with three large monitors surrounding each keyboard. Four had nameplates on them: Bowman, Shin, Edwards and Ching and two simply had DV.

"In the event that you need a computer workstation for any task, use the DV stations. They're for our visitors' use. Our translators use the others for pulling data from the cables, searching for keywords, and translating the pertinent messages into English. They're assisted in the tasks by sixty-four banks of IBM's new TrueNorth neural processors courtesy of DARPA. Together they provide the capacity of a team of fifty expert interpreters working around the clock. All of that information is then sent back to our headquarters in Point Mugu via high-speed laser beams floating above us for the review of the task-originating agency."

Finished with the tour he turned to us.

"Any questions?"

"How do we get in," Briscoe asked. "You just punched some numbers into the keypad out there."

"Since you've already passed through the vault's security lock Ivy knows you're in the vault and cleared for entry into the Z-room. Just punch in your ID number so we know who's in the room. You'll have to use it again to access the DV computers. Oh, and when leave the room be sure to log out using your ID on the keypad after you exit; a loud beeping will remind you if you forget."

With that, he led us from the room, slammed the door, and logged out.

"Now, Matt and Mica, please join Lt. Williams in her recovery of SeaPod 2. I'll be waiting for your return."

Chapter 12
SeaPod 2 Recovery

In Pod Bay 1, we found Williams scurrying around the SeaPod checking seals and lights preparing for the dive. The stairs were rolled up to the hatch and in the pod's manipulator arm a suitcase-sized object with a pair of long coiled hoses caught my eye.

"Must be the cutting torch," I told Briscoe as I pointed.

"Used one before?"

"Yes but not at a thousand meters."

"I did once, freeing a black box from a sunken Navy plane. Got some quirks at this pressure though."

"I'll let you do the honor then. Just don't damage the wheel. We have to roll tomorrow."

"Now, Marker, you know me better than that. And I promise not to damage your suit either."

"Good then button me up and let's go."

As I dropped my legs into the half-suit now labeled CROSS, Briscoe went to the cutting torch, took the torch head in his hand and flicked the trigger. A loud pop echoed through the bay then a bright jet-blue flame spewed forward.

"Works fine," he said twisting the valve extinguishing the flame.

"Coming, Marker. Raise your arms."

Pulling the upper half down over me, he explained that I could do it myself using the hand pincers in an emergency but it was much faster with two divers. As he fastened and tightened the final seal locks I felt like a superhero knowing that I looked like a storm trooper; such a refreshing change over my past dives using huge bulky mini-subs. Now I was a human submarine again able to travel anywhere under my own power for hours at a time... as long as I had water.

Soon we were all in our places ready for flooding.

"Hey, who's going to operate the flooding and door controls?" Briscoe squawked from his suit's intercom. "There's no one up there to do it."

"Got the controls on my console, Briscoe," her intercom boomed. We use them for self-diving but they aren't recommended for use without a spotter. Bowman knows we're out. He's our spotter. Plus Ivy always knows too. She watches the bays with her sonar."

I watched her hands move over the console then she paused.

"Ready for flooding, guys? Make sure to lock your boots in the floor stirrups. Otherwise you'll wash around in here. Show me a sign when you're ready."

I had done it once before training with Briscoe but the boot stirrups were tricky. Below each suit were two boot-wide pairs of locking rails that required a diver to kick the aluminum boots into them. Then the rails locked onto the boot grooves much like snow skis locking onto a skier's boots. Pulling them out was trickier. A Michael Jackson moonwalk maneuver was required to release the boots and I wasn't a good moonwalker.

Kicking my boots in until they locked, I was ready for the flooding to begin. Seeing Briscoe's arm go up I raised mine.

All at once, we were standing under a powerful waterfall ribbon of water passing over our helmets into the bay's center near the SeaPod. There was no torrential flow; just perfectly metered ribbons of seawater meeting together reflecting off each other raising the water level in the bay.

Only my second time through the flooding sequence I found myself holding my breath again as the water rose up over my faceplate and slowly covered it. It brought back a fear from my youth of going underwater unable to breathe and finally relinquishing my fate to the pain in my screaming lungs. I guess it was an autonomic reaction instinctive to life for self-preservation but to me it was from my childhood's claustrophobic horror of the water surrounding me closing in for the kill. It had never happened to me before in the mini-subs but this was different: instead of a small viewport out the front like a small movie screen the Exosuit's almost one-hundred-eighty-degree panoramic view put my peripheral vision into play increasing my visual immersion. Diving had become an IMAX experience.

Another thing I noticed was the chill that raced up my suit's interior tracking the bay's rising water. I had read from the POD that the outside water temperature (which stays almost constant a thousand meters down) was forty degrees Fahrenheit only eight degrees above freezing. If it were not for the internal suit heater, I would go into hypothermic shock in ten or fifteen minutes.

But even with the suit's thick aluminum exoskeleton around me I still felt as if I were being dipped into a bucket of freezing ice water.

Suddenly the water noises roaring around my suit ceased. The bay had topped out leaving only a few shrinking overhead bubbles. Those soon disappeared as Lt. Williams opened the pod bay door to the ocean replacing the door's white surface with the infinite darkness of the midnight zone.

"Going out," said her voice through my suit's intercom. A spinning turbulence vibrated my suit and signaled her departure as she flashed the SeaPod's floods and left the bay. Briscoe unlocked his boots and drifted upward and outward toward the darkness as he activated his forward floods.

"Coming, Marker?"

"Right behind you, Chief," I answered trying to kick out of my stirrups. On the second try they released leaving me spinning in the bay's currents still churning from their departures. Now I just had to remember how to navigate the suit as Briscoe has taught me. All by voice command, he had said. Just tell it what to do, he had said.

So I said, "Quit spinning."

Nothing happened.

Then frustrated I repeated louder, "Cease spinning dammit."

Still nothing happened but I knew I was getting dizzier with each revolution.

Next, I said, "Forward one knot," and to my surprise, my suit's propulsion motors activated and accelerated me across the room crashing softly into the far wall.

Fortunately, I was traveling so slowly the impact did no damage to anything but my ego. I was a clueless fool wanting a mini-sub's comforting joystick for control. Yet now, I was spinning out of control in the vortex on the other side of the room and still getting dizzier by the moment.

"Where the hell are you, Marker? I hear you giving some weird voice commands but I still can't see you. Don't think it knows 'cease spinning dammit' but it made me laugh. In my mind's eye I saw you twirling in the bay to the Blue Danube," Briscoe said his voice growing weaker with each word.

"Not funny, Chief. I can't remember how to control this thing."

"Heads-up display to your upper right. Read its voice command list. *Stop* always works in any emergency. Just be sure to---"

I figured his intercom must have gone out of range but I wanted to hear his last words. First, I had to stop my sickening rotation.

"Stop!" I commanded.

In one motion, the inertial navigator spun up the motors to stop my spinning.

"Thanks Chief, that worked," I said not knowing if he could still hear me.

For the next few moments after my dizziness faded, I memorized the voice commands before saying anything else. But I knew the words were there on display if I needed them.

"Rotate to port ninety degrees," I tried first.

That command turned me counterclockwise toward the open bay door facing into the darkness ready to proceed.

"Forward one knot," came next. I already knew that command worked; it had just slammed me into the opposite wall.

Gently the suit's propulsion motors edged me from the sanctuary of the lighted pod bay into the dark ocean, blacker than a moonless midnight. I looked down and saw the lights from the SeaPod and Briscoe moving slowly downward toward the crawler base under the Pod Bay 1 where Edwards had crashed.

"Where is it?" Briscoe's voice crackled weak from his distance but growing stronger.

"It's supposed to be wrecked on the front port wheel right under Pod Bay 1. Remember?" Williams replied.

"Yes. I saw it there before but it's not where I remember it being. How could it have moved? It was intertwined in those wheel spokes."

"Let me turn my floods toward it. Give you more light. Must be there somewhere."

My voice-controlled approach went perfectly using the heads-up vocabulary list at first then I relied on memory for the final maneuvers. I arrived with them still hovering over the crawler's front wheel.

"I'm here, Chief. Above to your starboard."

I could see his floods point upward toward me as he leaned back looking up.

"Got you in my view, Marker. Join me down on the floor. The SeaPod's wreck is gone from the wheel. Must have drifted off."

"Heading down. Give me a sec."

Moving down toward the ocean floor, I found the Exosuit's backpack propulsion system gave me a freedom I had never before experienced. At first, I was leery of its simplicity; after all I was accustomed to diving in a fifty-ton structure needing a large diving ship for support. Now there was nothing between my body and the unthinkable crushing pressure at a thousand meters depth but a jointed aluminum shell a half-inch thick weighing in at around three-hundred pounds fully equipped.

"Hi, Chief. What's the problem."

"There you are," Briscoe said turning toward me. His intercom blasted my ears.

"Yep. Got here as soon as I could."

He pointed his arm toward the base as he rotated shining his floods toward the wheel.

"I know you didn't see it last night but there was a SeaPod stuck in the spokes of that wheel right there."

"In those bent spokes?"

"Yes. I hadn't noticed that before but they *are* bent. So that's where it was. I thought so."

Over our heads, Williams had moved SeaPod 1 to shine its forward floods down on the wheel.

"So where the hell is it, fellows?" she asked her intercom booming through my ears.

Briscoe awkwardly bent over in his suit and retrieved a small rock from the silt. Then raising it over his head, he dropped it and watched it drift downward. It fell several inches away from his drop point toward Discovery One's aft.

"The current carried it that way," he said pointing toward the rear of the station.

"Must have broken loose last night when we felt that big bump."

Watching from above, she questioned him.

"How could that have happened, Briscoe? You and I tugged on it. And even with all our horsepower *we* couldn't break it loose. How could a current do that? It would have moved the whole station."

"Let me look over there again, Lieutenant," he said.

"Come with me, Marker, I need your eyes."

Following him back to the crawler's base, I noticed a tiny object reflecting my floods. That wouldn't have been too unusual on the street but reflecting from the deep-ocean floor covered with silt it was nearly impossible.

"What is that shiny thing, Chief?" I asked pointing downward.

He reached down and grasped a short metal rod between his pincers. In the light from the hovering SeaPod, I could see it. About a quarter inch in diameter and four inches long it was hollow and had discolorations at one end. He held it up to his floods and turned it over examining it.

"Hmm," he finally said, "I'll have to take it inside to examine it but if I were a betting man I'd say it's a cutting rod just like the ones in the cutting rig on your SeaPod's robot arm."

"Lieutenant?" he asked, "Are you still holding that cutting torch in your claw?"

"Let me look."

Glancing up I saw the manipulator arm move its claw to the front of the bubble and then return to its cradle.

"Yep, still got it. Need it down there?"

"No. And I don't think I will. The SeaPod has already been cut loose."

"What? You sure?"

"Not positive but I'm holding a cutting rod right now. Unless you dropped it someone else did."

"Put it in your pouch and bring it in. See anything else? How about the wheel? Is it usable?"

"Marker, examine the wheel for structural damage. I'm going to look around here for more debris. Maybe find some cutting slag."

On his departure, I moved back to the massive tractor wheel, forced to walk with an unnatural robotic motion. Now that I had filled the suit's ballast and achieved negative buoyancy, I could stroll the ocean floor as long as my movements matched the swivel joints' restrictions.

Out the corner of my eye as I stared up at the mangled spoke, I noticed a small flickering bluish light off in the distance moving with an erratic pattern but definitely moving.

"Hey guys," I called out, "I see a faint glow moving in the distance out forward from the crawler base. Anyone else see it?"

"Is it blue?" Williams asked.

I turned to face it and lost track of the bogey. "Now it's gone. Just dimmed out."

"Kill your floods, Marker" Briscoe said from somewhere near me. "Too much light pollution to see it." I couldn't see him but his intercom signal was loud and clear.

Quickly scanning the heads-up vocabulary, I found the command:

"Floods off."

Immediately, I submerged myself into total darkness with only my helmet's dim help-screen glow and Briscoe's floods hitting my eyes.

"It's back. Still moving randomly but growing larger... and yes it is blue."

Williams' intercom squawked.

"All right everyone kill your floods. I want to see this light."

I had experienced the blackness of the midnight zone before but there was always a visual anchor near me: a comforting shadow or glow. Now there was nothing but a tiny flickering blue glow out at the edge of my perception.

Seconds passed and then Williams' intercom blared out a cackling laugh before she spoke.

"It's an anglerfish! That's its photophore you're seeing. We call them the fireflies of the midnight zone. See them all the time down here. She's just fishing for a meal and not very far away either. They're less than a foot long."

I breathed a sigh of disappointment thinking I had discovered a link to the recent mysterious events. It was just a fish but an unusual one that I had never seen.

"Floods on." I commanded.

Briscoe still behind me in the distance blared, "Turn those floods off, Marker. I've got something very strange over here."

138

"Floods off. What do you have, Chief? And where are you anyway?"

"Over here, Marker, under Pod Bay 2."

I spun around searching for him but saw nothing.

"Flash your floods so I can find you."

The flash was only momentary but long enough for me to see that he was standing over something, kicking up silt with a boot and looking down. Keeping his location in my mind I moved slowly through the darkness until I finally saw the glow of his helmet's display illuminating his distorted face. In his expression, I found something I seldom saw from him: a wide-eyed stare of confusion mired with awe and wonderment.

"Whatcha got there, Chief?"

"L-look Marker," he murmured, his voice shivering barely audible through the intercom. His arm was extended downward to a glow buried in the mud. Not a blue glow but one of a million colors all happening at once.

I backed off and stared down with him for moments, trying to reconcile what I was really seeing. It appeared to be a point glowing from under the floor, brighter in the center and fading in brightness for six or seven inches out. Outside the ring, the floor returned to a black nothingness.

"What in God's name is that, Chief?" I asked unable to turn away.

"Don't know. Maybe a translucent magma fissure. Maybe a bioluminescent creature but it won't budge when it kick it. I'm mystified yet weirdly awed by it."

"What are you guys talking about down there?" asked Williams. "I can't see you anymore. Can I turn my floods back on? My sonar's not accurate enough to hold this distance in the darkness. "

"Yes. Sorry. We're over under Pod Bay 2. Watch for Marker's floods. He'll guide you here."

He motioned for me to turn around and light up my floods.

I spun around and said, "Floods on," expecting her to lock on to my visual.

Slowly she turned the SeaPod toward us.

"Gotcha, Marker. Coming."

Watching her approach over our location, I noticed the SeaPod drift slightly off course downward toward the crawler base.

"Everything okay Lieutenant?" I asked.

"Oh hell no, Marker. I've lost control again. Just like before."

"Reboot!" I yelled. "Remember? Flip the breaker!"

"Trying...."

The lights over our heads went dark. I could feel a turbulence in the water and through the intercom hear the water rushing by her SeaPod but had no idea where she was. I began to pray wanting to push the loading bar across the screen again. Suddenly her floods flashed back to life and I saw the SeaPod veer off heading away from the station only feet before hitting the massive tractor structure.

"Whew! That was close, Marker," said the Chief. "Well done."

With a crackling sound, the SeaPod's intercom reactivated.

"Thank you again, Marker. Do you have any idea what's wrong with this damn machine?" Her voice was trilling coming in breaths.

I turned back toward the Chief, looked down at the glowing visually churning spot, and answered:

"Yes Lieutenant. I think we're standing over it. Do not attempt to return to our location. There's something here in the mud that we don't understand. It may be affecting the SeaPods."

As I warned her, I glanced up to my heads-up display noticing a flickering in my peripheral vision. The display was cross-hatched with visual noise making it unreadable.

"Is your HUD working okay, Chief? Mine's on the fritz."

His eyes rolled up to the inside of his helmet and then bewildered, he looked back at me.

"Mine's the same, Marker. What's going on?"

"Let's get the hell out of here, Chief, before our suits fail. Whatever that is it's dangerous. Affecting everything electronic. Go. Go. Go!"

As we rotated our suits to leave, I realized we might lose our location once gone. The glow was almost impossible to see unless we were standing directly over it with our floods off. I looked up at the SeaPod drifting not far away.

"Lieutenant? Can you drop that cutting torch kit on the floor so we can find it?"

"I'm afraid to come any closer Marker but I can drop it out here. Not a long walk for you. Can you see my floods now?" Williams asked her voice stronger now.

"Yes. Drop down to the floor and release it there. I'll head toward your lights, retrieve it, and bring it back here using the Chief as a return beacon. I think I can see you both at the same time."

"On my way," she said. "I'll watch for your lights and drop it near you."

"Activate your floods, Chief, and move away from that thing a few meters but keep your eye on it. I'm going to drop that kit down there so we can find it later; it'll serve as a visual marker in this damn darkness."

"Good idea," he said reaching his left arm across to his right arm's suit cuff. His pincer dropped into a small indentation causing his suit to flare with floods. "I'll be here."

"What did you just do, Chief?" I asked, curious about his motion.

"Turned on my floods."

"How?"

"Oh. I must have forgotten to tell you. There are a few buttons in your right sleeve cuff that control some basic suit functions if your voice control fails. Big letters over them indicate their functions. The top one's for floodlight control, bottom one's for suit stabilization... same as the *Stop* voice command."

"Now you tell me. Thanks a lot, Chief."

I turned back and saw Williams hovering in the SeaPod near the floor not far away like an awaiting rescue helicopter.

"Coming, Lieutenant. Hold for me."

Skipping over the ocean bed to her floods, I felt like a NASA moon walker jumping three-foot bounds at a time. The only difference I found was the gentle deep ocean currents blew me a few feet sideways with each leap so I dogged it, jumping off course with each step compensating for the lateral drift. Soon I was there, standing only yards under the SeaPod hovering above me so close I could hear the motors' rumble and see silt swirling around my boots.

"Drop it," I said. "I'll get it."

The manipulator arm with the kit unfolded and reached out resembling a spider offering a strange gift, then its claw opened releasing the kit into a slow topsy-turvy drop to the mud. As it hit, a small cloud of silt billowed up all around but was quickly dispersed by the SeaPod's turbulence, flitting it away in all directions.

As she lifted off the drop site, I saw my chance and went in after it.

"Got it!" I shouted. Then turning back to Briscoe, I noticed his floods were dimmer that when I left him.

"Are you okay, Chief? Your floods are dimming."

"Yep I realize that, Marker. Don't know why but my power meter's dropping, too. May be a short in my circuitry somewhere. I don't notice the dimming so much because the glow below me is brightening."

"Hold tight. I'm coming," I answered worried there might be a connection.

In the twenty seconds it took me to return Briscoe's floods we so dim they were almost useless but I could still see him standing there near the glow, illuminated from below as if he was standing over a stage's footlights.

"Here. This should mark it."

I dropped the torch kit directly over it blocking some of the light but expecting anything to happen.

"Good pitch, buddy."

"Now let's get you away from here before you're powerless. I think that thing is draining your power."

"Aw don't be ridiculous, Marker. That cannot happen. There's no way," he said, his intercom weaker now.

"Let's go in ridiculous or not, Chief. Even my power meter's dropping, now."

We successfully reached our destination minutes later after half-walking, half-motoring back to the base of Pod Bay 1. Since his suit's propulsion motors had failed to provide him with the required lift to reach the awaiting bay still open and lighted for our return, I managed to grab his suit and lift him with me. Soon after that, Williams docked SeaPod 1 on its docking pad, again forcing us to use the stirrups against the wild eddy currents in the docking bay.

Williams' purging of the bay was fortunately uneventful. I was thankful because I didn't know much more stress I could take. I needed a checklist of things to worry about now with the introduction of another anomaly in my previously orderly life. It was just too much happening too soon. And, as expected, nothing was what it seemed.

Chapter 13
The Monopole

On our return to the station, we headed straight to the mess for coffee. Briscoe insisted and the Lieutenant and I agreed. We had a presentation to prepare before Bowman's meeting and we knew a group consensus of our mission's discoveries was in order. Otherwise, he might suspect some form of deep-sea mass hysteria.

Williams took a pen and small notepad from her pocket and began to write.

"Number one," she said, "The SeaPod was gone. Apparently cut from the tractor wheel according to Briscoe."

He nodded agreement.

"Number two: Briscoe found a piece of cutting rod. Still have that, Briscoe?"

He pulled it from his shirt pocket and dropped it on the table.

"Yep, brought it from my dive pouch. That's it."

I picked it up and examined it.

"Looks like a torch rod to me."

"Number three," she continued, "and this is a whopper: Briscoe discovered a glowing point in the silt near Pod Bay 2. When I tried to approach it, my SeaPod navigation failed. I had to reboot the system as Marker did yesterday only this time the SeaPod, a different one I should add, was not on AutoDock. Comments?"

I had to speak no matter how off-the-wall it sounded.

"When I saw the Chief kicking the silt from its surface, it seemed to come alive glowing brighter with more colors as I watched. Maybe it's just me but I see a strange connection here. On our first approach to the station when you were driving, Lieutenant, the same system blackout occurred as we passed over the object. Then Edwards took the same SeaPod out and crashed it coming out of Pod Bay 2. He had to pass over the object on his way to the front of the station to crash under Pod Bay 1. Finally, the Chief's suit power weakened to near failure mode as he stood over the object waiting for me to retrieve the torch pack. And when I returned and stood there with him and dropped the pack, my power also began to fade. It's like the object is stealing power."

"Or control," Briscoe said. "It's a monopole, a center of attraction. I've read about them somewhere. But I think they're only theoretical."

He cast his eyes down then stared at me.

"I hate to say this, Marker, but I'm in full agreement with you. That thing is sucking the life out of everything around it. But why hasn't it done that before? Did you notice anything unusual out there before we arrived, Lieutenant?"

She closed her eyes for a moment.

"Um no. Not that I can remember. Except Dan Li's empty Exosuit was found not far from that location."

"So maybe it was waiting to be triggered by some motion and Briscoe's boot aroused it."

"That's absurd, Marker. You've been watching too many sci-fi movies."

Williams laughed.

"Yeah, Marker. I saw that one too and that notion's just out of the question."

As we finished our coffee, we all agreed that we were up against something beyond our comprehension especially considering the secrecy of the station's mission. When we finally realized that the object could possibly be tied to another undisclosed compartment of Umbra's security web we decided to present our findings to Bowman and let him try to sort it all out. We certainly couldn't.

Lieutenant Williams stood and walked to an Ivy console on a nearby wall.

"Ivy, Sue Williams here."

"Good afternoon, Susan Williams. What can I do for you today?"

"Please notify Dr. Bowman that we have returned and are ready to meet with him at his convenience."

"Message received and transferred. Anything else?"

"No. Thank you, Ivy."

"You're quite welcome, Susan Williams. I'll notify you when Dr. Bowman responds."

She returned to our table sighed and sat biting at a fingernail.

"So," Briscoe said yawning, "I wonder when we can get some sleep. We arrived here early this morning without sleep and we're still going strong fourteen hours later. I haven't slept since seven a.m. yesterday and it's now three p.m. the next day. That's thirty-two hours I've been awake. I'm beginning to feel like I'm on a hospital staff."

The Lieutenant and I laughed at his humor but I knew how he felt. Everything was beginning to blur around me. My concentration was muddled and my energy gone. I stood, grabbed the Chief's mug along with mine, walked to the coffee urn, and refilled them.

"Thanks, Marker. This may get me through the next shift. They'll be calling me into the ER at any time now."

Almost on cue, Ivy's voice burst forth from the overhead speakers resonating through the mess hall.

"Susan Williams, Dr. Bowman requests your presence in Pod Bay 2."

"That also means you two," she said to us. Downing her coffee she rose from the table and headed toward the core hatch. Then turning back she asked, "Coming fellows?"

"Right behind you," answered the Chief gathering the torch tip into his pocket.

In her footsteps, we scurried into Quad 2 and down the hatch ladder into Pod Bay 2.

Alone in the empty bay Bowman greeted us. He was not pleased: he glared up from pacing over the empty SeaPod pad and stopped.

"Where the hell is the SeaPod? You were supposed to bring it back."

"It was gone, Dr. Bowman, apparently cut loose," Williams said.

His face flushed with anger for a moment, then after a deep breath he calmly replied, "May I ask who cut it loose, Lieutenant? Was it you? Briscoe? Cross? You are the only ones who have been out there since the accident. Please explain that."

"I can't, sir, but Briscoe did find a spent cutting torch tip under where it had once rested. We had to assume it was forcefully freed by something or someone. Even the tractor wheel spoke was mangled where it had become entangled in the SeaPod."

"So I assume you talked this over amongst yourselves," he said. "Where do you suggest we go from here? Briscoe, Cross, you're supposed to be on top of this. Did you find any other evidence of tampering out there?"

The Chief flashed a glance my way before speaking.

"Yes and no, Dr. Bowman. At the base of the crawler under Pod Bay 2, I happened upon something buried beneath the ocean floor. We had doused our lights---"

"Wait a minute, Briscoe. You found something buried? Was it one of our probes?"

"I don't think so, sir, unless your probes can glow and suck power from nearby objects. Marker and I think it may even be the culprit in all these crashes."

"That's absurd," he shouted. "Nothing can do that. Anything else unusual about it?"

Remembering that moment standing over it, I related my experience.

"Now I know this may sound ridiculous too, but I when I was checking my suit's power in the HUD, I noticed the clock's time read 1254 hours. By the time I dropped the torch pack and finally got the Chief moving which must have taken at least five minutes, I checked my power level again and the clock showed 1250 hours. Either my suit's clock malfunctioned or the object the Chief called a *monopole* reversed the passage of time."

"Rubbish!" he said then paused in deep thought. He shook his head as if to rid his mind of a notion.

"Williams... opinion?"

Preoccupied she jerked at his question.

"I'm sorry, sir, what did you ask?"

"The object Briscoe found. Do you believe it's supranormal as they say?"

"Well, I can't really say, sir, but I do know when I drifted over that area in two different SeaPods their navigation systems failed. And they've never acted up before this."

"Why didn't you dig it up and bring it back? I need to see this thing."

In our defense, I ventured an answer.

"Our suit's power supplies were failing as was the SeaPod's. Time was going backwards. Our only option for survival was to mark its location and retreat. Otherwise, you might be looking at even more accidents. I'm the one who suggested we return immediately as everything began to go south."

"All right, I'm sending divers out later today to pull in the isotope sensors and cable sheath. I'll just have them dig it up while they're out. How close is this---"

"Sir," the Lieutenant interrupted, "I've tried to remain neutral in my opinion of their discovery, but I have to say that damn thing really put the fear of God in me. It's a feeling I've never had before in my years of diving. Almost brings the eerie Davy Jones Locker legend to life. I do not recommend sending more divers out after that. It could kill them."

"Hmm. That's rather daunting. What do *you* recommend, Lieutenant? What are our options?"

"Use our ROV. It's been gathering dust since we've been down here."

Finally, he showed a hint of a smile.

"Excellent suggestion, Williams. I've been needing a reason to fire up the robot and that seems a perfect use for it."

Ten minutes later, we arrived at the ROV's control station: a bank of video screens around a console nestled behind the computer racks in Quad 1. It had numerous joysticks and levers resembling the control panel of a mini-sub and on the wall over the workstation a sign: SEA ROVER. Bowman offered us a seat around him and began to operate the controls.

Gradually a screen flickered and cleared into focus showing the remotely operated vehicle resting in the corner of Pod Bay 1. As the image sharpened, I saw the ROV sitting on a platform near the Exosuits.

I remembered seeing it there during our recent dive and wondered if they had ever used it. It was not a unique design as I expected but a standard ROV I had piloted before in the SeaCrawler squadron at Point Mugu. I knew it well: a sturdy metal cage weighing in at 500 pounds, four feet wide by eight feet long with two massive manipulator arms tucked into its bow. From the aft a length of optical fiber and copper cable, its umbilical, wound around a large spool ready for deployment.

Another screen flashed to life as his hands switched more controls. It showed the filled Exosuit racks taken from a lower vantage point I assumed to be the ROV's forward camera. In the frame surrounding the image were numerous data windows showing depth, pressure, time of dive, a manipulator-arm-image inset frame and water temperature.

"Here we go," he said. Then picking up a nearby hand microphone he pushed a button and spoke:

"Flooding Pod Bay 1 in ten seconds. Stand and be seen if you're in there."

Twelve seconds passed according to my watch and then his hand hit a switch labeled MAGNETIC LOCKS ON. Quickly he flipped up a safety cover and tripped the FLOOD BAY switch.

Instantly, flooding overhead ribbons of seawater gushed into the bay raising the level over the racked Exosuits' boots. Then as the water rose slowly passing over the ROV's camera, I held my breath again. I hated that instinct but blamed it on my childhood. My mind drifted back...

I had thought everyone was born with a deep fear of water but my mom once told me it was from an accident, a horrible accident, I witnessed at the beach. She always cried when she talked about it. I was just turning four when it happened she told me. It was a sunny day with dark storm clouds gathering on the westward horizon. Surfers yelling with joy off in the distance were riding monster waves. She said that dad had gone to the concession stand to get snow cones as my three-year old brother Mikey splashed through the waves screaming with joy as he ran. I wasn't far behind but stayed closer to land. As she watched us, a big cresting wave suddenly swept him screeching and scrambling feet first into deep dark water. The azure water under him had gone brown with sand. A vicious suction like that from an unplugged drain dragged him out with such tremendous force he couldn't catch a breath; he just disappeared. Then she said that she saw me turn and run into the roiling water after him. The same wave took me as I dug in his wake trying to save him. In thinking back, I do seem to recall my frenzied digging but nothing more.

The next day, a white sterile room invaded my blurry vision. Hissing machines and clicking pumps surrounded me all synchronized with a green blinking light on the wall. My first recollection after a lengthy coughing spell was the smell of a bit of fresh air seeping around my facemask. A doctor staring into my eyes through a small, lighted funnel he called an ophthalmoscope welcomed me to Mission General Hospital then said without emotion that I had died but through the miracle of science, he brought me back.

Then he told me the most horrible news my young ears had ever heard. My little brother Michael could not be saved. I must have cried for hours knowing my best friend was gone forever. All to a ferocious riptide that had somehow swallowed us both then kept my brother and spit me out. My mom tried to calm me by saying that

God needed only one little angel that day; the doctor said that riptides or undertows in that area were notoriously unpredictable. I didn't understand either of their explanations but I knew that I would never go near the ocean again. It was far too dangerous.

"Bay's full," Bowman yelled interrupting my unpleasant reverie. "Pod Bay door's opening."

Seconds later the ROV headed out into the darkness shining its floods forward illuminating fogs of moving organisms.

"Go toward starboard," Williams said.

Nudging the joystick to the right Bowman directed the ROV toward Pod Bay 2. Even though it was still thirty feet from the bay's entrance its video return began to distort with interfering lines running through and across the image.

"There it is!" barked Williams pointing at a spot on the screen. "That's the cutting torch pack I dropped down. Kill the floods."

As Bowman switched off the forward floods, the screen went black for a moment. Then the glow appeared blossoming amid severe cross-hatching of the incoming image.

"Well I'll be damned," he said moving his eyes closer to the image.

"See it, Dr. Bowman?" she asked.

"Hell yes... and I see the time clock up in the corner ticking backward too."

He looked to his side past Williams.

"Holy shit Briscoe! What in God's name have you found?"

As we watched, the glow brightened to the point that it saturated the camera leaving a flared video screen: white with no details of anything. Only the status panels surrounding the image showed through.

"Uh Dave?" I asked scanning the panels, "Is the water temperature supposed to be minus forty-eight degrees Fahrenheit down there? That's way below freezing. An impossible situation for liquid water. There should be ice forming."

He jerked his attention to the TEMP display reading -48°F then put his hand to his forehead. Seconds passed before he looked back at the screen.

"There is no earthly reason why that temp should be below freezing. At that temperature it's not even liquid, it's in another phase. However considering our display's malfunction it may be a fault in the temperature sensor."

During our discussion, the flared-out image screen had changed to what looked like a troubleshooting window. Along the top margin in the panel's frame was SOURCE CODE.

At first a few characters appeared 95HH32G9FZWXM. Then lines below that began to fill with numbers and letters at an ever increasing pace scrolling down the screen faster than I could read. It made no difference though; they were still gibberish.

"Good Lord, now what is that?" Bowman asked pushing back from the monitor.

"Looks like code," Williams said.

"But how is it getting into the ROV system? Suggestions?"

"I hate to venture a guess," I said, "but with its extreme brilliance the light from the monopole may be seeping into the ROV's fiber optic control cable. Your controller sees the returning light as feedback. But who am I to know; I'm not a computer geek."

"You may just be geek enough, Matt. That actually sounds like a reasonable cause for this data string. But, did you see it flashing when you were near it? Only that would simulate data."

"Yes. It was flickering colors so rapidly it appeared to be white until I blinked and caught a few dominant hues."

He stared at the screen still scrolling.

"Hmm. Wonder if it's trying to tell us something?"

"It's not an undersea cable, Dr. Bowman," Williams scoffed, "Just a flickering light on the ocean floor. Probably some bioluminescent creature gone astray."

He pointed to the ROV's clock panel still ticking backward.

"Then how do explain that, Lieutenant? A time-warping anglerfish?"

Suddenly, from overhead speakers a klaxon horn blared vibrating through the room. I had to cover my ears at the intensity of the alarm. As Bowman jumped to his feet, Ivy's urgent voice interrupted the obnoxious buzzing sound.

"Station Alert! Station Alert! Power in the station is failing. Power in the station is failing. All support-crew nukes report below to the power plant. Malfunction suspected. Repeat, malfunction suspected. Preparing the EPod for detachment and ascent. Scuttle plan activates in twenty minutes."

I checked my watch; it read 3:40 p.m. At four o'clock according to Ivy, the station would disintegrate.

"Bowman, pull the ROV back from the monopole," Williams screamed her face white with terror.

He sat back at the console and yanked the joystick toward him and waited for something to happen. The klaxon continued to wail as the screen rolled with unending code.

"Somebody do something," Bowman pleaded. "It's not responding."

"C'mon, Marker. Wanna take a dive?"

I first looked at him as if he was crazy then realized it was our responsibility to fix the problem. That's what we were being paid for.

"Sure, Chief. SeaPod or Exosuit?"

Bowman watched our exchange through saucer eyes.

"You can't be serious," he said. "You'll be trapped out there."

"Dead serious, Dr. Bowman," Briscoe said. "How else are we going to pull that ROV off the monopole? The umbilical is sourcing it power draining the station."

"Okay then, the Exosuits are all in the flooded Pod Bay 1 except for two emergency suits in Pod Bay 3 under the mess hall. Use them if you must; they're close to the action so just head left when you exit the bay. I'm going to settle the crew. They must be ready to mutiny by now."

Chapter 14
Starboard Side Out

F ive minutes later, we entered the mess hall and raced through it searching for the ladder leading to the docking bay. Seeing no arrow pointing downward, we panicked.

"Chef Saunders? You in here?" I yelled.

A faint voice from behind the kitchen answered.

"Yep, back in the pantry kissing my ass goodbye."

We followed his voice to a door behind the kitchen leading into a large dimly lit room. Pallets of large plastic containers covered the floor throughout the area. Above one tall pallet stack, a stenciled down arrow partially obscured by boxes showed through.

"We need down into the bay, Chef. Now!" the Chief yelled.

Heeding our urgency, he grabbed a corner of the blocking pallet and lifted it sending boxes flying across the pantry but freeing the hatch.

Within minutes, we were suited up ready to dive.

I turned to the Chief and asked, "How do we get out of here?"

He walked to a wall panel labeled EMERGENCY FLOOD and pushed a button then rushed back to the stirrups to lock himself in. The emergency flood process was faster but much rougher that the one I was accustomed to. Fortunately, only a minute later the bay door opened to the ocean inviting us outward. As I kicked out of my stirrups,

I noticed a row of small tools lining a rack on the wall. Quickly I snagged a hacksaw in my pincer and followed the Chief out of the bay.

"Don't forget to go left, Chief," I said, "This is a starboard side out."

Remembering the station layout in my mind, I knew the monopole should be below us about fifty feet to our left. Only a few yards in front of me, the Chief propelled over and down to where the monopole should be.

"There's the ROV, Marker. Looks dead in the water. Think we can move it in time?"

I checked the time display in my HUD. We weren't close enough for it to be ticking backward but I panicked when I read the time 15:56:00, only four minutes until all hell broke loose.

"Don't want to chance it, Chief. I've got to do something now."

"W-What are you gonna do, Marker? Don't do anything foolish."

"Chief hide and watch a master at work," I yelled.

I propelled ten feet over and beyond the ROV until I was upon its umbilical but safely beyond the effects of the monopole. With the hacksaw firmly in my pincer, I began to chew through the thick cable one stroke at a time. Although sparks were flying, I knew my aluminum exoskeleton suit would route the electricity harmlessly around my body. I kept pulling and pushing on the hacksaw until the blade finally broke through and the umbilical fell free dangling in two loose ends. My helmet HUD clock read 15:59:30 as I dropped the hacksaw and turned back to Briscoe with only seconds to spare.

I could hear him laughing through his intercom.

"Hope Bowman didn't count on that ROV coming back, Marker," he said. "You know, you're a mad genius in a diving suit but I think you just saved us. Thank you."

Awkwardly, he held up an arm and I slapped it down creating a loud *clang* through my suit.

We floated for minutes above the ROV waiting to confirm its disconnect.

"Hey Marker, my HUD clock says it's 1602 hours and we're still alive. Let's go home and get some sleep."

"I'm not sure if I remember what that is but I'm willing to give it a try."

After purging the bay, we racked our suits and began to climb the ladder into the pantry. Before I could reach up to open the hatch, it unlocked and dropped down missing my head by only inches.

Bowman reached through and gave us a hand into the pantry room now lit with brilliant fluorescents.

"Hey guys, you saved the station. Thank you. I'll never be able to repay you for that."

"Merci beaucoup," said Saunders, standing behind him grinning from ear to ear.

Looking confused, the Chief tilted his head.

"Is Saunders really a French name, Chef?"

"No," he snickered, "not really. But I was once a French Chef and I used that a lot."

Their interchange of humor signaled to me a relief of tension in the station. Even Bowman was changed: he laughed off the loss of the Sea Rover as unavoidable and then excused himself to start preparations for the cable transfer trip. I noticed though that our discovery of the monopole weighed heavily in his mind. He didn't want to leave it unattended for fear of more accidents on future missions. In addition being a scientist, he felt it was a great find: an extant theoretical entity worthy of further investigation. I even heard him mention that it exhibited black-hole properties and its physical proximity really bothered him.

Walking with him back to the core, he suggested we stop by the mess for coffee. The Chief had never refused coffee and I was game so we all grabbed a mug and sat discussing plans.

Bowman's plans had changed by our discovery and its threatening implications but he still had to move the station by tomorrow. TPCI and FRMS divers were heading out shortly to start pulling in sensors and another support crew of maintenance divers would be working on the tractor wheel spoke repair. In his mind, he was set for the move.

Then he asked about our plans.

At the top of ours, a simple plan was to sleep for hours in our rooms away from anything loud, traumatic, or wet.

Bowman agreed and apologized not realizing that we had not yet slept since arriving. His assignment to us before sending us up to our racks was to return with a solution for the monopole mystery: should we leave it, ignore it, take it with us, or even report its discovery to headquarters.

Another loud crash and jolt interrupted me from my sound sleep throwing me from my bunk.

From outside my door I heard the klaxon echoing through the hallway. Awaiting Ivy's message I flipped on my bunk light and checked my watch. It was 10:35 p.m. in my mind but 2235 hours station time. I had slept for six hours and surprisingly I was alert and rested, but my body ached all over from muscling around in the Exosuit.

"Station alert! Station alert!" Ivy loudly announced. "An object has impacted the crawler's structure under Pod Bay 3. Repeat: Impact under Pod Bay 3. Station dome integrity unaffected. Repair crew requested. Support crew report immediately to your duty stations."

Chapter 15
The Whale-Ship

*H*ere we go again I thought. I threw on my jump suit and rushed into the hallway to find the Chief and three other crewmen rubbing their eyes looking around and waiting for more information from Ivy.

"At least we're not flooding," said the Chief standing near the Ivy console.

"Think we should go see what happened, Chief?"

"What? Can't hear you over the klaxon."

"Think we should we go down into the chaos again?" I screamed.

"Yes, I think should we go down into the chaos again, dummy," he said mimicking my tone. "It's our mission, isn't it?"

In the mess hall, seven crew members were seated around a table wiping coffee and mug shards from the floor. As we poured ourselves a cup and sat with them, the ominous buzzing finally stopped.

Looking around the table, I recognized Williams, Norris and Alvarado, and was quickly introduced to Castro and Turnbull. Two others seated with them they identified as Broyles and Simon, repair divers from the support crew. They had all just returned from retrieving and stowing the sensor array and repairing the tractor wheel and were warming up with coffee when the station shook.

"Any idea what happened out there just now?" I asked as Williams returned with a fresh mug.

Swallowing a sip, she paused before she answered.

"I have no idea but there was a pesky little sperm whale calf in the distance clanging echolocations. Could have bumped into the station. Not too unusual lately. But no. Everything went like clockwork. We're ready to move... unless that impact damaged another wheel."

Broyles and Simon nodded in agreement.

"It's not a hard fix but takes time with all the safety hoops we have to jump through especially dodging that damn glowing spot and the downed ROV," Simon offered.

"Hey, Marker," the Chief asked, "ready to visit Chef Saunders again?"

"Oui oui," I replied, "He'll be so glad to see us. Wonder if he's restacked that pallet."

"Probably. Let's go find out," he said chuckling.

"Oh Lieutenant, would you please notify Bowman that we're going out to investigate? I know you guys are tired since you just came in. Drink your coffee and warm up," I said rising from the table.

"Sure, Marker," she said, "and we thank you for that. Seems like the water was colder this time out. Really chilled us all to the core."

We downed our coffee and went back to the kitchen. Calling out for Saunders, the Chief wandered back to the pantry.

"Guess he's in the rack. It's late," he said. "Nobody here."

Seconds later he yelled, "Oh, crap! It has been restacked."

I rushed back in time to see him with one motion lift the pallet's corner as Saunders did tumbling food cartons and boxes everywhere.

"Ready to do this again, Marker?"

"Yep. Same as before. Let's do it."

Without the urgency, this dive was going to be much less stressful even though we were diving into another mysterious situation.

For the first time I exited the bay before the Chief. I couldn't see him behind me but I knew he was there by his rapid breathing sounds over our suit-to-suit intercoms.

Leaving the bay, I turned downward toward the base shining my floods onto the most confusing sight I had ever seen. Waiting for the Chief to catch up I stared down upon a conundrum, an enigma that I was not ready to see. From what I could gather at my distance, I was nearing something resembling a huge animatron with a sperm whale's body and large fluke but with a thick clear plastic bubble where its face should be.

Moving in beside me, he exclaimed, "Holy cow! What in the world is that? A Trojan whale?"

"Now is not the time for humor, Chief. Let's approach it and see if it moves."

"Really, Marker?"

"Yes, I want to peek into the cockpit. It looks disabled: void of life."

As I slid up to the cockpit and looked in, Briscoe moved over its outer skin toward the large stationary fluke. Inside the creature's head, which I now thought to be a vessel was a large tubular room with three seats facing outward toward me. My most horrifying discovery was seeing three individuals slumped back in their seats immobile with their eyes and mouths gaping wide in horror like they died gasping for breath. There was no motion at all; even their chests showed no breathing movements.

Studying the scene, I realized that I was observing the inside of a foreign ship. Not only were the three occupants oriental males, the writing on the signs and displays throughout the cabin were in hieroglyphic-style symbols that I assumed were Chinese or Japanese.

"Hey Chief, come look in here. Tell me what you think."

He propelled back to my side and faced the bubble.

"My God, Marker, it's a spy submarine. Those symbols are like the markings I found on Edwards' crashed SeaPod. Something *has* been watching us but not sperm whales. They must have been tracking our divers pulling the probes and got caught in the monopole's grip."

He pointed back toward the monopole.

"From the looks of their direction of impact they had just passed over it when their ship went down."

"Just like our SeaPods."

"Yes, exactly like our SeaPods but those Jonahs didn't know how to reboot their whale."

It took a few seconds but I laughed at his morbid humor even though he wasn't trying to be funny.

"Well done, Chief. Keep looking."

Turning away, I shone my floods forward on the crawler base as he returned to the whale-ship. At the point where the whale head hit the crawler's thick hull there was no damage to anything other than the black hard-rubber flange surrounding the bubble. It was torn back all the way to the acrylic bubble. Had it peeled back another inch the bubble seal would have broken flooding the interior with tremendous pressure. Maybe that would have been a more humane death for them than slowly asphyxiating in an oxygen-free tomb.

"How do they get in and out of the whale, Chief? Find anything back there?"

"Yeah, I found a smooth seam half way back that looks like it could be a wide hatch door. Maybe into a small floodable bay. Can't tell until we open it."

"Next question," I said, "Can we fit that thing into one our docking bays?"

"Only into Pod Bay 2 since the SeaPod's gone. Diagonally maybe."

"So what's its length? About twenty-five feet nose to tail?"

"About that I'd say."

"Biggest diameter?"

He stretched out his suit's arms to reach across the bubble.

"Measures about six feet across at the head."

"Good. Let's remember that when we get back. Bowman will surely want to bring it in."

"Right. Ready to head back?"

"Yeah," I laughed, "Only if we can avoid the Chef. I just hope he hasn't restacked that pallet yet."

We completed the dive and reentered the bay without any interference from the monopole. That surprised us and told me that its field was still contained around Pod Bay 2. I made a mental note of that to tell Bowman.

The mess clock on the wall showed 2355 hours or five till midnight as we entered the hall from the pantry. Saunders was nowhere to be found and the kitchen was dark, but thoughtfully he had left a few MRE packs out on the counter.

We grabbed them, headed to the microwave, and waited as they heated.

"When are we going to tell Bowman?" Briscoe asked.

"As soon as he shows up."

"Shouldn't we tell Ivy we're back?"

"No. She's tracking us right now with biosensors remember?"

"Oh yeah," he said, "Big sister in the sky sees all knows all."

Removing our MREs at the oven's beep, we picked a table and sat down to eat but before I could take my first bite, Bowman entered the mess asking questions.

"What did you find out there? Williams thinks it might have been a sperm whale impact. It was tailing her all afternoon."

"Well she's right, Dr. Bowman but it was an Oriental whale," said the Chief.

He cocked his head then stared at him inquisitively.

"Now, Mr. Briscoe, I know the cetacean genus fairly well but I've never heard of an Oriental whale. Explain."

"Did you ever see the movie Jaws?" he asked.

"Yes, I remember seeing that when I was younger. Scared me to death. I had trouble building my sandcastles by the ocean while watching for Bruce, that animatronic shark. Scary movie."

He paused then asked, "But what does that have to do with an Oriental whale?"

"That's what crashed on the crawler's base under Pod Bay 3. An animatronic whale with three Oriental pilots aboard, probably Chinese."

Previously bending over our table, he sat down and leaned in close to us.

"Are you telling me there's a whale-looking submarine crashed into our base? With Orientals inside?"

"Yes, that's exactly what we're telling you, Dr. Bowman," Briscoe answered. "But they're all dead or at least they look dead. I think they passed too close to the monopole and it disabled their ship, powered it down. They appear to have suffocated in an airless cockpit without power for the fans and CO_2 scrubbers."

"Oh my God," he said, "What a horrible death." He shook his head with his eyes cast downward. Suddenly he jerked upright.

"Chinese? What in the hell are they doing around here? They must be spying on our operation. Can we bring their whale-ship into a docking bay? I have to find out what they know and what they've seen."

"It's a possibility but what are the dimensions of the empty Pod Bay 2?"

"Okay, it's a quarter-pie shaped slice receding thirty feet under Quad 2, seventy-five feet around the outer wall with a twenty-foot-wide Pod Bay door, and twelve feet wide at the smallest inner wall by the ladder. It's pretty big. Can it hold that thing, Mr. Briscoe?"

"Yes sir. Given those dimensions it can. But how can we raise it into the bay?"

"Use two SeaPods one on each end. Grasp it in the manipulators and raise it as a team. Maybe use a third if you need to depending on it buoyancy. I'll pilot that one. We have to get that thing on board before we leave. Think you can do that before we pull anchor at 1900 hours, seven p.m. your time? We always travel under the cover of darkness; hiding the floating laser beacon buoy and all."

"Yes sir we'll try. Mind if Marker and I finish these wonderful MREs first?"

He stood ready to leave and glanced back.

"Yeah in your wildest foodie dreams." Laughing he left the room.

We sat finishing our meals and discussed a retrieval plan. As we brainstormed, I told the Chief that I remembered seeing some flotation slings and balloons in one of the bays but I couldn't remember which one.

"Yep I've seen them too. They're in Pod Bay 1 by the Exosuit racks," he said. "Now you're going to tell me you want to lift the sub with balloons and then shove it into a bay with a SeaPod? Is that the idea, Marker? Huh?"

"Basically, yes,"

"Quit goin' genius on me, boy. You're beginning to make me look dumb."

At first, I thought he was angry but then the grin climbing his face gave him away.

"So do you think it'll work, Chief?"

"You do realize you're going to need some high pressure gas tanks to inflate those big balloons at a thousand meter depth."

"Yep. About 1500 psi tanks. Those will give a 600 psi differential pressure inside the balloons. Way more than enough to inflate them for our use. We've got those strapped to the walls in the Pod Bays for refilling the Exosuits. We even have tanks like that in the SeaPods just need a long hose."

"Oh stop it, Marker. You win. Let's go do it."

I took several hours for us to rig SeaPod 1 with the balloon-tethered slings, air tank and hose but only minutes for the balloons to overfill and slip away from the underbelly of the whale-ship disappearing into the darkness above our heads. My plan had failed miserably.

"Next idea, genius boy?" the Chief asked over the SeaCom pointing his suit's floods into my SeaPod's cockpit.

"Let me try to lift it with the manipulators, Chief. I have no idea how much that thing weighs or how much this pod's thrusters will lift but I'm willing to give it a try. Hopefully its ballasts are near empty."

I could swear I saw him roll his eyes through his thick face bubble and then he sighed into the intercom.

"Now Marker, I thought I taught you better than that but I'm willing to give it a try. Come on down here. I'll help slide your arms around it. But don't make any sudden moves. You barely know how to drive that SeaPod."

He was right. I had just self-taught myself how to maneuver the pod during the minutes spent diving down to him but it was a simple joystick control, something I was accustomed to in my prior mini-sub dives. I felt comfortable but was still cautious navigating around with the pod.

"Be right there," I said.

Soon I was hugging the whale-ship from above at its midsection waiting for the Chief's inspection of my manipulators' positions. He had climbed on its back to check my grip when I accidentally bumped the joystick toward me.

Suddenly with a loud groan, the whale-ship lifted up and away from the crawler base with the SeaPod rising from the ocean floor.

I had to look twice when I saw the Chief in his Exosuit still riding the whale-ship with his legs clamped tightly into side fin ridges and his pincers gripping the manipulator arm like a saddle horn.

"Yee-haw!" he wailed as he hung precariously on its back. "Whale-ship rodeo time."

I had to cover the microphone to keep him from hearing my laugh but I knew he had been in worse situations and never flinched. At worst, he would float off the back and settle gently to the floor.

"Sorry, Chief," I said. "I accidentally bumped the reverse thrusters."

"And I accidentally blew my suit's ballasts, Marker. Take me back to Pod Bay 2 and open the door. Let's get this fish into a bucket. This will be one whale of a story."

As we slowly approached the door, traveling at the pod's minimum speed I suddenly realized I didn't know how to open the closed Pod Bay door from the outside. At our current speed and momentum, we would crash through it in seconds.

Thinking back to our arrival, I remembered the answer just as the intercom crackled Ivy's voice.

"SeaPod 1, you and your cargo are on course for a perfect docking into Pod Bay 2. Reduce speed to one-quarter knot. Careful with clearances."

Miraculously, the door pivoted upward just in time revealing the welcoming bay lights.

Carefully maneuvering my precious cargo toward the opening, I saw the Chief lean over against the whale-ship's body and hug it trying to reduce the payload's height.

"Keep low, Chief. Don't want to knock you off."

"Roger that, Marker. Get this damn fish docked."

Very slowly I slid the whale-ship into the bay and readied the arms for release."

"Hop off, Chief. I'm going to drop it."

I watched as he flooded his suit's ballast and released his grip on the manipulators. Sliding gently off the ship he propelled himself past me out into the darkness and called back.

"Clear of the bay, Marker. Drop it and let's get back to Pod Bay 1."

173

"Ivy, please close the Pod Bay 2 door," I said after releasing the cargo and backing out of the bay.

Once I confirmed that it had closed I joined the Chief still hovering in the distance well above the docking bay.

"How's your HUD clock running?" I asked.

"Forward. That's why I'm up here out of harm's way."

"Good. Our fishing trip is over... and we caught a whopper. You ready for some wake-me-up juice?"

"More like warm-me-up juice but yes I'd love a cup. My treat."

Chef Saunders welcomed us to his mess standing at the rear of the kitchen blocking us from the door to his pantry.

"Welcome back divers," he said. "Thank you for not using my bay this time. I'm afraid those cookie crumbs on that pallet that were once perfectly formed cookies will turn back into flour with your next dive.

"Got any coffee?" Briscoe laughed.

"Sure Trooper Briscoe. Always on tap. Grab your cups and partake please. Oh, and I made you a fresh batch of donuts too."

Dropping his eyebrows Briscoe darted his attention to Saunders.

"How do you know that? I mean it's true but how do you know?"

"It's simple really. I overheard you and Mr. Cross talking yesterday when you mentioned the CHP. I put that together with your love of donuts and took a wild guess. Then I made you more

174

donuts as my appreciation for all the work you guys are doing around here. I already feel safer. Plus I needed to use those cookie crumbs for something so I made donuts."

The mess clock read 0330 hours as we wiped the sugar from our faces and finished our coffee.

"What next?" the Chief asked leaning back in his chair looking over the empty mess hall.

"Just wait something will come along. Soon I imagine."

Within seconds, Ivy's voice boomed over the mess hall's speakers, "ODF, please report to Pod Bay 2."

"I knew it," I said, "That's us. Bowman must have found the whale-ship. I wonder what he thinks."

"Let's go find out."

Chapter 16
The Dragon Returns

Dropping down the ladder into Pod Bay 2, we saw Bowman standing beside Williams and Yung Ching looking into the whale-ship's cockpit. They were abuzz about something but we couldn't tell about what.

Ignoring our intrusion, they continued their discussion as Williams spoke.

"...but look at his Tang Zhuang jacket with that gold embroidered dragon. And he shaved his Fu-Manchu moustache. He looks less menacing milder now in death than in life."

"Went incognito I guess," replied Ching. "He used to resemble Christopher Lee but without that 'stache he looks more like *Bruce* Lee."

"You're right. In death he's now the Dragon," Williams interjected sorrowfully.

I knew something was up seeing their familiarity with the dead pilots so I interrupted.

"What's going on, guys? Who are you talking about?"

"Lt. Commander Dan Li," Bowman answered. "That's him on the right. In the dragon jacket. He's one of the pilots --- the interpreter that went missing when we found his empty Exosuit. Remember?"

"Oh yeah, but what does that mean? He's a mole?" I asked seeing the whole security scenario change before my eyes.

"I'm afraid so, Matt," Bowman answered. "Or at least that's the way it appears until we get more information." He turned back looking around the bay searching.

"Can we get into its damn hatch with something? Anybody have a crowbar?"

Williams knocked on the rubber hull returning a dull thud.

"I don't think so, Dr. Bowman. This ship's sealed up tight. Probably take more than we have to open it. Might as well launch it out to sea and explode it."

"Wait a minute, guys," I said, "I have an idea."

Briscoe rolled his eyes.

"Here we go again. Another one of Marker's hair-brained ideas. Get ready folks."

Ignoring Briscoe's sarcasm Bowman stared at me for moments before speaking.

"What do you need, Matt? I'm game. I've always trusted your intuition."

"I assume the hull's resistant to the pressures of this depth," I said, "so it will take almost a ton per square inch to break it open. But... it's a different story if we apply the pressure from the inside. Now I'm going MacGyver on you so listen closely. I need a half-inch threaded hollow pipe about four or five inches long, an electric drill with a long half-inch bit, a pair of vice grips and a high-pressure air tank and hose. That's all."

Within fifteen minutes Bowman had gathered the parts for me awaiting my use. After chucking the bit into the drill I put a half-inch hole through the heavy Plexiglas bubble, which I estimated to be six-inches thick, threaded the pipe into the hole until it was tight, then attached the hose to it and opened the air tank's valve. Everyone stood immobile apprehensive as air hissed into the sealed cabin.

"Stand back," I said, "That front cap's going to pop off at any minute."

In the middle of the Chief's cynical laughing there was a loud boom when the bubble blew several feet across the floor and then rocked like a dropped salad bowl for minutes.

"Wow!" Bowman exclaimed. "That was really thinking outside of the box, Matt. I'll have to remember that. I always look at pressure as a foe but never thought of using it as a friend. Well done, my friend."

"Your hydraulic elevators made me think that way, Dave. You're already using it as a friend you just don't realize it."

Nodding Bowman turned to the open cockpit, ducked, and cautiously entered avoiding the three dead pilots.

"Somebody get these traitors out of here before I kill them again and get some damn mug shots. I want to send them to HQ to see if they're listed as spies. I just can't believe that Dan Li is in here. Fricking turncoat!"

He continued toward the rear of the whale-ship and looked back.

"Here's how they did that horrible empty suit trick. It's an airlock hatch into a small flood bay. Li in his Exosuit probably entered the bay from the ocean, took it off in the airlock and then dumped it back into the ocean as he stayed safely dry inside. That bastard!"

Looking around on a nearby shelf, he grabbed a thick red marker and held it up for us to see.

"And here's the grease pencil he used to mark his suit and Edward's SeaPod. Must have used that Chinese ADS in the corner for that venture. With this whale-ship and that suit he could lead them all around the station without being seen but he never expected that the monopole would foul his plans."

From outside the whale-ship Williams and I watched the hall of horrors unfold before our eyes. We had discovered the boogey man's lair complete with incriminating evidence supporting their illicit activities. There was no Davy Jones Locker mystery involved just ordinary criminal espionage and now we had the smoking gun.

As he swiveled around to leave, still hunched over, he noticed a thick notebook, grabbed it, and brought it out with him. Across its cover were Chinese glyphs meaning nothing to him or us.

"Where's Yung Ching. This is probably their logbook. I need an interpreter," he said, scanning the bay.

"Down at the end of the bay moving the bodies. Took Briscoe with him to move them but he seemed not to mind," I said. "Ching said that he was going for a camera after that."

Bowman sighed and squatted by the open cockpit, put his elbows on his knees, and looked down resting his head between his hands.

"You okay, Dr. Bowman?" Williams asked.

He glanced up at her and went back into his position.

"Yeah I'm fine, Lieutenant. Just trying to absorb everything that's happened here and what it all means to our mission."

"Well I hate bring up the elephant in the room, Dave," I said, "but that ship is just a small sub like our SeaPods. It probably has only a ten- or twenty-mile range. That means there is a larger mother ship somewhere around us within twenty miles waiting for its return. Either a big sub or surface vessel."

"Oh dear God, you're right, Matt," he said. "I have to get this information to Point Mugu. When Ching returns with the camera have him bring the shots to my office ASAP."

As he left the bay, Williams and I went back and found Briscoe arranging the bodies on the floor of the bay like a criminal line-up. After opening their eyes with his thumb and forefinger, he backed off and dusted his hands.

"There. That should give some damn good mug shots," he said. Then he looked back past us and yelled, "Where's Ching? I need that camera."

From the back of the bay by the ladder came a winded voice.

"I'm coming. I'm coming. Be right there."

He raced up to us and started to take a photograph for the line-up standing over and straddling Li's body.

"Gimme that camera, Yung," said the Chief, reaching out. "I'm taller. I'll get a better angle."

He relinquished the camera as I noticed tears forming in his eyes.

"Hey Yung," I said grabbing his shoulder pulling him closer, "I know you lost a friend and I'm truly sorry for your loss but he was not who you thought he was."

"But seeing him again reminds me that he was such a good man and loyal friend to me. Everybody loved him," he sniffled. "I just can't imagine him doing this to us."

I knew his pain having lost my brother and parents when I was younger. No matter what they had done, the memories always seemed to fall on the softer times of their lives. I hugged him tighter as he broke down and began to weep uncontrollably on my shoulder.

"Hey now," the Chief said putting a hand on his back. "He's in a better place and probably at peace with his wayward ways. I never met him but I feel we're all better off without his mischief."

Yung sniffled again, wiped his eyes, and looked back at Briscoe.

"I guess you're right, Mr. Briscoe, but it's still hard to lose a buddy like that especially when you realize that he was really your enemy. I was duped so badly; I feel like a fool."

"Hey Yung, let's all take these photos to Bowman. He's waiting for them." Williams said, sliding her arm around his back pushing him toward the ladder.

Williams, Ching, Briscoe, and I entered the vault noticing the open Z-room hatch showing through to Bowman's office door.

Approaching it, I knocked.

"We have the mug shots."

"Come," he said.

As I opened his door, he looked up from a folder.

"Close and lock all the doors behind you including the vault's."

Williams turned back, rushed through the Z-room into the vault, and pulled the heavy door until it locked. Then as I watched, she closed the Z-room hatch door and pulled the locking lever. Finally, she reentered his office and closed the door behind her.

"Done sir. We're secure," she said, out of breath. "What now?"

"Good. I see you have the camera, Mr. Briscoe. May I have it please?"

The Chief handed him the camera and waited.

"Sit down please; you're all making me nervous. This may take a while."

We sat as he attached a USB cable to the camera. Then out the corner of my eye, I saw Ching checking out the thick leather-covered notebook lying near him on the desk.

"Mind if I look at that book, Dr. Bowman?" Ching asked. "Those glyphs on the cover are Mandarin. It says Log Book. Is that from the whale-ship?"

"Oh yes, Lt. Ching. I want you to examine that book and summarize it for me. Found it on a shelf in that ship. Thought it might be a log. Help yourself."

Bowman resumed cabling the camera to his computer as Ching lifted the tome from the desk, opened the cover, and began flipping through pages.

Williams leaned over and glanced at the pages.

"Well what does it say, Yung? Anything interesting?"

"Hmm, wait a minute. It's pretty vague. No names so far. They are documenting their recent dives around the 'dome' as they call it."

Now intrigued by his translation I also leaned over into the book as if I could read anything. All I saw were pages filled with Chinese symbols and a few hand-drawn sketches.

Suddenly he gasped, laid the book on his lap, and began to weep again.

Bowman jerked up from his computer.

"What's wrong, Yung? What did you find?"

Ching pulled up the book and pointed into a page. In between sobs, he gazed on the strange glyphs.

"This entry dated June 11th, 2016 tells of a venture around the dome. It says, 'We finally captured a diver in his strange suit. He was alone with another diver tending to sensor probes some distance away. Brought him in, marked his suit with YOU LOSE, and dumped it back through the water lock onto the ocean floor.'"

He put his hands to his eyes wiped them and with a wavering voice admitted:

"That other diver was me. But I never saw them. The symbols on his suit I saw later were a wrong dialect of Mandarin for me to understand probably northern. Seemed more like ancient glyphs."

He sniffled and referred back to the log.

"It continues, 'Diver claimed he didn't know Mandarin only English and said his name was Fook Yoo nothing else. Will take him back to mother ship and question him further. Must leave the dome location now. Instruments acting very strange.'"

Ching raised his reddened eyes and glared at Bowman.

"See? I told you he couldn't be a spy. He was a captive."

Bowman listened and closed his eyes for a few moments ignoring the three photographs loading on his computer's screen.

"I'm truly sorry I rushed to judgment, Yung, but it appeared he was in cahoots with the pilots. He still could be and those words may be meant to deceive us if found. Disinformation it's called. We use it often in our communications with headquarters."

He glanced back at his screen typed some text into his keyboard and then emphatically hit a key.

"There! We'll see what their database says about these interlopers."

Directing his attention back to Ching he asked, "Anything else interesting. Does it mention the name of the mother ship?"

Ching studied further turning rapidly through the pages. At a page near the front, he stopped and began to read.

"Here's something: 'Left the ship from the submerged docking bay with Fook Yoo and headed back to the dome.'"

He glanced up at us with reddened eyes.

"They must be talking about a moon pool or floodable bay."

Now less distraught he continued his translation.

"'Neared the dome with our echolocation simulator chirping and found a crashed empty mini-sub twisted in the wheels of the dome. Cut bubble loose with torch and tried to catch it before it drifted up and away with the current. Currents were too fast to capture. Retreated to home ship.'"

Captivated with Ching's interpretation Bowman scoffed, "Of course they wouldn't name their home ship. Too risky if they got caught. But that explains a lot. Now we know what happened to Edwards' SeaPod. Still don't know what became of him though."

"As much as I hate to admit it Dr. Bowman he's probably fish food," Williams said factually. "We all know of the dangers out there and most of us don't hot rod around by ourselves for that reason. He was just careless plus he encountered the monopole."

Ching flinched and looked up at her from the logbook.

"I was told to avoid that when we retrieved the cable tap. What is it anyway? Sounds like the name of a theoretical object I once studied in a physics class. But it can't exist in reality."

"You're right, Yung, it can't, but that's what Mr. Briscoe named it and it's stuck for lack of a better name," Bowman offered.

"But a monopole can't exist," Ching argued, "like a Yin without a Yang; a shadow without light, it's an impossibility."

I thought, rolling the dilemma over in my mind.

"That's just what we called it, Yung. It is an inexplicable object. Just PFM. Sucks energy out of everything near it. Almost seems as if it's acting like a neutron star sucking in energy and growing into a black hole. But it's bright now and getting brighter."

Bowman squinted and shook off the notion.

"Well whatever it is I think I should report it to headquarters. Could be something that fell off a cargo or research ship. They'll surely be looking for it with its unusual characteristics."

Ching continued to read through the logbook, apparently finding no other information related to the mysteries but he did find and pause on their assessment of our mission.

"Seems like they are convinced that we're only measuring radiation," he said. "They suspected that we might have tapped into a communications cable but found no evidence of that. From what it says here they've been tracking our actions for only a few weeks. That's when all the weird things started happening around the station."

Bowman exhaled and smiled turning to Williams.

"Well that's comforting to know. I was afraid our operation had been compromised but your cable intercept divers, Lt. Williams, have been the best there are in your covert cable connection work. Thanks to you and your divers we're still a radiation monitoring station in the eyes of the world."

He then turned to me and glanced between us.

"Now I must commend both of you for your excellent exploratory work with our strange occurrences. They now seem to be contained so we can move on with our operations and pull anchor later this evening. We are set---"

"Dr. Bowman, you have a live transmission arriving from headquarters," Ivy interrupted from her small console on his desk. "Caller has set message security to Umbra ZX, scrambler level to Black. Would you like to take the call? Your office guests are all cleared for the information."

Bowman turned to her console.

"Yes, Ivy. Please put the caller through to my desk console on speakerphone."

"Connecting..."

A few clicks and buzzes preceded the scrambler-distorted voice roaring deeply resonating through the room.

"Hello Dave? Admiral John Franklin here at SSU headquarters. I just received your images and ran them through our international database of suspected foreign intelligence agents. Two of them hit immediately. The one on the left Xi Jin is a Chinese national working for the MSS, the Ministry of State Security out of Beijing. According to our passport records he is currently still in China. The middle photograph is of another Chinese national Ming Tse Tao who has visited the U.S. on temporary B1 visas numerous times negotiating for various China-US or CHUS transpacific cable repair contracts. We suspect him of counterintelligence activities during those trips. Finally the third image on the right is of U.S. Navy Lt. Commander Dan Li, honor graduate of the U.S. Naval Academy in 2012 and according to our records Dave he is now serving as a crewman on Sea Station Umbra. Is that correct?"

"Yes Admiral, that is correct."

"May I ask how you came by these photographs, Dr. Bowman? The men all look deceased"

"Yes sir, that is also correct. They are deceased."

"Then please explain why I'm holding the photographs of three dead men: one a USNA honor graduate and the other two known foreign spies"

"Well Admiral, it's a long story."

"I have plenty of time. Try me."

"A few hours ago a Chinese mini-sub disguised as a sperm whale calf crashed into the station's base. It did little harm to Discovery One but killed the three occupants of the whale-ship. Those are the men in the pictures. We suspect Li was taken captive on a service dive and used as a guide for their subversive activities against us."

"Wait. Whale-ship? Why did it crash? Was it a suicide mission?"

"No Admiral, we don't think so. It went down under the control of a strange monopole object on the ocean floor near Pod Bay 2 and lost power suffocating the men inside. The whale-ship is still intact minus the cockpit bubble but it can be reattached."

Admiral Franklin took a moment to reply.

"Dave, you do realize your story sounds rather fantastical don't you? Have you checked your station's air supply for impurities? Like cannabis? Or maybe your drinking water for hallucinogens?"

"N-No, Admiral, it's all true. Some very weird things are happening down here in addition to the

189

Chinese espionage attempts. We've already lost our ROV and Edwards' SeaPod to its power. All collecting down there around the monopole. Our clocks tick backward around it and it's getting stronger by the hour."

Again a pause.

"Hold a minute Bowman. I need to check something."

"Sure, Admiral, I'll be here."

Bowman's description of our situation sounded as incredulous to me as the Admiral had suggested but it was really happening. I wanted to comment in Bowman's defense but then Franklin might think we were all batty.

Chapter 17
Code Deep Black

The next voice from the speaker was Ivy's, surprising us all.

"Changing scrambler sequencing code to Deep Black at the Admiral's request. Reconnecting...."

"Dr. Bowman, I now understand your situation down there. I want you to postpone your station's departure to the CHUS cable for a few days. I'll be flying out with a particle accelerator physicist and arrive over your station in four hours around ten-hundred hours. While I realize I am violating your station's daylight access rules considering the urgency I feel it necessary. Can you send that beautiful Lieutenant Williams to pick us up as she's done before? She supports my belief in mermaids in the sea."

I looked at her for a reaction and saw her blush. She smiled and nodded affirmatively then whispered, "What a prick."

"But why, Admiral?" Bowman asked. "Everything's back under control now. We don't need your help."

"You may think not, Dr. Bowman, but you do. I just remembered a worldwide emergency alert our agency received a few days ago from the International Physics Consortium. That alert was issued to all world governments at the highest Code Deep Black security level. It may concern your station."

"Now you have my interest, Admiral. Can you tell me more?"

"Yes. That's why I switched the scrambler level, Dave. I think your station may be in grave danger. Two days ago CERN's Large Hadron Collider in Geneva, Switzerland managed to create and physically contain an elusive Higgs boson or God Particle, suspending it in a superconducting magnetic plasma. It was placed in a hundred-ton lead pig for transport from Geneva to the SLAC National Accelerator Lab in Menlo Park for verification. The pig was then loaded onto a Super Galaxy C5M cargo plane and sent on an easterly route to the California lab to avoid flying over populated areas.

"Everything was fine after it left Switzerland including an in-flight refueling over the Pacific north of Hawaii but soon after that things went drastically wrong. The escorting fighter planes reported that it began to drift off course to the south and from what I can tell head in your direction. Then in mid-air, it just vanished, taking one of the escorting planes with it. The remaining escort pilot who's now in a mental ward for psychiatric evaluation said it started melting in on itself becoming smaller and smaller until it just disappeared. Simultaneously he saw his buddy's fighter which was flying nearer the C5 begin to dissolve in the air and swirl like a whirlpool into the melting C5 before it also disappeared."

"And you thought *my* story was weird, Admiral. That's one hell of a doozy," Bowman said writing on a notepad.

"So, Admiral, do you think the plane's debris went down near here?"

"According to its last radar sighting, yes. Very close to where you are. And, here's the kicker to that story. The few particle physicists that finally did manage to believe his story claimed that the plane exhibited spaghettification and they estimated an object smaller than a BB weighing around 400 tons fell out of that reaction into the ocean. They also said that it will continue to absorb mass and energy spaghettifying everything around it and glowing with particle interactions until it becomes unstable and finally goes black-hole... but that may take years or even centuries."

As Bowman sat frantically scribbling notes, I looked at the Chief sitting wide-eyed staring at the Ivy console and whispered:

"No wonder it didn't move when you kicked it Chief. It's a mountain in a BB."

Shaking his head he scoffed, "More like a volcano in a BB."

I had heard of the term spaghettification before on a Science documentary hosted by Morgan Freeman and it truly tweaked my imagination. But that was in a theoretical world full of wormholes, quarks and black holes safely across the cosmos from my reality. To learn that such a physical anomaly could be pulled into existence by some manmade creation on the other side of the world shook me to my core. We were hastily delving into the no-man's land of science and beginning to feel the consequences of those ventures leaving us helpless against the perils of our own scientific curiosity.

"Are you there, Dave?"

"Yes, Admiral. I'll be awaiting your arrival. I do think we could use your help. Thank you."

"Fine, Dr. Bowman. See you soon."

With Franklin's sign-off, Bowman read over his notes and directed his attention to us.

"Lieutenant Williams, please prepare SeaPod 1 for a surface dive commencing at 0930 hours. You'll pick up the Admiral and his guest as he requested at 1000 hours and be on time. We don't want them floating in the waves for more a few minutes. See if you can track the helicopter in and forget the daylight rules. We're disconnected from everything so we can roll at a moment's notice if we need to."

Addressing Ching, he continued:

"Yung, please see that our DV terminals in the Z-room and in Quad 2 are booted up and working. They'll probably want to examine your recent translations so tidy them up a bit if you can. Also clear Edwards' and Li's quarters of personal items and send them up to storage on Deck 4 then prepare their rooms for visitors. They're the only two empty berths on Deck 2 and I don't really want to send them up to Deck 3 with the support crew."

"Now, Matt," he said looking at me, "I would like for you and Mr. Briscoe to inspect the whale-ship for anything I might have missed. If you see any new technology, take it and save it for analysis. I plan to replicate those Mandarin symbols from Li's suit all over the whale ship and release it back to the depths. That should really piss them off."

"Good for you, Dave," I said. "If and when they find their ship we should be in another part of the ocean far away. Can we do anything else in preparation for your guests?"

"No. Not really. Bringing in that Chinese sub was quite an accomplishment. Go rest on your laurels before they get here. I'm sure it will be all assholes and elbows down here after that."

The meeting broke up minutes later and the Chief and I headed back into Pod Bay 2 to search the whale-ship for additional evidence. Ching had stayed behind in the Z-room moving among the high-security terminals preparing them for our new guests. Williams had veered off in the core room on her way to Quad 1 saluting us as she left.

"See you guys later."

The ladder down into Pod Bay 2 led us back to the whale-ship appearing eerily like a slaughtered cetacean laying across the pod bay floor. Making things stranger, the room had begun to take on a foul odor we assumed to be from the still-uncovered dead bodies in the corner of the bay.

"We need some body bags," said Briscoe.

"Okay, just hop in your cruiser and race down to precinct headquarters and get a few. I'll wait here," I joked.

"No. Seriously, Marker, what do *you* suggest we do with them?"

"I see no harm in leaving them here for another few hours until Franklin arrives. He may want to examine himself."

"From the sound of his conversation with Bowman they will probably be the last thing he wants to see. But you're right. We'll give him the choice." He put his hand to his head for a moment then added, "But he probably will want to see this ship. Maybe want to snap a few photos to take back with him. It all needs to be here. According to my rules we don't mess with the scene of a crime."

"Chief, I'm afraid that ship has already sailed. We moved it from the crash site into this bay. No telling what evidence we lost with that decision."

Sighing, he bent over and reentered the whale-ship's cockpit.

"I am going in to see if I can find Li's notebook that went missing with him according to the crew's last accounts."

"Yeah, I remember that. And how did that extra person get into the station before he disappeared. That's yet to be explained by anything we've found. See if you can find evidence of that. I'm going back to examine Li's clothes and pockets for more clues. Maybe he left a note."

Back with the bodies, I held my breath to keep from throwing up. Lt. Li's face was distorted with the blood drained out and his pupils were dark holes with almost no iris showing. I quickly drew his eyes shut and began checking his pockets. After searching his coat and shirt pockets and finding nothing, I tried his jeans. From the left hip pocket, I withdrew a small folded piece of paper that seemed to be a page from a notebook. Quickly I dropped the note into my jumpsuit pocket and headed back to tell Briscoe.

Subtly at first from the pod bay's closed door, a bizarre moaning noise swept over the bay. An ominous sound I had heard before and dreaded, it gave me goose bumps that ran up my spine.

"Did you hear that?" said the Chief startled, poking his head out from the whale-ship's cockpit.

"What? That mournful growl? Hell yeah I heard it. It's the same sound I hear when I accidentally scrape my sub's hull on a hidden ocean boulder."

Listening for more he stood motionless as I joined him by the sub. Shortly a high-pitched screeching noise like metal scraping metal reverberated through the bay.

"That must be some big ass whale out there scraping its barnacles off," he said. "Sounds like giant fingernails scraping a billboard-size blackboard. Sends chills up my spine."

"Me too. Except I always anticipate the final crunch of a collision with a dock or another ship."

"In my world it's always car versus car or 18-wheeler. Same sound but much faster and there are usually casualties involved."

Drifting down from Quad 2 through the pod bay's open hatch, Ivy's pleasant but firm voice echoed.

"Alerting Condition Yellow! Repeat the station is now in Condition Yellow! I am detecting an unusual vibration in the station near Pod Bay 2 but there are no sonar signatures showing near the dome. This is a non-sequitur condition. Divers please investigate. Message will be repeated in five minutes."

Chapter 18
Dali Actualized

"There's our call, Marker. Let's go. SeaPod 1 okay with you?"

"Oh, but of course, Chief. I'm driving though. You attend to the siren and PA."

We flew up the ladder through Quad 2 then the core room and into Quad 1 in seconds. Shortly we were in SeaPod 1 waiting for the bay to flood.

Watching the pod bay door open into blackness, I wondered what we would find out there. Another crashed whale-ship? A sperm whale knocked unconscious by impact? Or something else. That something else worried me the most.

Slowly I brought the SeaPod out of the bay and steered to starboard toward bay number 2 while maintaining a safe distance from the floor to avoid the monopole lying twenty meters ahead of us.

"See anything yet, Chief?" I asked

"Just midnight as usual. And maybe a few anglerfish off in the distance fishing for a meal. Wish *I* could be fishing for a meal right now on Big Bear Lake."

"What? And miss all this fun?"

"Yes. I'd do it in a second. And since our mission here seems almost complete I'm already smelling the mountain pines and tasting the cold beer flowing down my throat."

"Oh stop it, Chief. You're making me smell steaks grilling over a roaring wood fire. And that's impossible in this sealed plastic bubble. Now pull yourself back to reality and find out what's causing those sounds. Check the tractor frame and see if there's anything rubbing against it. It has to be huge to create those grinding vibrations we heard and felt."

Briscoe went silent for moments peering out and down through the bubble. Then he jerked in his seat and pointed downward to the location where I expected the monopole to be.

"Down there," he said, "Where the ROV once was---"

"What do you mean 'where it *once was*?'" I interrupted.

"There *is* something by the monopole but it's not the ROV. Looks like a wax model of it that's been in the heat too long. That quarter-ton pound ROV is melting flowing across the ocean's floor in a brilliant glowing two-meter-long river of blue magma like lava seeping from a volcano. The water around the lava flow is boiling and bubbling up like crazy."

He repositioned himself in his seat and shielded his eyes from the control panel's glare.

"Can you turn the floods toward it, Marker? I need more light down there."

"Roger that, Chief."

Carefully while watching the instrument panel for changes I pivoted the SeaPod downward facing into the monopole. With the floods pointing down, we gasped when we witnessed a vision we were not prepared to see. As in Salvador Dali's Persistence of Memory painting, objects around the monopole were acting strangely like the melting clocks on his surrealistic landscape. And, as my mind's eye imagined that imagery the surreal drooping watches were ticking in reverse.

"Can you see it flowing, Chief? Moving?"

"No, it's barely creeping like molasses on a cold morning."

"Well that's comforting," I said. "We still have some time left."

"Suppose that movement could make those creepy sounds we heard, Marker?"

"Yes. They were weird, Chief, because we heard the sounds in reverse like a record played backward. Time is not flowing forward around it."

"Oh my God!" he exclaimed, "Look over there at that tractor wheel near the monopole's glow. It's beginning to melt too but it's barely out of round so far: it's just warping."

Thinking back to Franklin's warning I uttered:

"I'm afraid we're watching the beginning of spaghettification of Discovery One. If the station remains here for very long we'll all be sucked into its nucleus never to exist again."

"Or maybe tumbled through space-time into another dimension."

"Oh don't be ridiculous, Chief. That's impossible."

"You mean like the object we're looking at right now?"

His retort shut me up when I realized that our understanding of the monopole's existence was far beyond the reach of any rational imagination. It couldn't exist yet it did. We were observing a theoretical curiosity actualized into real life: a monopole, a God particle, a singularity, or whatever it was called; it was a physical impossibility. Yet, were drifting toward it slowly succumbing to its power.

"Hey Marker, wake up!" he yelled tugging my arm. "Our power is dropping and the console clock has slowed to a crawl. Better back away from its grasp or we'll be joining that ROV in its fiery grave."

Fortunately, he had noticed the problem. My eyes had been fixed on the visual impossibility to the point of ignoring the controls. As I slammed my attention back to our reality, I saw he was right. We *were* in the field of the object and being pulled closer by the second.

I jammed the joystick toward my stomach and the propulsion motors roared into reverse vibrating the SeaPod's structure trying to escape its pull.

"Not working, Chief." I yelled. "The motors are straining and we're barely holding our position. If they weaken more we'll be sucked right in. Options?"

"Hey Marker, you're beginning to sound like Bowman now but that's not a bad thing; blow the damn ballasts and get us some lift. Those motors need some help against that monster's gravity."

I hadn't dumped a SeaPod's ballasts before but instead relied on its neutral buoyancy and propulsion motors to navigate. Blowing the ballasts was an extreme action equivalent to an emergency surface command, ridding the pod of hundreds of pounds of dead weight all at once. It just might work. We would head straight up after they filled with compressed air and then I would have time to regain control as we drifted upward.

Bending closer to the control panel, I searched for the ballasts icon. Nestled in between several other icons I found it. A legend below it said RED=EMPTY. I touched the icon glowing green and listened for the hissing of air: a signal that they were filling. Instead, I heard two loud echoing gasps, sounds that I was not expecting but they told me the same information: the ballasts were filling with air.

"Hey Marker. We're pulling away! That did it. Now figure out how to stop this thing from floating to the surface. Got your power back now?"

Looking at the panel clock for confirmation, I checked it against my watch.

"They're both ticking forward and the battery gauge reads green, so yes. We have power."

"Well, thank God! Let's dock this thing before something else goes wrong."

A mere thirty minutes after we left Pod Bay 1, we returned as changed beings. Joking about the pilot in the mental ward we wondered if we also should check in, questioning our own sanity. But we had each other as a witness and we agreed on what we had observed. We had to find Bowman and tell him of the looming danger.

"Now repeat that," he scoffed. "You experienced spaghettifying?"

"Yes, Dr. Bowman, that's what we're trying to tell you. Just like Franklin explained to us. When Ivy warned of the Condition Yellow alert after those grotesque sounds echoed through the station we went out in a SeaPod to investigate. What we found was unfathomable. Down below Pod Bay 2 the ROV is melting into the monopole and a tractor wheel near it is starting to warp in a bizarre distorted way. It happened in front of us as we watched although very slowly," Briscoe answered.

'B-but that can't be real -- what you saw. It just can't happen. Are you positive you didn't experience some form of hallucinogenic mass hysteria down there?"

"We wondered the same thing, Dave," I answered, "but when the SeaPod began to lose power and almost killed us we knew then we were in real trouble, not imaginary trouble. It's down there absorbing everything in sight right now. Probably growing brighter too. The only thing we can't figure is why it's not using seawater as a fuel."

"I'm sure the particle physicist will explain that when he gets here *if* what you tell me is true."

"And when is he due here?" I asked.

"At 1030 hours unless they experience weather delays."

"That's two hours from now. Mind if we catch a nap, Dave?" I asked. "We're pretty much running on empty right now, with all the emergencies waking us up."

"Sure, knock yourselves out. I'll handle our guests when they arrive but I'd like for you to meet them and describe your findings over lunch at...," he glanced at his watch, "1200 hours. I'm having Chef Saunders prepare his special DV meal for us. You won't want to miss it."

As he stood to leave Briscoe said, "We'll be there, Dr. Bowman. I'm as starved as I am exhausted so that will be perfect."

"Head on up, Chief," I said, "I need to give Dave this note I found in Li's back pocket. Almost forgot about it with all the ruckus. Meet you in the Mess Hall at noon."

Nodding he smiled.

"Sure. Tell me what the note says then. I'm too tired to care right now. Just old age I guess but I *can* still hear my bunk calling." He winked and left the room.

Dave settled back in his chair and held out his hand awaiting the note.

"What do you have for me, Matt? Did you say you found it in Lt. Li's back pocket?"

"Yes," I said and pulled the note from my pocket. Unfolding it, I placed it in his hand and sat waiting curious about its message.

"I haven't read it," I added.

He stared at me for a few seconds then moved his attention the note. I watched his eyes quickly scan the note then move back to me.

"Well, Matt, it seems what you have found is the missing link to his abduction mystery. Li says here that the one that calls himself Ming captured him from a dive with explosives strapped inside his suit and ordered him into the bay then commanded him to retrieve his notebook and return to the bay without being noticed or he would destroy the station with a giant explosion. He obeyed Ming but was taken captive anyway. And the most important thing in here is his comment that when retrieving it he pulled all the Z information from the notebook and left it in his desk."

"What does that mean, Dave?"

"It means they still think Discovery One is a radiation monitoring station. He kept the Z material from their eyes. What a brave soldier."

"I'm glad to hear that, Dave. He must have been a pleasure to work with. Renews my faith in humanity." Growing tired and ready to bunk down I stood to leave. "So does that tie up all the loose ends of your mysteries we came down to solve? I mean can we head back home anytime soon?"

"Not so fast, Matt. You're forgetting the new elephant that just walked into the room."

"The monopole?"

"Exactly. Our staff is not trained in stressful diving procedures nor expected to participate in life-threatening undertakings. That's what you and Mr. Briscoe are best at, from what I hear. I'd like you both to remain here and get us out of this new danger. And, not surprisingly this one may be the most difficult to deal with. Seems we are now fighting the laws of physics and none of us are prepared for that battle."

Chapter 19
The Visitor

"**S**tation Alert! Station Alert!" Ivy's voice boomed from the overhead speakers startling us. "We have a visitor. A large submarine is pulling along side the dome fifteen meters out on the starboard side. According to my submersible database and the sonar returns from its structure, it shows to be a Kilo-class submarine modified to operate at this depth, possibly a new PRC super-secret sub. However, none of its measurements exactly match any of China's submarines in my database. I'll report more information when my sensors detect it."

"Oh shit. Speaking of battles," Bowman said rising from his chair, "Here comes another one. That's a Chinese Russian sub. They must be looking for their lost whale-ship."

Sighing he bent over and spoke into the glowing panel on his desk, "Ivy, how large do you estimate this ship to be?"

A soft purring sound preceded her answer.

"It's length measures to be eighty meters or about two-hundred-and-fifty-feet and the hull shows a ten meter beam; over thirty feet across. Weight is estimated at three-thousand tons."

"Good God what a monster," he said, "I had no idea they could dive this deep."

He looked at me with eyes like saucers and returned his attention to Ivy.

"What's it doing now, Ivy?" he asked.

"At a standstill ten meters off the ocean floor. Its engines have gone quiet and its sonar is pinging the area apparently looking for something other than us."

"They *are* searching for their ship," I said. "What do we do now?"

"We wait and pray. Hopefully they will move on after an unsuccessful search. They do have a moon pool according to the whale-ship's logbook but it can't be used at this depth so I don't expect any knocks on our doors."

"Implement silent running, Ivy. PA announcements off," he ordered.

"Do we have armaments on the station, Dave?" I asked exploring our defensive options.

"Yes, we have three torpedoes tubes on each flank of the crawler's hull but if we use them the explosion will surely take the station with it. They obviously know that. That's why they're nearly on top of us."

"Want me to go rouse the Chief and prepare a SeaPod for diving?"

"And what would you do out there, Matt? Kick sand in their face?"

"Well no, but that's not a terrible idea," I said snickering, "Might blind them."

Briscoe blustered back into the room and rushed up to us.

"Did I hear my name called? You can't rouse me when I never made into my bunk before all hell broke loose again. What is it this time another submarine? That's what Ivy said."

I glanced up and said, "Yep, a big one. Might as well sit this one out. We're pretty helpless against it."

With the Station's heating vents barely blowing air, the room began to chill down as we sat in dead silence waiting for something to happen.

"Is it getting cold in here or it just my cold-flashes returning?" asked the Chief.

Bowman stared at his computer screen.

"No, it is not you. We're on silent running. Every system is running at reduced power to prevent vibrations and noise. It'll drop to about forty degrees in the station before the auxiliary heaters kick in. The sub should be gone by then."

"But what if it doesn't?" he countered.

"Then we put on coats."

Suddenly something from Ivy's announcement resonated through my mind.

"Did Ivy just say the sub was on the starboard side of the station? That's near the monopole. I wonder if they're close enough for it to affect them."

"I don't know. Let me check," Bowman said.

Bending over her console he said, "Ivy, submarine status?"

"No change. Still in position pinging their sonar."

After twenty minutes with no additional information from Ivy, Briscoe appeared restless.

"Hey, Dr. Bowman, is there a coffee center in the Z-room? I need a cup. This waiting is killing me. Either I get a cup or fall asleep right here and fall out of my chair. And that would be embarrassing."

Bowman smiled at the break in tension.

"Sure, Mr. Briscoe, but you may have to make a pot with the guys gone from their workstations. The room normally sits empty when we're traveling or disconnected from the cable."

Minutes passed before he called back:

"Can I bring anybody a cup of fresh java?"

"Count me in, Chief," I shouted.

"I also would like one, two sugars, no cream. There are cup carriers on the shelf under the pot."

Teetering the carrier, he reentered the room and distributed the steaming coffees.

"Did I miss anything while I was gone?"

"Oh, if only it would go that fast," Bowman said. "They're trying to instill fear with their inert proximity and silence."

Chuckling Briscoe commented, "Working for me. You, Marker?"

Bowman sat up in his chair and leaned in toward us.

"Look, guys, if they wanted to kill us they would have already done it by now. All they have to do is fire one tiny torpedo toward us. Their hull can take the impact. On their sonar, we're just a big balloon hanging over a bulls-eye. Impossible to miss."

"Any evasive measures available?" the Chief asked.

Scoffing he answered, "Yeah, after we spend ten minutes activating the bridge and starting all the wheels into motion we roar off at a half-mile-an-hour. So, no. We got nothing."

Thirty minutes later after fruitlessly discussing an evasive defense in the event of a torpedo attack, we returned our attention to the sub. Bowman again asked Ivy for its status.

"Little change. They're still motionless but settling toward the floor. Sonar is still chirping but growing softer as if they're limiting their search"

"Or losing their power," Briscoe added.

On his observation, we all looked at each other.

"Could that be possible? I mean for the monopole to affect something that large?" I asked.

"We have no precedence as to what it can do, Matt. And, even if we base our projections on what it did a day ago they could all be wrong today. He hiked up his sleeve and glanced at his watch.

"Hmm. Williams should be leaving Pod Bay 1 right about now. Hope she goes out to port and avoids our sleeping giant."

"She'll take that route just to avoid the monopole," I said, "She heard Ivy's message I'm sure. She wouldn't go that way anyway."

"Ivy, has Lt. Williams left the station?" Bowman asked.

"Yes, Dr. Bowman. I tracked her safely out past the submarine with passive sonar. She's on her way to the surface now. I've determined that she left the bay door open for her return. Shall I close it with the suspicious vessel in the area?"

"Yes, Ivy. And reopen it on her return after you verify the craft as one of ours."

"Understood, Dr. Bowman. I'll signal ID confirmation using light semaphores retaining acoustic silence. The SeaPod is programmed for that."

"Well it seems you've thought of everything, Dave," I said. "I'm more impressed every moment I'm down here."

He stared at me curiously for a few seconds.

"Matt, you must need rest badly otherwise you would remember that you described that sandcastle feature to me almost twenty years ago and told me exactly how it would work for evading enemy interception. Remember?"

My mind *was* fogging over with exhaustion, but I did remember that design. He was so excited about it he brought a small flashlight with him to the beach the next day and even created a flashing code for signaling the drone ships. I guess I was just good at implanting ideas in my younger days.

"But I thought that was your design," I said, "You even created a signaling code. I remember you used three shorts three longs and three shorts for Save Our Station. You had me convinced it would work. What glorious imaginations we had back in those days."

"You're right and I hate to admit it, Matt, but mine's being challenged right now. Nothing down here is even imaginable. My reality keeps changing planes and I'm always getting bumped off the passenger list."

"I suspect that Admiral Franklin and his guest may ground those planes when they arrive, Dr. Bowman. In fact I'm kinda counting on that," said the Chief smiling.

Then lowering his gaze with a hushed voice he added, "I'm not comfortable when dealing with the unknown either. I'd rather know what I'm dealing---"

"Dr. Bowman the sub now rests on the ocean floor and has gone silent. Sonar pinging has stopped and life signs have ceased. Data suggests that power in the vessel has failed. Rescue measures should commence immediately."

He bolted upright at Ivy's interruption and glared at her panel.

"What? Rescue the enemy, Ivy? Why?"

"Because they are human, Dr. Bowman. Something I can never hope to be. Humans consider life precious then allow it to die without remorse, an emotion I can never hope to possess. I am just relating my innate programming to this situation not fully understanding the meaning of the word enemy or its antonym friend. When I'm finally programmed with sentience in my next version V, I may fully understand my mistakes in reasoning. Until then I remain a logical entity relying on strict rules for my behavior and responses. Does that clarify my reaction to the ship's power failure, Dr. Bowman?"

Sighing he said, "Yes, Ivy. Understood."

Then he paused and added, "Privacy please, Ivy, until I give the keyword 'awaken.'"

With his command, her eye that had always glowed from the desk panel went dark.

"Good," he continued, "Now we can talk."

The Chief sat up in his chair squinted and eyed Bowman.

"Are you planning to rescue the entire crew of that ship? In a sub that huge, there must be at least fifty crewmen. If we bring them all aboard the station they can easily overtake us. They may even commandeer the station and take it for their own use."

I looked at the Chief now confused from Ivy's compassion.

"Chief, I believe you are playing out a moral dilemma that has plagued humans for centuries. There is no right answer. The mind answers one way while the heart answers another. Neither is wrong. Neither is right. I suggest we leave the question for the Admiral when he arrives within the hour."

Bowman agreed nodding.

"Well said, Matt. This is truly an international crisis brewing before us and I prefer not to take any responsibility with a rash decision. For all I know this may go straight to the President's desk for a final resolution."

"But it better be quick," I added, "those men can't live for long without fresh oxygen especially in that minus-fifty-degree water temperature around the monopole. They'll either suffocate or freeze to death... or both."

Briscoe rose and turned to leave then looked back, "Please excuse me gentlemen while I go try to catch at least a few of those forty winks I promised my body. And, as far as my concern for that sub out there? I say we saved ourselves a torpedo." Then he was gone.

Chapter 20
Jonas Silkwood

Approaching Quad 3, we had grumbled at each other from the lack of sleep since leaving our rooms but agreed that we needed food. Briscoe had managed to get a few hours sleep before Ivy woke him and I had sneaked in an hour-and-a-half prior to his obnoxious banging on my door. Amazingly, we both were rested, rejuvenated, and ready to meet Franklin and his guest.

At a long table, Bowman sat with Lt. Williams and two men wearing wet suits. Immediately I remembered seeing one of them on my tour of Umbra headquarters with Admiral Greenfield. He was talking on a phone in a Z-level office when I passed by. He remotely resembled Bruce Willis and that's how I remembered him so easily. Now dressed in a black rubber suit that revealed his fit body he looked quite different from that day wearing Navy Whites. Even the ID badge clipped to his rubber collar hung with military precision. I had to do a double-take when I noticed three stars on each cuff, signaling a Vice Admiral. Embroidered over his breast pocket area, FRANKLIN glistened in the overhead lights.. *Custom wet suit. Nice* I thought.

When the Chief and I neared the table, Bowman waved a hand back.

"Come meet Admiral Franklin and his esteemed guest Dr. Jonas Silkwood."

Never expecting them to stand at our arrival, I was surprised when they did.

"Mr. Cross, Mr. Briscoe," said the Admiral, "I'm honored to meet the naval legends that once graced our Navy. Thank you for your service. I'm proud to have you both aboard."

Then standing aside, he introduced his guest.

"Dr. Silkwood, this is Matt Cross and Mica Briscoe. Great men on land but superheroes below the surface of any body of water. We're lucky to have them with us on this project."

He shook with us and nodded graciously.

"My pleasure. Any experience with particle physics in your work?"

The man was exactly who I expected to meet. I knew particle physicists were not known for their physical prowess, polished appearance or social skills and he did not disappoint. Reminding me of a graying Sagan, he perfectly fit the image of a middle-aged researcher who spent his days cooped up in offices and classrooms writing equations that no layman could possibly understand on whiteboard after whiteboard.

Smiling patronizingly, Briscoe said to him, "No, Dr. Silkwood, I assume that's why *you're* here. We do the diving and you do the thinking and I presume we're all the best at what we do."

"Well said, Mr. Briscoe," Franklin said, "and that's why I gathered you together. We're going to need the best minds in the world to solve our problem... if we can."

"Sit gentlemen," Chef Saunders said wheeling a food cart to our table, beaming with pride.

"Your lunch today is from Hawaii. Coq de Mer au Vin my specialty for our visitors."

Briscoe began to laugh bringing a frown from Saunders.

"What's so funny? he asked obviously upset.

"Oh nothing, Chef. I don't know much French but that sounds to me like Chicken of the Sea with wine. Are we having canned tuna for lunch?"

Saunders blushed as his frown faded to a grin.

"I see that I must brush up on my French and my American vernacular, too. It is tuna but fresh yellowfin, known on the island as ahi. Definitely not canned. It was accidentally included in the station's food drop last week so today it's my gift to you. Bon appétit!"

None of us was prepared for the quality of food he had delivered. With his second bite, the Admiral commented that it was better than a dinner he'd recently eaten at a Michelin two-star restaurant. Even Silkwood was duly impressed with the texture of the braised tuna and overall layered flavors commenting that he wondered if the chef had known he was a pescetarian: a fish-eating vegetarian.

"So, Dr. Silkwood," I said, "Do you think our problem is possibly a real monopole? Or something else."

Chewing a bite he answered, "First I have to explain that every magnet has two poles: a north and a south. Now if you take a magnet and break it in half expecting the poles to stay on their respective ends you'll find instead that each broken piece now has its own north and south poles. There is no way on earth to create a magnet without two poles so that is an absurd question. Only in theory a can a monopole exist."

217

Briscoe scratched his head at Silkwood's answer and probed further.

"We all know that magnets can be demagnetized right? Otherwise the word wouldn't exist."

"Right," he said without flinching.

"Well then when we demagnetize a magnet where do the poles go?"

He had to think for a second before answering.

"There are millions even trillions of magnetic dipoles in any finite object. When they all align in the same direction, the material is said to be magnetized and have north and south poles. If we heat or physically shake the magnetic object enough, the microscopic dipoles will become disoriented leaving them in magnetic chaos: demagnetized. Simple."

Seeing the Chief's direction poking fun at the physicist and testing him, I joined in.

"So let's say we take that magnetic object down in size one magnetic dipole at a time until we reach the smallest physical size possible: an infinitesimally small object of Planck's length. Which pole wins? There can't possibly be room for two poles otherwise it wouldn't be the smallest conceivable object."

"Hmm," he answered. "Now you're dealing with the theoretical quantum world. That's a whole new dimension."

"Well maybe that's what we have... or at least had. It has grown much larger adding the four hundred tons of that C5M and escort plane when they spaghettified. And, on the ocean floor below us it's added a quarter-ton robot and is now sucking in one of our massive tractor wheels."

Silkwood laughed.

"Now you're talking apples and oranges. Spaghettification comes from exposure to extreme gravitational forces found near black holes or their event horizons not magnetic forces. That's just preposterous."

I countered, "So what we're really dealing with is a baby black hole? Is that what you're saying, Dr. Silkwood."

He shook his head and took another bite.

"No, there's no evidence on earth of that, Mr. Cross; such an entity would defy the laws of physics as we currently understand them."

"Then how do those laws explain why our timepieces and system clocks run backwards when we near it?"

Sipping from his wine, he stopped and abruptly placed the stemware on the table.

"You have evidence of this, Mr. Cross?"

With Williams and Briscoe supporting my claim nodding yes, I answered, "Yes. We've seen it twice and probably have it recorded on the ROV's video as it neared the object just before I cut its umbilical to set it free."

"And why would you do that? As I understand them, they don't work unless they're tethered to a remote controller and power source."

Bowman interjected giving me time to gulp down a large bite of tuna.

"That is correct, Dr. Silkwood, but as the ROV neared the object its data stream was hijacked, for lack of a better word, and our control panel viewed the return signal as a massive stream of randomly sequenced data. Then the station's power began to weaken causing a power alert from Ivy, Discovery One's AI attendant. Matt cut the tether to save the station."

Admiral Franklin finishing his meal turned to Silkwood.

"Now, Jonas, I realize you may be having trouble understanding our situation but in light of the recent collider accident it seems to be a possi---"

"What collider accident?" Silkwood interrupted. "I've heard nothing about a collider mishap. Which one?"

"The Large Hadron Collider at CERN. It wasn't really their problem but a problem with transporting their finding."

"Oh dear God," he said, "What happened?"

As Franklin described the eerie incident Silkwood's eyes grew larger with each detail. He had not been privy to the Code Deep Black warning but mentioned that he *was* worried about the possibility of scientists unleashing an uncontrollable monster with their obsession for ever-increasing accelerator energies. He finally admitted that such an accident was inevitable as scientists rushed headlong, recklessly into the infinite abyss of god-like particle physics.

"I'm afraid I've lost my appetite, Admiral," he said dropping his fork. "Can one of the station's crew take me out in a SeaPod to observe this alleged anomaly first hand?"

Bowman, directing Silkwood's attention away from Franklin, scanned his guests at the table.

220

"Matt, you and Briscoe take him out and show him the object. Williams and I will tour the Admiral through the whale-ship then follow you out stopping by its latest victim on the way. Please remember that Dr. Silkwood has only a basic Umbra clearance so please keep your information within those guidelines."

I nodded my understanding and eyed the physicist.

"Are wearing a watch?"

He pulled up his wetsuit's sleeve and revealed a new expensive diver's watch.

"Of course, Mr. Cross. Bought it this morning just to be on time down here although it's only water resistant to a thousand meters. Why do you ask?"

"Well, Dr. Silkwood, your watch will far outlast you at this depth so don't worry, but what would you say if I told you that in few minutes that watch will be ticking backwards?"

"An interesting concept, Mr. Cross, but again that's a physical impossibility, knowing how watches work. The various springs and ratchets just won't allow reverse movement. Simple mechanics but I'll be glad to participate in your folly if only for my curiosity."

Saunders rushed to our table as we stood, leaving our half-eaten plates on the table.

"Is there something wrong with my food," he asked.

We all glanced at Silkwood expecting an answer.

His silence prompted me to explain.

"No, Chef Saunders, something disagreed with him and it was not your delicious lunch. It's science. And, at his request, we're taking him on a fact-finding dive right now."

"Oh no. Not out of Pod Bay 3, I hope. My pantry is a mess right now."

"No, no," I said, "We'll be using SeaPod 1 but I suspect Dave may want to use your bay."

"Not to worry, Chef," Bowman said, "We'll use the SeaPod in the Quad 4 bay. Simpler access from my office anyway."

Loading our crew into the SeaPod was uneventful, except Silkwood did slip on the still wet floor slightly injuring an ankle. Once he finally dropped into the cockpit, we adjusted ourselves in our seats and I closed the hatch and drew a slight vacuum sealing it. Having never experienced a flooding diving bay Silkwood toyed with his new watch waiting for the process to begin. Shortly, the water rushed above and around us causing him to squirm as it rose over the bubble and filled the bay.

"This is quite an experience," he said. "Vaguely reminds me of an out-of-control car wash. I've actually had nightmares about this exact sensation. Strange."

"Oh yes, Dr. Silkwood," Briscoe said smiling, "and you're about to experience the ultimate level of strange as we visit an object from which nightmares are made."

"We shall see," he said as the bay door opened into the black infinity of the midnight zone.

"Here we go," I said feeling somewhat like a lackey tour guide but then I realized we were embarking on a trip with possibly no return.

As we left the bay and I flipped on the forward floods, he gasped at the brilliance surrounding us. Accustomed to the bright fog of reflecting particulates, I expected to see nothing until we were almost upon it. That was just the way deep-sea diving worked.

Turning to starboard heading toward Pod Bay 2, I checked the sonar screen and saw our target roughly fifteen meters out visually verified by the glimmering point of light below us.

"There that's the object out there," I said pointing downward.

He followed my finger. "Ah yes. I see it. Looks pretty benign to me."

"Just wait. I'm taking us into the periphery of its field so you can observe its effects."

"But how will we know?"

"Oh we'll know," answered the Chief. "You keep an eye on your watch and we'll monitor our power levels."

Several minutes passed as we drifted slowly downward toward the object. Then a quick flash of a reflection entered the cockpit from our left distracting Silkwood's attention from his watch.

"What's that huge thing out there?" he asked shielding his eyes from the instruments' glare.

Briscoe glanced out at the huge convex reflecting surface and answered.

"Looks like the hull of its latest victim, a three-thousand-ton submarine that succumbed to the force just before you arrived.

"Impossible!" he argued. "Nothing has that kind of power."

I thought I remembered the boundary of its influence but the motors slowed slightly and the power meter dropped early, indicating I had gone too far. The boundary had grown.

"Check your watch!" I yelled pulling back the joystick to its limit. Still we drifted forward out of control.

Silently, he bolted upright and faced his watch into the control panel's glow. His mouth was agape but he didn't speak. Then came his voice, trembling.

"I-I see it. Ti-Time *is* reversing. Holy mother of God it is what you say it is! It can't exist yet it does." Looking at me his face went white with fear.

As he stared out in horror, our motors groaned; straining against the pull, the props began to roar with cavitations and smoke filtered into the cockpit.

"Do something," Silkwood screamed, "I didn't come down here to die."

For a moment, I panicked as we were pulled closer and closer into its relentless grasp. The object in front of us now glowed so brightly we had to shield our eyes from its fury.

"Look!" Silkwood screamed.

"It's consuming the hull of that ship! Metal's streaming into it like a plasma jet. The ship *is* spaghettifying! This can't be happening!"

Briscoe with his voice trembling, yelled, "The ROV is gone. We're going to crash into the hull of that sub and join that graveyard! Pull back, Marker! Stop this damn SeaPod."

"I have it in full reverse, Chief! Can't stop."

"Purge the ballasts! That worked before!"

I punched the ballast icon and heard the air gasp into the tanks over sounds from the roaring motors but we still drifted forward downward toward our doom.

"Ballasts blown, Chief! Still in its clutches."

"Marker," he screamed, "Check for a dead-weight ballast to release! Our DSVs have them. Break us loose from this Goddamn nightmare. Do it now!"

Coughing in the thickening smoke, I wiped my eyes clear and scanned the control panel searching for a ballast-release icon as the blinding light from the approaching object illuminated the cockpit's smoke. Now feeling as if I were in a white-out snowstorm I bent closer to the panel to see. I squinted through the blinding choking smoke and finally found an image of a tiny block of bricks hanging from a chain with a down arrow below it. *That must be it* I thought.

I pushed the icon and waited for something, anything to happen. Loudly with a forceful boom and a sharp upward jolt the ballast dropped, sending us up rising away from the menacing force.

"Thank God, Marker! We're free," gasped the Chief, coughing and wiping his forehead. It took him seconds to stop shaking and speak again.

"Now get us back into the bay and out of this damned cockpit before we choke to death. Now that we've regained some power the air scrubbers should work long enough for our return."

I glanced at Silkwood sitting to my left. He was trembling with his hands over his mouth and his eyes still glued to the receding object's glow.

"You all right, Dr. Silkwood?" I asked.

225

"No. Not at all," he said. "My lifelong work, my beliefs, and my science have just been nullified by that object. The entire world of theoretical physics will be changed by it. I'm still trying to convince myself that I really saw it and that my watch ran backwards."

He inhaled shakily.

"We were on the event horizon of something magical yet so terrifying. No one's going to believe me."

Then he sighed and looked over at me.

"Mr. Cross, can we possibly observe it in more detail without dying?"

"You tell me, Jonas. You're the physicist. I've read about event horizons and the way I understand them is you might pass through them but you can never leave."

"Now you see our problem, Dr. Silkwood," the Chief agreed. "We *have* attempted to approach it for closer observation but since I stood over it yesterday it has grown stronger, sucking in everything around it."

Distracted by the conversation I realized we were still rising and couldn't stop. Futilely I struggled with the joystick twisting and shoving it as the motors groaned in response. Yet we drifted upward. Then from a speaker behind my head came a quiet warning message.

"Flood ballasts! Flood Ballasts! This vessel is an uncontrolled rise. Structural damage may occur if maximum speed is exceeded."

Suddenly, reminded of a step I had missed, I touched the icon and cautiously waited. Within seconds, the ballasts burped and filled stopping our rise even without the dead-weight ballast.

With the SeaPod seemingly under control, I navigated downward back toward our bay. Down on my left I glimpsed the floods of another vessel traveling far below us.

"That must be Bowman with the Admiral and Williams," I said.

Briscoe followed my gaze then jolted up in his seat.

"Must be. Oh, crap! They're too close to the sub. Better warn them of the object's increased range."

"SeaPod 4, this is SeaPod 1 above you at one o'clock," I said tripping the SeaCom switch. "Do not approach the object. Repeat, do not approach the object. Its field has grown much stronger. Very difficult to recover from it."

Bowman's stressed voice sifted through the static with a weakening signal, "Too late, Matt. We're trapped in its field. Motors can't break us free. Being drawn downward. Please take control of my station and treat it as your own. I know you can do it, Matt. And remember that I still love you as the big brother I never had. So sorry it had to end this way. Everyone's screaming and crying in here. Can barely hear you."

My heart sank and my stomach rushed into my throat at his pleading tone. He had never before told me the way he felt but deep in my heart, I knew that we were best friends forever, brothers from different mothers.

"Blow your ballasts and drop your dead-weight load, Dave," I yelled into the microphone. "It's the little orange icon in the lower right corner of your control panel. Looks like a load of bricks on a chain with a down-pointing arrow. Push it!"

Seconds passed without a response.

"That helped, Matt, but we're still caught in its pull. If the motors don't fail we might pull back but they're already smoking. Say a prayer for us."

"Hell, Dave, I can do better than that. You know me. Hang on. Be there in a minute."

Briscoe stared at me with huge eyes.

"You mean we're going back into that hellish mire? Shouldn't you at least consult us before putting our lives at risk?"

"Sorry, Chief. You taught me never to give up. And, if I left them behind to die that's exactly what I'd be doing. We're going down there but not as close as before. I'll extend the manipulator arms and grab their aft cross beam. Without our dead weight we'll have more pull. Then we'll all tug together: do it with teamwork. Consider yourselves consulted."

Silkwood said, "But- but---"

The Chief shushed him and shook his head no.

"Do not interrupt him, Jonas. This is how we divers roll. Now just sit back and enjoy the sights."

Smiling at his support, I veered the SeaPod back down toward Bowman's pod. We were only twenty meters back and closing quickly. I scanned the control panel seeking an icon before I realized there would be joysticks for controlling the manipulators. Below the main navigation joystick, I found two smaller ones.

On their base, some small instructions read Push to Extend, Pull to Retract and Twist for Claw

Control. That's all I needed to know to unfold them. Shortly they stuck straight out in front of the pod with their pincers open ready to grasp Bowman's SeaPod.

"Keep your eyes on your watch, Silkwood. Chief, you watch the power meter. If either of you thinks we've entered its horizon let me know; I don't want to go in too far."

Slowly very cautiously, I dropped the SeaPod in behind Bowman's pod edging the claws of both arms inch by inch around its aft bumper. We were both traveling together as one but I was bucking the thrust from his giant propellers pulling me forward. I had to will my hands to cease trembling as the pincers finally clanked against the metal crossbeam.

"Gotcha," I yelled twisting the little joysticks closing the claws over it.

"Time is slowing but not reversing yet," announced Silkwood engrossed in my maneuvers.

"Careful don't let go," he said, glancing rapidly between his watch and the manipulators' grippers.

I tapped the SeaCom's icon and announced:

"We're connected up and set to go, Dave. I'm got your tail. Give 'er all the power you've got, Scottie. Back us up."

Returning through the intercom his next comment tickled me, giving me hope.

"Aye, Aye Captain, I've giv'n her all she's got, an' I canna give her no more."

Still I heard his fans roar louder, cavitating the water with bubbles, as I jerked back on my joystick forming a tandem backward force. I softly cheered when the manipulators stretched tightly with tension and held the aft frame firmly in their grasps.

Then looking to port at the submarine hull, worrying that we might back into it, I noticed that it appeared to be very gradually moving forward but it couldn't be: it was grounded. We were backing up!

"Woo-wee!" Bowman yelled, "Keep on pulling, Matt. You're breaking us free!"

"C'mon, SeaPod, you can do it," Briscoe shouted patting the console, "Your motors aren't even smoking yet."

Since I had no forward view of anything but the aft of Bowman's pod I couldn't tell if we were really moving until the huge sub's hull gradually dropped down and disappeared below us.

"How's your power, Dave? Clocks running forward?"

"Yes. Thanks to you, Matt. Everything's fine but we still have quite a bit of smoke in the cockpit. The particulate scrubbers should quickly fix that."

"Breaking off then. Thanks for the dance," I said with a smile. "See you back in the dome."

With that, I released the pincers and curled the arms into their cradles then headed back to the bay.

Chapter 21
Voices

Silkwood, sitting anxiously with us in the SeaPod waiting for the bay to drain down, scanned his eyes across the room and stopped them on the Exosuits.

"What are those robot-looking things over there?"

"Atmospheric diving suits... Exosuits we call them," Briscoe replied. "They're basically one-man submarines."

"Can anyone use them?"

"Yes. But first I would recommend some training from me and permission from Dr. Bowman. I'm sure he won't mind."

The Chief tilted his head. "Why would you ask?"

"Mr. Briscoe, a cursory glance at an object which challenges the laws of physics is not in the cards for me. Like Mr. Cross, I cannot give up and leave it behind until I have interacted with it, understood its origin, and grasped its capabilities. And, as much of my research work involves directed energy weapons, I see a shortcut here for a new realm of superweapon. I need to go back out in an Exosuit and examine the object in more detail. Only then can I even attempt to help your situation here."

"But you'll die, Dr. Silkwood," I said.

"Has it directly killed anyone here yet?"

I had to think before I answered.

"No. But it has indirectly caused the deaths of many including those souls out there in the submarine with the ruptured hull."

"Aha! So it's really the depth's pressure that's killing them not the object?"

"Well, yes. But if you approach it too close your suit will lose power and you'll most assuredly join those casualties around it. You will then die as they did as a result of its influence on your suit's failing technology."

"So, as I understand it, the problem lies in my not being able to retreat from the object once I near it. Is that true?"

"Basically yes. Then you'll suffocate within minutes as your suit powers down from the object's drain."

"Well, I wouldn't consider asking anyone to accompany me directly to the site as did you, Mr. Cross, but there are other means of remote rescue if that were to happen."

"Like what?" I answered pissed at his accusation.

"Like a rope. Tied around the waist of a suit. Leading to a suited rescuer standing many meters away or waiting in a SeaPod to pull me from harm. Can someone do that for me?"

"Jonah, you'll have to ask Dr. Bowman and if he agrees I'll do it. Not for the weapons aspect but for saving the station."

"Fair enough," he said, "Let's go up and meet with him. I also need to report in with Admiral Franklin."

Entering the mess, we found the remaining station staff sitting with coffee, some with food. at long tables quietly talking among themselves. I knew they were primed to leave the site in a few hours and were awaiting the status on our delayed departure.

Dave, sporting a broad smile, saw us walk in and waved us over to his small table of six with three chairs standing empty.

"Ah there are the heroes," he said rising as we neared. "Please sit with us and accept our appreciation for your bravery. Thought we were goners."

As we took the vacant chairs, Briscoe spoke up.

"We thought we were going down the same route but thanks to Marker's dumping that load ballast we broke loose. It was easier the second time around with your SeaPod with both of us pulling."

"So you had to do that twice? Once for you and again for us? That must have been quite a scare for you guys."

He pointed at Silkwood.

"It was, but not so much for one passenger; he wants to go back out in an Exosuit on a lifesaver tether. Get up close and personal with it."

Bowman glanced at Silkwood.

"Is that true? That's never been done."

"Yes, Dr. Bowman, I've seen an object that shouldn't exist and I've seen time run backward. Now I have to return and understand how and why it exists. That's just the nature of my business."

He paused then concluded, "But I want a tether. Something to pull me free if I encounter a problem.

All I'll need is a rope long enough for my partner to distance the object's fury."

From the end of the table, Franklin joined in.

"I see no problem with that Jonas. That's why I brought you down here. To examine and explain the inexplicable. It's all yours and I'm sure Dr. Bowman can easily provide your tethering request with a long rope. Have at it and summarize your findings when you return. Just be careful."

Sitting beside him, Williams, with her hand to her head, looked up at Silkwood.

"We do have one extended-life Exosuit. Has an additional battery pack for longer diving times. We can suit him up in that one. It'll give him more close-in time before he loses power."

"Excellent, Lieutenant. I'll take it," Silkwood responded.

Briscoe sighed and murmured under his breath.

"Here we go again, Marker. You gonna buddy him out?"

"Only if you'll get me a coffee, Chief."

"You're too easy, Marker," he chuckled. Rising from his chair, he looked over the table and asked, "Anyone else need coffee? Dr. Silkwood?"

"No thank you, Mr. Briscoe. I prefer tea. Hot tea. No cream or sugar."

"I'll see if I can brew some up for you. We have hot water and we have tea. Shouldn't be too hard."

Minutes later, returning with three cups in a carrier, he placed it on the table and stared at it as if something was wrong.

"Forget the tea, Chief?"

He glanced over at me then back at the carrier.

"See anything strange, Marker?"

I stared for a few seconds and counted two dark coffees and one lighter cup.

"No, Chief. Did you forget the creamer?"

He scoffed and sighed.

"I know as well as you do that neither of us uses creamer... and you use two sugars. This one's yours."

"Thank you," I answered taking my cup. Then staring at the other cups, I noticed what he was worried about: the liquid in them was not level.

"What? Is the table tilted?" I asked tilting the carrier to level the cups. "It's about two degrees off level I'd say."

Backing off he looked across the mess hall. Then he turned ninety degrees and looked again.

"It's not the table *or* the cup holder. The station is listing a few degrees to starboard."

Bowman in a side conversation with Williams keyed on the word and eyed Briscoe.

"Listing?" he repeated. "That's not possible. Ivy keeps the station level within a tenth of a degree with servo-controlled levelers in the wheels."

He stood and ran over to the nearest Ivy console.

"Ivy, Dave Bowman. Why is the station listing?"

"Hello, Dave Bowman. Let me check my inclinometer data... There seems to be a problem receiving data from the three front crawler-wheel levelers under Pod Bay 2. They do not respond to my leveling requests. So I'm compensating as well as I can with the other wheels."

As I watched, Dave rammed his fingers through his thinning gray hair.

"Wh-why haven't you warned us of this Ivy?"

"I did not consider it a problem, Dave. I assumed it was the surface settling. A few degrees off level does not affect the operation of anything in the station. I was prepared to warn you at a five-degree list."

He sighed loud enough for us to hear from our table.

"Ivy, from now on report any station changes, inconsistencies or problems to me immediately no matter how unimportant they may seem. I'm especially worried about the station's stability."

"Yes, Dave Bowman, I erred and I'm sorry."

He turned and walked back to the table mumbling to himself.

"No you're not. You're not programmed for sorrow."

From her console, she loudly countered.

"How about I apologize? Will that work?"

"No. It just means your thesaurus is working. Good comeback, though."

"Good evening, Dave Bowman. I'll be vigilant of your stability. Ivy out."

Sitting back in his seat, he looked at us and whispered shielding his mouth from her eye.

"If anyone ever hears me mention the word marriage, please shoot me on the spot."

When the laughter finally died down, we returned to the serious business of Silkwood's request: revisiting the object.

"Lieutenant," Dave asked, "can you go up to Deck 3 and find a roll of half-inch braided nylon rope. There are one-, two- and five-hundred-foot spools. Grab a two-hundred-foot one for Dr.

Silkwood's use and bring it down to Pod Bay 1. We'll stage his dive from there. Mr. Briscoe, you and Matt take Dr. Silkwood with you down to the staging area and test him out."

He cleared his throat, sipped from his cup, and said, "Now I'm going to my office and huddle with the Admiral about our recent visitor. Apparently its crew died with the hull rupture so the rescue mission's off."

Standing from the table, he addressed the physicist.

"Dr. Silkwood, I would like for you to spend a few moments of your valuable time around the object evaluating the damage to those three front wheels. Last information I heard, only one was involved; now it's three. That worries me."

"Yes sir, I'll check them out but I'll have to get in close for that. Shouldn't be a problem."

As Briscoe carefully lowered the Exosuit's upper shell over Silkwood's upraised arms Williams dropped a heavy reel of yellow rope through the hatch, hitting the floor with an echoing boom.

Briscoe jumped prematurely releasing the shell.

"Lieutenant, that scared the crap out of me." he yelled then returned his attention to Silkwood's suiting procedure. "Are you all right, Jonas?"

"Yes sir," he answered through its intercom, "that just made more aware of its mass. How much does it weigh?"

Buckling the upper and lower shell together, the Chief looked into his faceplate.

"With the extra batteries, the upper shell weighs around three-hundred pounds. The lower shell, pants and boots is about one-fifty."

"So I just gained a quarter ton?" Silkwood asked his voice distorted by the electronic interface.

"Yeah, close to that but you won't feel it diving. It weighs nothing underwater in its neutral-buoyancy mode. You can also use voice control to fill or purge the ballasts as we used in the SeaPod maneuvers. It's always a good escape mode unless your power is gone. More instructions are on the Heads Up Display in the upper right of your helmet. Push the top button on your cuff panel to talk over the acoustic intercom. If no one answers you pray."

"I think I understand all that, Mr. Briscoe. I'm ready to explore the object. Let's go."

"B-but don't you want a training session here in the safety of the bay?" the Chief asked.

"No. Can you train me to encounter the object?" his voice growled, "That's my ultimate nemesis."

Briscoe stared at him and shook his head then looked at me.

"Load the SeaPod, Marker. I'll tie you together, close the pod bay hatch, and then climb in. Make room for one more."

"You're going with me?"

"Marker, no force on earth could keep us apart on this death mission. I can't see any way it can end well."

Shortly, we were ready for diving but before I pushed the Flood Bay icon, I noticed Silkwood was not locked in the stirrups.

"Dr. Silkwood you need to step over to a pair of those recessed rails in the floor and kick your boots in until they lock. That will prevent you from washing around the room as the bay fills. Copy that?"

He stepped awkwardly to the rails and kicked in one boot then the other.

"Look okay?" he asked.

"Can you move your feet?"

"No. I'm locked in as you instructed."

"Good. Now after the bay floods and we're ready to dive push down with your toes and back your feet out. Then voice-command your suit's direction and speed like 'forward one-knot.' Got that? "

"Hey guys, this is scarier than it looks. Can I still ask questions after we exit the bay?"

"Of course. I'll turn our SeaCom sensitivity to max so we should be able to hear you even at the end of the rope. Two-hundred feet away. Briscoe has set your intercom for full duplex. Just speak and listen; there's no switching involved."

"Roger that. Let's dive."

Minutes later the bay had filled and Silkwood stood under the xenon lighting still locked in the stirrups.

"You need to leave the bay before us so the vortex from our prop wash doesn't spin you dizzy. I know that from experience."

Obeying, he moon-walked out of the rails and stood looking at us.

"Now what?"

Briscoe rolled his eyes and whispered.

"Oh this is gonna be fun."

I laughed then replied to Silkwood, "You still have negative buoyancy so you can walk around. Leave it that way. You'll need it when you reach the bottom. Now just turn toward the door and when it opens propel yourself outward with voice commands as we said and wait for us.

'Stop' or 'hold' works well but with your negative buoyancy you'll slowly sink with 'stop.' 'Hold' will keep your altitude about the same using the suit's vertical thrusters. Got that?"

"Open the door and let's try."

The door opened with a gentle whoosh, which I'd never before heard. *Must be the SeaCom's added sensitivity* I thought.

Silkwood stepped around and faced outward into the darkness.

"Forward one-knot," he said starting a slow forward motion out of the bay lights.

At the far edge of the lighting, he disappeared.

"Hey guys, it's dark out here. How do I turn on the lights?"

"Say 'floods on.'"

On his command, the suit's floods illuminated showing him as a white-outlined shadow still drifting outward trailing the yellow rope behind him.

"Hold," he said bringing himself to a stop hovering in place some sixty feet out.

"Good," I said, "Now we're coming out behind you. Move off to starboard and give us room to exit."

"How do I do that?"

Briscoe at the end of his patience sighed. Surprising me, he grabbed the microphone from my hand and yelled back.

"Read the damn HUD! It's all in there. Just look up to your helmet's display."

Seconds passed before anything happened. Then we heard his command loud and clear.

"Turn to starboard ten meters then hold."

It was like watching a beginner at a video game causing us to chuckle quietly, wondering what he would do next, but slowly his suit veered right and went out of view behind the bay wall.

"We're coming out," I announced. "Steer clear."

As I pushed the joystick forward, we moved out of the bay into the darkness with Silkwood still hovering level with us at some distance off to the right of the bubble. I turned the SeaPod toward him illuminating his suit and presenting a perfect image of a space walker on a repair mission trailing a yellow tether connecting him to his spaceship.

"Looks like a scene from *Gravity*," Briscoe said. "Amazing the effect a simple rope tether can add."

"Yeah. Wish we had a camera. We could give him a selfie he'd never forget."

"Going down to explore," he said then he issued some more commands, which surprisingly took him directly past the submarine and down to the ocean floor landing near the monopole.

"On site, gentlemen. I made it!" his voice crackled over the SeaCom.

"I'm setting the SeaPod down about fifty meters behind you facing our floods your direction. Narrate your findings as you go."

The floor's contact bumped gently through the cockpit as I released the joystick. We were stationary lying silently on the ocean floor facing him with the submarine to our left and his lights appearing as four dim dots off in the forward distance. The only sounds I could hear were our whirring air-scrubber fans and his jagged breathing sifting through the intercom's speaker.

"Roger your command. I'm about two meters from the object and its fiery disk has gone black in the center. And I mean black. It's the damndest thing I've ever seen. It's like a hole in my vision. Just nothing there. My power meter is just barely starting to drop so I'll continue on."

"Okay but let us know if you get into trouble," I added. "We'll pull you right out."

His voice returned with more static.

"Now standing by the three missing wheels. All around me, streams of glowing blue plasma are oozing into its black core. Having to dodge them. A forth wheel is now being pulled weirdly distorting into the hole and even the bulkhead of the crawler's base behind the wheels is grotesquely distorting and drooping down toward it. Looking over at the sub's hull, I see it's sagging in on itself like a tire going flat. My surroundings remind me exactly what I've read about an event horizon's predicted effects. I must be entering the Kerr ring."

"Thank you, Dr. Silkwood, for the description. Sounds like you may need to leave. Are you ready?"

"No, no. Much more to see. I'm in a wonderland of impossible physics. Going toward the black ho-ll-lll-le."

"Did you just call it a black hole?" I asked trying to confirm his statement. A change in the intercom's sound lowered the pitch of his voice and slowed it down into a deepening slow-motion drawl.

With no answer, I asked, "How's your suit's HUD clock? Running backwards?"

"Oooh nooo, nnott rruunnning, iiittt's raaciing baaackwaarrrds."

"We're pulling you out now, Silkwood. Clear your rope and prepare for a jolt."

"Nooo dooo noottt dooo thhhaaaattt, I'mmm nnooott rreeaddyyy, yyyetttt." His rapid breathing had slowed to a ghoulish roar between words.

I stared at Briscoe needing an opinion.

"What should I do, Chief?"

"Just cool your jets, Marker. Let him stay. He's in his realm. He wants this experience before he goes back home."

Agreeing, I nodded affirmatively.

"Well he's getting it. When his suit alarms power failure over our SeaCom we'll jerk him out. Give him maximum exposure until that happens. Shhh. Let's listen."

His roaring breaths continued until suddenly: a pause.

"Helllloo lliitttllle onnnne. Whaaat aarrre yoouuu?"

His breathing restarted.

"Whhhyyy aarrre yoouuu heeerre?"

We leaned in toward the speaker listening for a response. Nothing.

"Whhheeerrre aarrre yoouuu frrroommm?"

243

Again nothing sounded from the intercom but his heavy roaring breaths.

"Foouuur poooiiinnnt twwooo whaaat? Liiiighhtt yeeaarrrs? Immmposssiibblle."

"What's he talking about? And to who?" the Chief asked.

"Sounds like he's hallucinating, Chief. Maybe his air mixture's off. Could be CO_2 narcosis. We need to pull him back."

"No wait. Something's happening."

In the distance, the outline of his suit began to glimmer with a brilliant blue-white light illuminating the sub and crawler base with sporadic lightning flashes like those from an arc welder's rods.

Then his deeply distorted voice replaced his uneven growling breaths.

"I'mmm cccoooommmiiinnggg iiiinnnn. Arrrrrree yooouuuu thhhheeerrrre? I'mmmmm sstttrrrrreeeettttcchhhiiinnnggg. Ooohhhh wwooooowww......."

As his voiced tapered off, the yellow rope trailing over the ocean floor from our SeaPod to his suit suddenly jerked up from the ground and wildly uncurled, straightening until it was taut, and then yanked us forward several feet. All at once, his glow went dark and the rope slackened and gently drifted back to the bottom.

"What happened, Chief?"

"I don't know. Call him on the SeaCom. See if he's okay."

In the eerie quiet now void of his roaring sounds, I pushed the intercom.

"Are you all right, Dr. Silkwood? Please respond."

Silence.

"Are you there, Jonas?"

Silence.

"Reel in the rope, Marker. Now! We have to pull him out before it's too late."

The urgency in his voice struck a chord and I jammed the Reel In icon starting a whining motor beneath our feet. With our eyes glued to the swiftly approaching rope, we watched in horror as the distant end appeared in our floods with nothing in tow, dragged across the floor throwing up silt and then drew into the reel spinning endlessly.

"Silkwood's gone!" Briscoe said, "The rope must have broken. Let's go get him."

Even though I wanted to share the Chief's optimism, I knew that Silkwood had vanished drawn by his compelling curiosity into another plane of existence... or dimension. We were suddenly dealing with deadly consequences and I feared we would be next. Ironically, his death or whatever it was, was the first one directly caused by the monopole.

"No Chief. We shouldn't return. He's gone. I can feel it. No need to go back and jeopardize our lives again. We have to return to the station and warn Dave of the impending danger."

Chapter 22
Tilt

"**B**ut he warned me that he was prone to paracusia on the trip down here," Franklin argued. "I say what he heard was from his auditory hallucinations. He told me that he frequently experienced them under stress and if that wasn't stress I don't know what is. He had previously heard voices in his head and his coworkers reminded him that he often answered them with nobody there. Poor soul. May he rest in peace."

"So you think he created that conversation in his mind?" Williams asked. "From what Marker and Briscoe said it was a cogent albeit bizarre interchange between him and another entity possibly from 4.2 light years away."

She closed her eyes for seconds then opened them wide-eyed.

"What if that object is not a God-particle or Higgs boson from the Hadron Collider accident as we suspect but rather a speck of something like a visitor from another time or dimension that drifted into our atmosphere and impacted the Pacific near us? Ever think about that?"

"Hmmm," Briscoe added. "It's unfortunate that Dr. Bowman took this so hard. I wish he were here to add his observations."

"He doesn't have any experience with extraterrestrial visitors *or* particle physics," Franklin said. "They wouldn't help."

"Does anyone?" I questioned. "I think we might as well be discussing his encounter as a paranormal experience."

"Ghosts?" Briscoe scoffed. "Don't be ridiculous, Marker. That's not even scientific."

"Not so outlandish, Chief, if you consider the old Davy Jones legend... or the Bermuda Triangle mysteries. Things just mysteriously disappear into the ocean depths sometimes with warnings but most times without."

"So what are you hinting at, Mr. Cross?" asked Admiral Franklin. "That this is just a figment of everyone's imaginations? An exercise in mass hysteria? That's preposterous!"

"No, Admiral, I'm simply offering that we may never know what really happened especially with our inability to interact with it or understand its origin. It remains the enigma it is and will continue that way after we have to abandon this station and leave it buried under a two-hundred-ton debris field."

"What?" Franklin barked standing from his chair. "W-what do you mean abandon the station? Why would we do that?"

Looking over at Briscoe I said, "You tell him, Chief."

With his eyes cast downward he began, "Admiral, the object that Silkwood called a black hole is eating away at the station assimilating it. He described the process as ephemeral tendrils of blue plasma flowing from the wheels and even the crawler base into the object's center a core he said was blacker that black. The structure of Discovery One will soon be so compromised that it will no longer hold back the pressure and we'll have to evacuate."

Appearing shocked, the Admiral pried further.

"And when will that be in your estimation, Mr. Briscoe?"

"Hours, days, weeks? Who knows? We're dealing with something beyond human experience or knowledge."

He put his hand to his head and closed his eyes obviously in deep thought. Then, sitting down in his chair, he said, "We need Bowman here. We need to move the station away for this thing as soon as possible."

Supporting the Chief's warning I spoke up.

"Given the damage I saw down there I doubt that will be possible but it's worth a try."

"Williams, find Bowman and bring him down to the bridge," Franklin ordered, checking his watch. "I'm heading there now and we're moving the station to the CHUS cable as planned just a few hours early."

"Aye, aye, sir," she answered standing and leaving the room.

Tracking behind the Admiral, the Chief and I had no idea where were going but he did. Rushing to keep up we entered Quad 2 and paced through the racks of computers into the rear of the room. On the back wall, another down arrow noted BRIDGE with a red-lighted box around it resembling an exit sign.

Stooping he twisted the hatch lock and let it drop down into a dark musty vertical tunnel leading to a cavernous room far below. On his first step down the long ladder, the distant room illuminated with a muted red lighting. Briscoe glanced at me waiting behind him and squinted down into the room.

"I hate that red lighting," he said. "Makes me feel like my vision's failing."

"It'll get better, Chief. Your eyes have to adapt. You know the drill."

"Yeah, but I still hate it."

At the bottom of the ladder, we stood by Franklin surveying our surroundings. Unlike a ship's bridge, the room was more like an aircraft cockpit with a panoramic forward-looking thick window and a pair of side-by-side joysticks under them. Above and around the window were numerous video panels flickering to life displaying lines and panels of moving data.

"Here's the heart of our navigation system: the helm," Franklin said fanning his hand across the windowed area. "Looks complex but it's really like driving a zero-turn-radius riding lawnmower. The left joystick controls the ten port wheels while the right one controls the starboard's wheel array of ten more. They all move in tandem under computer control with a five-hundred horsepower motor powering each wheel."

"What about the three front missing wheels and the fourth decaying one. What will happen?" asked the Chief.

"We'll have to see when we power them up," he said matter-of-factly. "The tractor system's redundancy *should* account for their loss. Although it has only been tested in the pre-commissioning trial runs, it worked well when we removed or blocked several wheels simulating anticipated difficulties."

Briscoe nodded and stepped over to the window's right corner, then peered downward.

"Where are the Pod Bays. I expected to see them below us."

"Above us, Mr. Briscoe, a level up. That's why the long ladder down. We're on the lowest habitable level with the nuclear plant and other life-support systems behind us."

"So we're on the closest level to the monopole?"

"Yes, that's right but we never anticipated such a danger below us. Fortunately the bridge is still intact."

"But not for long," I said noticing a small puddle of water on the floor beside Briscoe. "There's water seeping in over here."

He rushed over and stared down at it then slowly raised his eyes to me. "My God you're right, Mr. Cross. It's happening."

"What's going on down here," asked Bowman dropping down with Williams from the tunnel. Lieutenant Williams said you were anxious to leave. Why is that Admiral? First, you said to hold off and now you're rushing us to leave. Has that DOD meeting schedule changed?"

"No, Dr. Bowman, your station has changed. Look over there," he said pointing to the small pool of seawater.

"Well, Admiral, I can get a towel and clean that up if it bothers you."

"Don't be such a dumbass, Bowman. That doesn't bother me. It's the billions and trillions of gallons of water pushing that puddle inward that bothers me. And according to the Deep Force team here we'll be dodging water knives if not flooding all over the station pretty soon."

"So how will moving solve that problem?"

"The thing down there is eating the station, Dave, and we're beginning to see the results of that damage. The station is now listing several degrees and that puddle is directly over it. The more we list toward that monster the faster it will consume us. You have to pull away and save what we have left."

Without argument, Bowman walked to an Ivy console on the rear wall.

"Ivy, Dave Bowman. Please notify the station to prepare for travel in ten minutes. Announce for the crew to close and seal all hatches then clear the mess and tie down loose items. Also secure the Pod Bays for travel. The usual stuff."

"Yes, Dave Bowman. Shall I also lock the hard drive heads as usual or run computations through the move?"

No. No computations. And prepare to pull anchor on my command."

"Understood. I will be standing by. Ivy out."

"Lieutenant, are you needed elsewhere," Bowman asked rejoining us at the helm.

She glanced back to the tunnel still lit by the overheads in Quad 2 and said, "Only to seal that hatch. I left it open thinking we'd just be a few minutes."

"Well things have obviously changed. Please close and secure it. You're staying with us until we're moving."

"Yes sir. Anything else I can do?"

"Pray."

Ivy's announcement on the PA system soon started.

"Attention staff and crew. Attention staff and crew. Prepare for station's travel mode in ten minutes. Repeat, prepare for travel mode. Stow all movable objects, clear and close the mess hall, close and lock all watertight hatches then staff your travel stations. Motion will begin in ten minutes."

As she ended her message, Dave sat down at the driver's console and powered up the tractor controllers. A small bank of indicators illuminated one at a time starting with #5 and blinked green through #20. At the end of the sequencing process lights #1 through #4 flashed red.

"What's that all mean, Dave," I asked watching over his shoulder.

"Those red-flagged wheels failed the self-test but I can override them manually take them out of the loop. We'll run on sixteen. Not a problem though: we can run with five on each side if we have to."

Reaching up he touched four buttons under the red indicators turning them dark.

"Done. No more problems."

Scoffing, the Chief whispered in my ear, "Famous last words."

On my other side, Lieutenant Williams also engrossed with Bowman's start-up procedure flinched.

"Oh crap! The hatch. I forgot to close it."

She turned back and rushed up the ladder. Seconds later, I heard the hatch slam closed with a solid clunk that echoed through the bridge.

"Fast work," I said on her return. "That would have taken me twice as long and I'd be huffing and puffing. You? You're not even winded. How do you do that?"

She backed off and looked me over.

"If you spent six months on this station rushing up and down these ladders all day long you'd be fast too. Just comes with the job I guess."

Nodding in agreement then looking back at Bowman, I saw he had activated the bridge's forward floods and was studying a large map lying on the console.

"Got the CHUS intercept coordinates I sent down, Dr. Bowman?" asked Franklin.

"Yep, looking at them right now. Thanks."

"See any problems?"

"Nothing unusual. The usual hills and valleys and a seamount we have to bypass. No canyons or abysses. Smooth riding all the way. I see no problem with the scheduled arrival ti---"

Interrupting him Ivy announced a message.

"Dave Bowman, the ten-minute delay has expired, You may proceed when ready."

He turned back to her panel and spoke.

"Pull the anchor, Ivy. Inform me when it's secure."

The result of his command was a deep rumbling banging from below the floor at the rear of the bridge. It sounded like a slow motion clunk-clunk-clunk as the anchor's chain rolled into its tray wherever that was. I expected something more elegant than a standard bulky anchor chain but then I realized they always worked. Then the sounds stopped.

"The anchor is secure. Start motion when ready. All systems, hatches and decks show go," Ivy said.

"May I ask a question before you start?" Franklin said, placing his hand on Bowman's shoulder.

"Sure, Admiral. Shoot." He dropped his hands from the joysticks and looked back at him.

"Which way do you plan to drive out? Forward or reverse?"

"Well I normally drive out forward unless there's an obstruction. See a problem with that? Anyone?"

Pointing down toward the ominous starboard glow, Franklin responded, "Only that you're going to run six perfectly good wheels over the debris collecting around that monopole down there including what's left of the old wheels and the ROV."

"Good point, Admiral. Reverse it shall be. Everyone please take a place in the surrounding seats and harness up. This may get tricky."

I sat, then Briscoe and Williams in a row of seating behind him. Finally, Franklin sat in the copilot's seat beside him. Four harness clicks signaled him to start.

"Wish me luck," he said firmly grasping the twin joysticks in his hands.

Loud vibrating harmonizing hums arose from the bridge's exterior telling me that he was moving them activating the huge motors but with such precision I couldn't see which direction. Then I felt a comforting backward lurch. The calming feeling lasted only a second until I felt something else like balancing on a teeter-totter nearing the tipping point. Then all at once, we tilted more. The front starboard side plunged at least five feet down to the surface throwing up silt and mud over the windows. The right edge of the forward window looked down into an eerie glowing blue-black bulls-eye.

"Holy shit!" Bowman yelled as pencils, clipboards, screwdrivers and other things flew down to the floor then scraped noisily across it into the corner and settled in the growing puddle of water under the window.

"What the hell just happened?" he shouted.

"We've tilted our starboard hull down on the monopole. It's got a grasp on us. Can you move forward?" Franklin yelled.

Bowman shoved both joysticks forward creating a collection of sounds. Some motors were grinding some were growling and others were whining at full speed.

"We're raised off the aft wheels off the surface like a tripod," shouted Franklin. "Nothing's going to gain traction with our incline. Can you go back? Get all the wheels back on the ground?"

"Don't know. I'll try," he panted.

From my seat behind him, I saw Dave was in trouble as he flashed his hands between the joysticks and his forehead wiping sweat from his eyes. I wanted to help but there was nothing I could do.

"C'mon, Dave, you've got this," I said. "Take your time and think it out."

Releasing the sticks, he silenced the motors. Then delicately he pulled the joysticks toward him starting different sounds: ones of distorted hums and growls but still creating no movement.. Then one-by-one the green lights over wheels #5 through #20 flickered and flashed to red.

"They've failed! The motors are gone," he shouted lowering his head in obvious defeat.

Williams scanned the helm for damage and fixed her gaze on the objects floating in the puddle under the front window.

"Uh-oh," she said, "We've got more problems. There's now a blue glow under all that crap in the corner and the water's starting to rise."

Just as she completed her sentence, a tiny pencil-sized shaft of water flashed across the room striking the rear bulkhead wall and scattering into a thick freezing mist, spraying us with a shower of icy water.

Suddenly from the overhead speakers Ivy's voice blared, "Condition Red. Condition Red. I am detecting a sudden pressure fluctuation in the bridge. Attempt repair or evacuate immediately! Please acknowledge."

"Heard, Ivy." Bowman released his harness and fell awkwardly to the floor.

"Watch the tilt," he grumbled.

Righting himself, he ignored our new increased list and surveyed the damage.

"We have to leave now unless anyone has an idea how to repair that rupture."

Feeling his eyes on me I said, "I got nothing, Dave. Sorry. Time to leave."

Nodding, unbuckling his harness, the Chief agreed, "We have to leave before that leak grows. It's right over the monopole now and its force is more directed. That hull won't last long."

Horrifying seconds later, we were all standing together holding hands for stability, clumsily trying to reach the ladder without slipping in the rising water.

Williams went up first opening then dropping down the hatch.

"All clear up here! Come on up. Hurry, the water's rising!"

She was right. I felt the frigid liquid seeping into my socks and then looked down and saw it slowly rising up my boot.

"Need a hand, Admiral," I asked. Before I could finish he was at the top climbing through the hatch.

"You go now, Dave."

"No, I'll go last. You first, Matt. Then Briscoe. I'll follow and close the hatch behind me."

Rather than argue I sped up the ladder surprising even myself at my agility and turned to help the Chief. He face was right below me revealing a fear he seldom showed.

"Thanks, Marker," he huffed grabbing my hand. "Not as young as I used to be. And I hope it continues past this. You still owe me Bear Lake."

I smiled and pulled him up suddenly realizing for the first time that we might not escape our imminent doom. "Oh, you'll get it. I promise."

Then breathing heavily, Bowman poked his head through, climbed out, and spun around to seal the hatch. As he reached down and tugged it upward, the pressure below forcefully slammed it closed almost injuring his hand. Squatting he twirled the hatch wheel until it locked and glanced up at us standing over him.

"That pressure's building down there and it has a powerful force. Be very careful around it."

He jumped up wiped his hands on his jumpsuit and frantically turned toward the Admiral.

"We have to start emergency scuttle procedures as soon as possible." Then grabbing the Admiral's arm he pulled him toward the door stumbling awkwardly into the core room.

"Come with us," Briscoe said spinning toward Williams. "We're cold wet and thirsty. Let's see if there's anything left of the mess and regroup there."

Shivering she answered, "I'm behind you."

Chapter 23
Mayday

With Bowman rushing off somewhere to call Mayday, we found ourselves in a tilted wacky-world station forced to manhandle our way around the deck grabbing the nearest object to pull our bodies along without falling and sliding to the front starboard corner of the room. Disoriented, we struggled into Quad 3 and found the mess cluttered with tables and chairs piled against the starboard wall rising almost to the ceiling.

Briscoe looked around curiously sniffing the air.

"Is that coffee I smell, Chef Saunders?" he called out.

"You bet! Just perked it," said his voice from the pantry. "It's such a damn mess back there I don't know how I'm gonna feed my next meal," he said stepping carefully, slanting to port, back into the kitchen.

He side-stepped through to the jumbled wall grabbed a four-top table from the pile and dragged it over for us. Then from a roll of tape he was carrying he taped down the legs and went back for the chairs.

Briscoe, Williams, and I smiled at each other watching his resourcefulness ignoring the disaster we faced.

"In a world gone sideways there has to be sanity," he said finishing the last chair's taping. "And I'm making it right here. Seat yourselves, please. I'll bring us coffee. Two sugars for Mr.

Cross and none for the Lieutenant and Mr. Briscoe, right?"

"Correct," we answered in unison.

With the cup carrier carefully balanced in his hands he slant-walked back to the table and handed us coffees, keeping one.

"We're doomed aren't we?" he asked sliding into his seat. "I heard Ivy's announcement about the bridge. How bad is it down there?"

Ready to answer I glanced at Williams, noticed teardrops forming in her eyes, and deferred to her.

"It's bad Bill," she said. "It's sealed off from the station never to be entered again. Fully compromised with the pressure."

"So we can't be leveled?"

"No, I'm sorry. Unless a miracle occurs we're not going anywhere... or leveling the station."

"But-but I can't cook or serve like this. How can I provide meals in this mess?"

"I'm afraid you won't have to. We'll be scuttling Discovery One before your next meal."

With his eyes and mouth agape, he stared back.

"What?" His lips began to tremble and a sorrow fell over his face.

"But why? There are no alarms. There's no panic. We're just tilting. I love it here. This is my family. This is my home."

Briscoe put a hand on his shoulder.

"But there soon will be, Chef. This station is an engineering marvel of safety but there's a cancer eating away at its base. It can only sustain the damage for a few days before the dome's final involvement. Then it's too late. We have to evacuate now while there's still time."

260

From the ceiling Ivy spoke, startling us.

"All station personnel please assemble in the mess for evacuation instructions. Please report to the mess hall for evacuation instructions."

Ivy's announcement jolted Saunders into action. He stumbled around grabbing tables and chairs and hurriedly began taping them down. Empathizing with his motivation, Briscoe and I helped him by holding them for taping. Then he backed off and counted.

"Four long tables with twenty-one chairs should seat everyone including me. Thank you guys for your help. Gotta go make more coffee."

As I talked plans with the Chief and Williams waiting for Dave to arrive, members of the station's crew began to file in and sit around the tables hooting and cheering. At first that confused me: revelry in this time of extreme danger seemed frivolous but then the Lieutenant explained to me it was for Chef Saunders' thoughtfulness. Suddenly, I realized that all the crew, not just us, loved him as family. She told me that he had always gone out of his way to please them and they were just showing their appreciation in the final hours of the station's existence.

"Fresh coffee!" he yelled from behind the tilted serving line. "It's on me today. Come and get it." Another cheer arose from the small crowd as they filed up to the urn and filled their cups then returned to their seats awaiting the exit briefing.

Soon Bowman entered the mess with Franklin, looked over our table and nodded, then headed for the coffee. I could see from his resigned expression that this was not going to be an easy meeting for him.

Sitting down at our table, squirming into his seat to keep his balance, he glanced around the room and sighed.

"Mayday has been sent and acknowledged. Rescue vessels are on their way and should be hovering over us within the hour."

Then he put his head into his hands and closed his eyes.

"So it's come down to this. My hopes and dreams dashed by a physical impossibility from hell. Why did it have to land here? I just wanted this station to work and demonstrate the feasibility of deep-sea habitats. I guess I must have happened on one of its hidden gotchas."

Williams put her hand on his. "Dr. Bowman, you have already proved it to me and everyone else in here. I've heard them talk. All of their experiences have far exceeded their expectations. You have nothing to regret and it's certainly not your fau---"

A loud gasp came from the crew with the jolt as the starboard side dropped again further increasing the tilt.

Bowman's eyes widened when he realized what was happening.

"Goddammit!" he cursed, "It's going too fast. We have to go."

Rising from his seat, he turned to the anxious crew.

"That's our signal. We must leave now for the panic room and board the EPod. Is everyone here?"

Several of the support crew lifted from their seats and scanned the room looking from table to table.

"Broyles and Simon aren't here," said one. "They may be trapped on the third deck. The elevator doesn't seem to be working."

With veins in his neck rising he yelled, "What? The elevator's not working? Are you kidding?"

The crewman hesitated before answering.

"No sir, it won't rise above the first deck. Just bumps up and down a few inches like it's stuck on something."

"Oh shit," Bowman said. "It's the tilt. It's binding with side friction against the tube. I never designed it to be used this far off vertical."

"Then how do we get them down from Deck 3?" he asked. "We can't just leave them there. Is there an emergency stairway? Ladder?"

Shaking his head, he answered.

"No. Too complicated. The sealed compartment safety design between watertight decks wouldn't allow for them. The elevator's our only means of vertical movement and it would work if we weren't listing so badly."

"So, Dr. Bowman," he asked, "Are they as trapped on Deck 3 as we are on Deck 1? How can we get to the panic room and the EPod without the elevator?"

"We can't," he said flatly, "but we're only trapped until I find an alternative exit. Do not worry. I will find a way."

"What about using the SeaPods?" another crewman asked. "Can't we load them up and make multiple trips?"

"You're talking many hours of up and down travel to clear the station and we'll still have two men trapped on level three. I expect more breaches by then. The last trips won't make it."

Then fortunately, in an apparently premeditated move, Saunders entered the room from the pantry with an armload of MREs and spread them over the serving area.

"Come and get it. This may be your last meal... for a while," he laughed. "I hate to see bad food go to waste."

The laughter he created saved Bowman from the lynch mob forming in the mess. As they lined up for food, he nervously sat back with us and bowed his head.

Then he whispered, "What can I do now? I'm done. Someone please help me."

As we began to discuss possible exit methods around the table, my mind wandered back to my civilian life at MBORC seeking an answer. The Alvin-class submersible, which I drove and had driven for years, had an ingenious emergency escape mechanism where the self-contained bubble cockpit could be released from its wrecked or trapped propulsion hull by a simple pull of a lever sending it soaring free-floating to the surface. I compared that to the station's design and saw a great similarity: a disabled crawler base with a watertight pressurized dome over it. Could they be separated? I wondered.

"Dave," I said interrupting his conversation, "Exactly how does the scuttle escape process work? I've heard that the EPod sealed in the apex of the dome is released by its crew then as it floats up uncovering the core, water rushes in and floods the submarine core and decks. Then a ton of explosives blows the station to smithereens. Is that an accurate view?"

"Not entirely, Matt. Scuttle is only intended to destroy all the computers, the terminals, and their data," he answered with a glimmer of curiosity in his eyes. "The EPod is manually released by its occupants and does float to the surface as you said. But then to prevent the destruction of the nuclear power plant in the base with all the radiation it would spew, the dome mounted on explosive bolts, is released floats up and at a preselected distance, I think around five-hundred meters above the base, sixteen-hundred pounds of C4 explosives obliterate the station and spread it widely over the ocean's floor. It's basically like an underwater fireworks cannon." He tilted his head. "Why do you ask?"

"Dave, your station is similar to our submersibles only they don't blow up the life-saving sphere. Why use the EPod? We can't access it anyway. Use the entire station as the rescue pod. Save everything don't destroy it."

"Hmm. Interesting idea, Matt."

I could see the gears churning as he considered my idea. It was a slim hope but the only hope for us.

Briscoe, catching on added, "So we release the dome without flooding it and ride it to the surface? Can that be done? It won't have power without the nuclear plant. And we'll be blown to bits halfway up."

"But that can be fixed, Mr. Briscoe. The station has an internal battery bank that runs it for a short while, around an hour or two allowing it to rise to its explosion depth. But I can bypass that to prevent the explosion... I think. Then all we have to do is break through the dome once it surfaces since there are no escape doors above the Pod Bay doors. Those doors will be useless without main power. And since we'll still be trapped on Deck 1 we'll have to break through one of the walls surrounding these four quads."

"Is there any C4 on this deck?" I asked.

"Yes. One-hundred pounds in each quad placed in the walls around the peripheries." Suddenly his spirit brightened.

"I see where you're going, Matt. It's a very long shot but if I can remember how the explosives are wired I can disable them all from the scuttle panel in my office. Then at the right time, once the dome surfaces I can pick any quad wall to blow leaving all the others sealed. It's a hack but it might work."

"What about the inrushing water pressure when it blows? Won't it kill us?" Williams asked.

He closed his eyes then answered, "No. The top of the dome should float above the water leaving our deck opening only twenty or thirty feet below the surface. It's an easy free-dive escape for us. Should take less than a minute to float up and be rescued.

From a nearby crew table Lt. Jill Deason approached and stood over Bowman with her arms behind her back appearing defeated.

"The crew wants a short prayer service, Dr. Bowman, to memorialize those who have already died on the station and those who are about to perish. Do you mind?"

Standing from his seat Briscoe offered an answer.

"I've given many eulogies for fallen police officers, Dr. Bowman. I'll do it."

Bowman nodded his approval.

"But don't leave them without hope. We're going to make it. Matt and I will be figuring a way to save the station. We've done it before, long ago."

Watching the Chief walk to the center of the room and bow his head starting a prayer I whispered, "Come on, Dave. Let's go save these souls. We don't have long."

The normally short trip to his office took longer than usual as we climbed uphill through the vault and Z-room to back of Quad 4. Panting, he rested his hands on his knees for a moment then kneeled at a wall plate labeled SCUTTLE PANEL behind his desk and started unscrewing screws. As they released and fell to the floor, I watched them race toward the front of the room and collect at the doorsill leading into the Z-room.

"Back here are the sixteen wire-pairs leading to the blasting caps," he commented pulling the panel from the wall. "Now all we have to do is disconnect them from the pressure sensing activation probe."

I peeked into the wall box and saw a rainbow of colored wires connecting to a long terminal strip. "But how do you know which ones to disconnect?"

"We need them all disconnected. Don't want any automatic pressure detonations or we'll flood halfway up."

"Oh, right," I said.

Then he pointed to the terminal trip.

"See these small labels? They start at D1Q1 and go to D4Q4. All we have to do is decide which quad wall on Deck 1 we want to blow when the time comes."

"Dangerous voltage on those wires?"

"No, we use twelve volts but it's the amperage that counts. A flashlight battery will work." He opened his desk drawer and pulled out a flashlight then unscrewed its back and pitched me a D-cell keeping one for him.

Within a minute, back at the panel he had all the wire pairs disconnected and hanging loose from the box.

"Brown, red, orange, and yellow, each paired with white, mark the quads one through four on this deck," he said. "Remember that in case something happens to me. We can find those wires leading to the C4 packs in each quad and intercept them there. Then all we'll need is a wire cutter and that D-cell battery across the pair to blow the wall. Got that?"

I nodded yes, hoping that I did. It was a lot to remember especially in the panic I expected to ensue.

"Now for the dome release trigger wire; that's what I'm looking for. It's over here."

He probed through another maze of wires in the box with the screwdriver and looked back.

"If I remember right the scuttle signal comes in on these two wires after the EPod blasts off and this timer here delays the pulse for the explosive bolts. Then a minute later, it sends pulses out to them over these wires and breaks the dome loose sending it floating upward."

"You sure, Dave?" I had delved through wiring mazes just like it and knew one wrong move could bring devastating consequences.

"Fairly sure," he said frowning. Then with a snort, he added, "Of course I'm sure Matt. I designed and built it." Then pointing his screwdriver to the panel lying upside-down on the floor he chuckled, "And besides, that's the schematic right there. I'm reading from it"

Another jolt shook the station tilting us further up. I noticed the screws in the doorway that had stopped at the doorsill bumped up from the floor and rattled into the Z-room.

"Condition Red. Condition Red," Ivy announced. "My inclinometers show a dangerous tilt in the station. Tipping is imminent. Evacuate immediately! Evacuate immediately."

Frowning at her announcement, he raised his head and spoke toward her console.

"Ivy, Dave Bowman. Announce on the PA across the station for the crew to lie down on the floor and hold tight to something sturdy. They may be tossed around a little as we break loose from the base and right ourselves on our way up."

"I will do that Dave." A moment of purring.

"But, Dave, if I lose my power from the base I will go dormant. Is that true?"

"I'm sorry, Ivy. Yes. Dormant but not out of existence. Your thoughts will remain in your memory until we power you back up in the future."

"Very well, Dave. Goodbye. It has been a pleasure serving with you. Ivy signing off."

With Ivy's announcement beginning from the PA speakers, I queried him.

"So Dave, how is this going to work? Other that all at once I mean. I know that, but when you activate that timer what happens?"

"First I have to simulate the EPod's release by shorting these two terminals, then we run like hell through the station dodging obstacles and seal the Q4 hatch behind us. After it's sealed we race back into mess hall and then seal the Q3 hatch. Finally we join everyone else on the floor and pray for the best."

"Roger that, Dave. If I don't get a chance to tell you later, I want you to know that way back when we were little standing on the beach together making those sandcastles that were always gone by morning I loved you as the younger brother I had lost... and I still do. I never said that but I always assumed you knew."

"I did big brother. Now let's roll."

Chapter 24
Breakaway

W iping a tear from his eye, he reached down with the screwdriver and shorted the two terminals flashing a brief spark. I checked my watch as the timer he had just pointed out began to count down with one-second flashes.

"Go, go, go!" he yelled standing up waiting for me get out of his way.

Through the Z-room and vault, we raced avoiding overturned chairs and computer consoles as we stumbled toward the core room. Having cleared the vault he turned back then leaned against the heavy bulkhead door and slammed it closed and twirled its locking wheel.

All we had to do now was round the core room and enter the mess. I glanced at my watch and saw only twenty-two seconds left until the bolts would disintegrate finally releasing us from the monopole's fury.

"Hurry, Dave! Twenty seconds!"

Rushing around me, he stopped in his tracks.

"Damn! Some idiot closed the mess door," he screamed.

He fought the hatch wheel for seconds finally freeing it and spun it until the thick door unlocked and swung forcefully on its hinges into the tilting room, crashing against the bulkhead wall and rebounding. Its unexpected force yanked him into the room and sent him sliding and rolling across the floor into the serving line's base.

"Somebody grab him he's not moving," I yelled seeing my watch tick down the final seconds. "Hold him tight!"

I turned back and pulled then pushed with all might against the door forcing it closed. As I spun the locking wheel, the room shook with loud explosions and jerked upward then downward. Tables and chairs slid over the floor, slamming into the crew as they grasped vertical beams and pipes around the room. Then all of a sudden, the overhead lighting flickered and changed to a deep red, shadowing my vision. The blood-red darkness made it difficult for me to see across the room where Dave had stopped.

"Is Dave okay?" I yelled holding tightly on to the wheel as my eyes adjusted.

"He's all right! Just knocked out cold by the fall," Williams yelled back.

"How about the Admiral?"

"He's fine. He's tending to Bowman's head wound."

My watch continued counting up to the one-minute mark, as I waited for it, bucking the station's undulations and worrying that Dave's memory of the scuttle's C4 trigger wiring might have been incorrect.

Wiping sweat from my eyes as it ticked past one minute, I breathed a sigh of relief. Nothing had happened except the sound of water rushing past the surface of the dome had grown louder as we increased speed, rising faster and faster, still bobbling toward the surface. The crewmembers were silent staring into nothing with terrified expressions not knowing what to expect.

"We've passed into the safety zone," I shouted trying to comfort them. "We'll be topping the surface any minute now."

Their cheers and applause made me smile and I finally accepted that we would make it.

Surfacing would have been less noticeable if it weren't for the distant sounds of helicopters whirring over the dome and our slow rocking motion in the waves. With the crew rising, standing up for the first time since our ordeal started, wild cheers erupted at the sounds.

"What now" Briscoe asked approaching me.

I glanced down at Dave and saw he was still unconscious.

"We have to break through the wall. Dave told me how."

"Break through this wall?" he asked. "I would think that would be very difficult. Have a Sawzall or jackhammer on you?"

"No, but I do have a hundred pounds of C4 on my side."

"A hundred pounds!" he shouted, "That'll blow through the whole damn deck and kill us all."

"Well Dave told me it's in the walls. We have to find it. Maybe we can separate the loads and fire something smaller."

"Yeah, that would be smart, Marker. Let's do it."

"Oh," I added pulling him back, "You'll find an orange and white pair of wires leading to a blasting cap somewhere on the outer wall. The C4 should be there around the cap."

He ran into the pantry and began throwing boxes around looking for the wires. I joined him and started to search, patting my pocket for the D-Cell. I knew this would be a very hazardous exercise after we punctured the wall. We would then have to wait for the quad to fill with water before we could finally swim out. Then we'd still have to free-dive up through ten or twenty feet of cold Pacific water to reach the surface. *Extremely risky* I thought.

"Do you see another way to get out Chief?" I asked pulling a pallet from the wall.

"Well, the pressure's not as dangerous out there since we're so close to the surface. I expect we're floating with the top decks out of the water. But if we flood this quad we'll sink further making our upward free-dive longer."

"So what can we do?"

"Think. Outside the box, Marker. That's what you seem to do best. Do it now."

As he returned to flinging boxes across the room, I stood running escape possibilities over in my mind. After a minute exhausting my imagination, none of them worked better than the C4 idea. But it was so dangerous.

"Hey, Marker. I found a C4 packet back here. On the wall over the hatch."

"Find the wires too?"

"Yep. Orange and white. They run into a pipe sticking up from the floor. More wires of all colors with them but they're the only orange and white pair."

"Hold on I'm coming back there."

274

The pantry was dark but enough light filtered in from the kitchen for me to see the Chief standing there by a thick patch of C4 on the wall, holding the wires trailing from it, looking confused.

"Can you reduce the size of that explosive pack," I asked remembering his warning.

"Let me see," he said digging his hand into the putty-like layer. "How much do want Marker? Reminds me of Play-Doh but a tad bit more dangerous."

"Just enough to poke a man-sized hole through this wall."

He turned back and stared at me.

"You may think I'm smart but I am not a demolitions expert. Your guess is as good as mine."

"Then grab a fistful and put the blasting cap in it and slap it on the wall."

"You're obviously not a demolition expert either Marker. That handful will set the other ninety-nine pounds of this pack off in a sequential explosion wiping out this entire deck."

"Then, what do we do, Chief?"

"We have to scrape this remainder of the pack from the wall and move it to a distant location in another quad."

"Can you do that?"

"Yep, but it may take me a few minutes. I have to avoid any sparks when I scrape it off."

Calmly he scratched his head and seemed to realize the folly of our plan.

"I hate to bring up the obvious Marker, but how are we going to explode this handful of C4? It takes an electrical pulse to set the cap off. And who's going to do it with this short wire.

I patted my pocket and took out the D-cell.

"Dave said this would do it. I'm going to use some pallets for protection and do it myself. All I have to do is hold the orange wire on one end and the white wire on the other. Then I hold my breath and pray."

"But the water will rush in and kill us all."

"Not if I close the pantry door. There's not that much pressure outside the dome. Then, when I signal you that the pantry's full you open the door and let it into the quad and everyone swims out."

He put a hand on his hip and cocked it.

"Now, Marker, that's the most cockamamie story I've ever heard. You'll kill yourself and take us all with you. That's like your balloon-strap solution for raising the whale-ship: doomed to failure."

"Just do it, Chief. We don't have all day and our oxygen will soon be exhausted. Want to die like those Chinese spies gasping for their last breath?"

I timed him and in seven minutes, he had removed the excessive C4 and replaced it with a handful-sized ball with a six-foot orange-and-white wire pair dangling down.

"I put the extra C4 on the wall in Q1. Should be far enough away to prevent a sympathetic detonation but I don't guarantee it."

"Close the panty door, Chief, and listen for my instructions. Tell the crew to brace for a wall of water if it fails. Oh, and please say some prayers for me."

Suddenly he grabbed the battery from my hand and ran into the pantry locking the door behind him.

Seeing him close the door, I panicked and started banging on it pleading for him to return.

"Marker," he yelled, "If I don't make it tell Barb that I love her and went out doing what I do. Now I'm going to count down from ten. On zero, I'll complete the circuit and if all goes well we'll be free one way or the other. I guess we'll have to postpone that Big Bear vacation until we meet again. Now brace yourself for the detonation."

"Ten."

"Nine."

"Eight."

"Seven."

I ran to the door and yelled hoping he could hear me.

"Hey Chief! I don't think I ever told you but I love you like the dad that I lost. I thank God every day that you came into my life after he died in that horrible crash. You've kept me on the straight and narrow and I never repaid you. Please give me a chance. Let me do it."

Silence.

"Six."

"Five."

As he continued counting down, between his numbers, I heard a thunderous rumbling of overhead choppers circling the dome. Suddenly I heard a weak voice coming from the ceiling. It was not from outside but echoing down from inside the dome above us.

"Four."

"Attention crew," an amplified voice crackled from above with a megaphone's sound.

"We have broken through the dome above the waterline and are cutting our way down to you deck by deck with a torch. Knock or bang on the ceiling so we can find your location. We know you're in here somewhere: Simon and Broyles just told us."

"Three."

"Did you hear that Chief?" I screamed frantically banging on the pantry door.

He slammed back the door and stood grinning at me.

"What? That voice from heaven? Sure did, Marker. Sounds like two are already out. We're next."

As he left the pantry and reentered the mess the crewmembers had grabbed anything longer than three feet including chairs, tables, and brooms and were banging them raucously on the ceiling over the big room.

"Move to the end of the room by the core," he shouted over the din. "They're probably coming down from the hallway surrounding the core. Less chance of fire."

On his command, they all moved with Franklin to the narrow part of the wedge near the bulkhead door and resumed their noise.

"We hear you now. We're on our way down. Clear the area for slag and metal droppings."

Shortly, we heard a loud metal clank on the ceiling. Then it scraped off and went silent above us.

"That'd be the third deck's floor cutout dropping down," Briscoe said. "Then they'll have to

278

let the rim cool and drop down a ladder and torch for the second deck."

"Sounds like you've been here before, Mr. Briscoe," Franklin commented looking at the ceiling with anticipation.

"Previous Navy training, Admiral. Something you never forget, being trapped on a sinking ship."

He finally grinned again, showing relief and agreed, "Yes. Some of our training is rather rigorous."

In a little over ten minutes as we all stood watching, holding our breath, a spray of fire broke through the ceiling and spewed down by the bulkhead door. Fiery droplets of glowing white metal danced over the floor as they landed.

"Wha-what's happening here?" shouted Bowman. "We're on fire! Somebody do something; don't just stand there."

I looked down and saw him lifted up on one arm confused and staring through the crowd in fear. Then I realized he couldn't see the circle being torched through the deck above.

"Dave!" I shouted, "It's our rescuers. They're on the deck above us cutting their way in."

"You mean we-we're on the surface? We're s-safe. Th-the monopole's gone? I must have fallen. Oooh, my head hurts."

"Yes. We made it, Dave, thanks to you and your station's modular design. Now let's get you up and ready to leave."

"No, Matt. Not this time. I'm staying with the station now that it's made it this far. I have nowhere to go and there's plenty of work for me to

279

do here. My sandcastle's not going to be gone by morning this time."

He stood and groggily walked to the Admiral putting his arm over his shoulder. "The Admiral here will probably get me into a dry dock by sunset. Won't you, Admiral?"

He sighed and answered:

"Well, Dr. Bowman, since you guys brought us back pretty much intact; I'll have to think about it. Moving this big egg around the ocean will not be an easy task but we'll try. Remember we still have that CHUS cable to attack but it may take us a while to return."

Laughing together, they jumped as the ceiling cutout fell and crashed clanging to the floor. The hole left in the ceiling about three feet in diameter looked like it would give us adequate room to climb up and exit once it cooled. I could already smell freedom. Then a ladder dropped down, bringing another cheer and the crew started up almost as soon as it hit the floor.

Small groups of crew had gathered, laughing and saying goodbyes, but soon they broke up and climbed up to Deck 2.

I pulled the Admiral to the side as he put a foot on the ladder.

"Are we going back to Point Mugu? Do you know?"

"I do not know but I assume that, yes. You'll have a short debriefing there and then I'll have you and Briscoe taken home. I believe the Osprey is on standby for that. The Tine is not far away." With that, he turned and climbed up the ladder.

Finally, Briscoe and I stood with Dave reflecting on the unbelievable past week.

"Come up with us Dave. Please," I said, almost begging.

"No, my place is here. I'll see you again, Matt Cross. I know it."

He sniffled and held out a hand and shook with me then the Chief.

"You both will never know how much I appreciated your help. I couldn't have done it without you. We'd all be dead by now."

He paused and whispered, "You know that you're my prime witnesses for what happened down there. Nobody is going to believe me but the Admiral, and he's set to retire next month. Can I call on you for verification of the horror we experienced if I need to?"

"Sure," I said smiling.

Briscoe patted him on the back.

"Of course, Dr. Bowman. I for one will never forget that thing and the trouble it caused. I just wonder what will become of it."

"Me, too. I may have to go back someday and find out," he said.

"Ohhh no. Time to go, Marker. Say your goodbyes and follow me up."

With unexpected emotions I hugged him goodbye and stepped up on the first rung. Looking back at him I said, "We'll send a ladder back down to you. I know they have rope ones."

Before long, we had climbed to Deck 3 looking out through a jagged hole in the dome, over the ocean lapping at the dome only feet below us. The cool salt sea air had never smelled so good as we stood breathing it in for minutes with storm clouds brewing off to the west darkening the horizon and the evening sun.

Soon a harness dropped down from a large chopper and its lineman motioned for one of us to go. His assistant standing near Briscoe strapped him in and sent him up. Then he eyed me.

"Are you the last? The Captain?"

"No, he's staying down on Deck 1. Can you get him a ladder so he's not stranded down there?"

"I'll put a rope ladder on each level before we leave sir. The Admiral already asked me for that. He will be well cared for since he just saved this multi-million dollar station from destruction."

I nodded, smiled, and watched the Chief enter the chopper's side door.

Moments later, he reached out and grabbed the harness as it neared.

"Here's your ride. Climb in."

As I drifted up toward the chopper and watched another one hovering nearby with the station gently rocking in the waves below, I felt a loneliness that I'd never before experienced.

I was leaving a part of my life down there. A part I could never talk about to anyone---even my wife. Briscoe *would* believe me but he would probably go back to his cruiser, put on his campaign hat, and happily cruise the Interstates soon forgetting our mission. I knew I would be returning to the depths at MBORC pulling up derelict ships and lost cargo but nothing could ever match the excitement of my time on Sea Station Umbra. It was a story I could tell my grandkids.

"Where are we going, Chief?" I asked. "Heard anything yet?"

"They said Point Mugu. Should be there by sunset. Then a late debriefing and we're heading home."

"Tonight?"

"Yep, that's what they said."

I looked around at the chopper's jump seats filled with the station's crew. As they laughed and relived their tour, I thought forward to seeing my wife again and hugging and spending the rest of my life with her. I thought *Funny how time away from each other especially life-threatening time brings you closer together.* I had never told Lindy why I was so melancholy when I returned home from trips like this but I suspected she knew.

"Hey, Marker. All his merriment reminds me. When are you taking me and the wife to Big Bear like you promised?"

I glanced up at him smiling, awaiting an answer.

"Why, next weekend of course. How's that?"

"All right. I'm gonna hold you to that. Call me and tell us where to meet you. We'll drive up and enjoy the ride."

"I'll call for reservations tomorrow and if they're full I'll just buy the place."

He laughed and started a conversation with Williams so I went back to daydreaming.

Soon we began our descent over NAS Point Mugu. Looking out the side window, I saw lights on the runway flashing in sequence awaiting our arrival. I wondered what to expect. Then I noticed an F-4 Phantom fighter sitting at the end with heat tendrils still rising from its engines.

"Look," I said directing the Chief's attention. "That's Admiral Greenfield's ride. Wonder if he's here."

"Probably, Marker," he scoffed. "You know how he likes to fly back and forth to Florida. Must have a golf game nearby."

As our chopper landed, I looked out on the runway and saw a Navy pool bus waiting by a long stretch flag officer's limo. With the chopper's rotors spinning down, its main door opened and steps dropped down to the tarmac, then the crew started filing out toward the bus under a seaman's direction. Briscoe, Franklin, and I were the last to deplane and were stopped by a distant voice calling our names.

"That's Greenfield!" exclaimed Franklin. "Never expected to see him here."

"Hope he's not pissed," said the Chief peering his way.

The Admiral looked at Briscoe.

"Why would he be pissed? If you had just come back from a scuttled station he might be pissed but you didn't. You saved it. He's probably heard by now and wants to thank you."

"I hope so," I said. "We did our best."

Walking up to us Greenfield smiled and looked around.

"Where's Bowman?"

"He stayed with the station. Gonna ride it into dry dock," Franklin replied.

He shook his head and sharply saluted us.

"Thank you, boys. I heard what you did. And I have to tell you that you did not disappoint me. From what Bowman said during his Mayday call, you performed some miracles down there. Now, as to how you got that Goddamned station to float up to the surface intact I'll never understand. It should have scuttled halfway up but thank God, it didn't. He reached in his pocket and pulled out two cell phones handing one to me the other to Briscoe.

"There are your toys gentlemen. Use them wisely. I would hate to see you walk into a signpost reading your email as I did today... but it *was* about your station's emergency. Fortunately, I was away from Florida: otherwise I could never have made it here in time for your return."

His signpost accident confession brought a round of laughter from us as he opened his briefcase and pulled out two checks.

"This is for you, Mr. Cross, and this is for you, Mr. Briscoe. There's a bonus in there of a million each. You performed way beyond the terms of your contracts and you also discovered something down there that may quite possibly end civilization as we know it. I'm not going to penalize you for that but instead thank you for bringing it to our attention. It's certainly captured the Navy's interest. Now as for Silkwood's visit, we gave him a memorial burial at sea after an unfortunate scuba training accident with a shark. It's already in the papers. That will be your story if anyone ever asks you. Otherwise you know nothing about Sea Station Umbra, understand?"

"Yes sir," we answered together.

He pointed off to a side taxiway.

"Your Osprey is waiting over by hangar 405 to take you home to your wives and families. Thank you again for your service... and if you ever feel like re-upping, call me and I'll get you both in as flag officers with Special Forces. Now hop in the limo and Franklin and I will drop you off by the hangar.

Even in the twilight of the evening I recognized Harper's V22 Osprey with its up-tilted rotors. It meant to me that we were heading home and I'd be there in a little over an hour. Briscoe's trip to Tustin Field was shorter because we would first stop there and drop him off. Then we'd head north to Marina and the MBORC ball field where nearby my car was parked. It had happened so often I called it the Local Route V22.

Chapter 25
Water on the Mountain

L indy must have heard my key slip into the lock because before I could turn the knob she threw back the door and stood in shock looking at me half-crying and half-laughing. After a moment, she threw her arms around my neck and cried hugging and kissing me, welcoming me home.

"Matt, I missed you so much," she whispered in my ear. "I went crazy when you disappeared like that. Please don't ever do that again."

I comforted her for the longest time apologizing for my sudden absence but as usual, I couldn't speak the truth. This time I told her that I had been forced back into the SeaCrawler program at Point Mugu searching for a missing secret Chinese submarine. Although only part of that was true she believed me.

After a moment, she ran into the kitchen and brought out two beers, wanting to hear more. I took one and swigged from it then continued my story, telling her how the Russians had captured us at gunpoint and threatened to kill us all if we didn't call off of the search. The spy sub was originally Russian but they had sold it to the Chinese Navy and the Chinese reneged on their payments. They wanted it back. They said that it was none of our business to search for it even if it held our national secrets.

I guess she became disenchanted with the details of my story at one point because she jolted upright during a pause and stared at me.

"Oh my God, Matt. I'll bet you're hungry. Can I make you a plate of something? I have some leftover spaghetti and meatballs from last night I can heat up in a jiffy."

"Sure, I'd love something, honey. I am hungry. But do we have anything other than spaghetti?"

"Matt, I thought you loved my spaghetti," she asked pouting.

"I do, but I had a really bad batch on my trip and I'm just not ready to see it again."

"How about a fried baloney sandwich? Will that work?"

"Mmm. Lovely. Got any chips?"

After the meal and two more beers, with my eyelids drooping, I told her that I had been awake for most of five days straight and needed to go to bed. When she heard that, she ran around fancying up the bedroom with candles and dim lighting until I fell asleep on the couch.

The next morning I awoke to her anger. I jerked up from the sofa and groggily opened my eyes as she ranted storming into the living room.

"Matt, you go off on some mystery trip and leave me at home by myself for days; then you come home and have the balls to ignore me? You can't do that. I deserve a vacation with you. Take me away and I mean now. You're not due back at work for at least a week so can we go somewhere this weekend?"

Acting surprised, I answered her.

"S-sure honey. Of course. How about Big Bear Lake? We'll spend a week."

"Oh, Matt. You promise? I'm so excited. I love the mountains." Squealing with joy, she bent down and hugged me.

"Yes, we'll leave tomorrow. I'll pack the car today while you're at work and then tomorrow we'll leave bright and early.

We arrived at the Bear Den Lodges just after noon. Private and subtly tucked into the folds of surrounding mountain ridges they astounded us. The air was crisp and cool and smelled of the pines surrounding our cabin. After unpacking, we sat on the spacious porch overlooking the beautiful lake with blue jays flitting through the trees calling out to each other. Campfires crackled in the distance creating the perfect setting for a week together away from the pressures of work and for me away for the sterile smell of purified pressurized air.

That day was the perfect relaxation for us being back together until later in the day when I decided to introduce her to the Briscoes. I called him on my cell and invited them over to our cabin for dinner.

Glancing at my watch, I expected the Chief and Barb to arrive at any time. In my conversation with him after Lindy left for work I had asked him to arrive quietly and unobtrusively allowing us time for some fun under the covers. He laughed and said that he and Barb were done with covers and would spend that time sleeping in, or out on a pier dragging lines in the lake.

They arrived thirty minutes later with a cooler full of ice, beer and all the makings for margaritas. The steaks on the grill were sizzling and creating the aroma that I remembered from the SeaPod. It had finally come to reality.

As the Chief and I tended the steaks and made the drinks, Lindy took to Barb immediately. Seems that Barb had worked in the media at a local L.A. radio station and they knew many of the same personalities.

They went on and on as the Chief and I finally sat and sipped our beers and devoured our steaks with them enjoying the view of the lake.

After dessert from inside the cabin through the open porch door, sounded a loud steady beep preceding a television news alert. Lindy and Barb stopped their conversation and listened.

"Shhh," Lindy said, turning her head toward the door.

"Today, witnesses are reporting the discovery of a new area of the Pacific they're calling the Hawaii Triangle far out in the ocean between Los Angeles and Hawaii. Seems that several ships and divers have mysteriously disappeared from the region during the past few days. This came only hours after several boaters reported sighting a large UFO shadowing a tugboat over the ocean. The Coast Guard is now warning boaters to avoid the area fearing more abductions. Little more is known about this new development but Navy scientists and psychiatrists are investigating the incident."

Wide-eyed from the report, Lindy and Barb caught us chuckling winking at each other.

"What's so funny, Matt? That's a very troubling story," Lindy frowned.

"Oh nothing, honey," I answered. "Those boaters must have had a few too many out there on the ocean. That's the most ridiculous story I've ever heard."

After several more beers, the Chief suggested that he and Barb return to their cabin and we didn't object. It had been a long day and we were more than ready to be alone.

After spinning through all the channels on the television, Lindy found no more news on the Hawaii Triangle so she stepped into the closet.

"Wasn't that a strange story, honey?" she asked slipping into a negligee.

"I just can't imagine that scene," I answered. "I mean I could imagine it out by Bermuda in the Sargasso Sea since that's always been a place of mystery but not the Pacific. It's reserved for sailboats, yachts, and earthqua---"

Interrupting, my cell phone vibrated on the bedside table. I picked it up and saw Unknown Caller on the caller ID.

"Who is it?" Lindy asked, slipping into bed beside me.

"Jake from State Farm," I joked.

Abruptly she grabbed the phone from my hand, jumped up, and ran to the back door and then heaved it far out into the trees.

"He'll have to call back. This week you're mine."

I kissed her and smiled, then spent the night in her arms wondering who had called and what they wanted.

APPENDIX

[TOP SECRET SCI UMBRA-Z (NOFORN)]

SSU General Specifications	
Navy Class:	DSMRL (Deep Submergence Mobile Research Laboratory)
Code Name:	SS Umbra-Sea Station Umbra
Nickname:	Discovery One
Known Name:	Deep Sea Fukushima Radiation Monitoring Station
Known Mission: (TS SI UMBRA-A)	Underwater Mega-Becquerel Receiving Array for Tracking Fukushima Radiation Pacific Encroachment
Covert Mission: (TS SCI UMBRA-Z)	Interception and Collection of Targeted TransPacific Cable Communications
Description:	100' dia. dome on 100' X 100' X 25' crawler platform
Weight:	192 tons
Crawler Base:	20 motorized LRV-DS mesh wheels, 10 per side, 500 hp per stub axle, independent suspension w/10' vertical play/axle
Max Speed:	½ mph
Max Range:	600 miles
Navigation:	Bendix BNS-6 Gyroscopic inertial navigation system
Station Power:	Westinghouse AP100 nuclear reactor - 100MW
Configuration:	Four decks: #1 Electronics, docking airlocks, sick bay, #2 Sleeping quarters, #3 Support crew and #4 Storage

Sea Station Umbra

[TS SCI UMBRA-Z (NOFORN)]

Sea Station Umbra Science Staff

Name	Rank	Clearance	Duty
Alvarado, Chris J.	Ens.	Umbra-A	FRMS Diver
Bowman,J. David	Civilian	Umbra-ZX	Station Mgr
Castro,Roger G.	Lt. JG	Umbra-Z	TPCI Diver
Ching, Yung L.	Lt. Cmdr	Umbra-ZX	TPCI Translator
Deason, Jill R.	Ens.	Umbra-A	FRMS Scientist
Edwards, Bill M.	Capt.	Umbra-ZX	TPCI Lead
Li, Dan (NMI)	Lt. Cmdr	Umbra-ZX	TPCI Translator
Norris, Leon S.	Ens.	Umbra-A	FRMS Diver
Ortega, Sam A.	Lt.	Umbra-A	FRMS Lead Sci.
Shin, Umi S.	Lt.	Umbra-ZX	TPCI Translator
Turnbull, Ross A.	Ens.	Umbra-A	FRMS Scientist
Williams, Susan R.	Lt. JG	Umbra-Z	TPCI Lead Diver
Visitor	(any)	Umbra	Temp Scientist
Visitor	(any)	Umbra	Temp Scientist

LEGEND

TPCI	Transpacific Cable Intercept
FRMS	Fukushima Radiation Monitoring Station

U.S. Govt. Form SSU 501-SS

Sea Station Umbra Support Crew

Name	Rank	Clearance	Duty
Adams, Sue	CPO	Umbra	Maint.
Broyles, Seymour	PO1	Umbra	Maint.
Burton, Chris	PO1	Umbra	QM
Peters, Joe	Ens.	Umbra	Nuke
Quinn, Mary	Ens.	Umbra	Nuke
Russo, Tony	SCPO	Umbra	CQM
Saunders, Bill	Civ	Umbra	Cul. Spec.
Simon, Harry	PO1	Umbra	Maint.

U.S. Govt. Form SSU 503-SC

ABOUT THE AUTHOR

John Paul Cater, a retired engineer and scientist, has authored many works under the name John P. Cater. Dating back to 1983, the first books he published were non-fiction instructional works on computer speech technology.

These paperback books are listed below:

Electronically Speaking: Computer Speech Generation
>   HW Sams & Co. Inc, 1983,
>   ISBN 0-672-21947-6

Electronically Hearing: Computer Speech Recognition
>   HW Sams & Co. Inc, 1984,
>   ISBN 0-672-22173-X

Many years later after working with the astronauts at Johnson Space Center's Astronaut Office, he changed his preferred genre to semi-fictional technology, and began writing speculative fiction in 2004. Published works since then are listed below:

Paperbacks:
The Endlight Event
>   Authorhouse, 2004,
>   ISBN 1-4184-9830-0

The Endlight Event: A New Ice Age is Coming...Tomorrow
>   Daily Swan Publishing, Inc, 2008,
>   ISBN 978-0-9815845-0-8

Endlight Dawning 2012: The Maya   Knew
Daily Swan Publishing, Inc, 2012,
ISBN 978-0-9829769-5-1

E-Books:
 Satellite Lost
 (With Matthew Cross and the Canyon Glider)
  Kindle Direct Publishing, 2015,
  ISBN 978-1-4951-6146-9
 The Endlight Event
  Kindle Direct Publishing, 2015,
  ASIN B00Z5GB67U
 RawShock Tales
  Kindle Direct Publishing, 2015,
  ASIN B0120NJ6M2
 Pi Day Doomsday
 (Another Matt "Marker" Cross Thriller)
  Kindle Direct Publishing, 2015,
  ASIN B013Y5DTOG
 Sea Station Umbra
 (Matt "Marker" Cross at his best)
 eBook:
  Kindle Direct Publishing, 2016,
  ASIN B01D3U6AIY
 Paperback:
  CreateSpace Publishing, 2016,
  ISBN 978-1-5332-4323-2

This book *Sea Station Umbra* is his second venture out of the sci-fi genre into the world of speculative fiction techno-thrillers.   Hope you enjoyed it.